EXCESSIVE
JOY
INJURES
THE
HEART

BOOKS BY ELISABETH HARVOR

FICTION

Women and Children (1973, reissued as
Our Lady of All the Distances, 1991)
If Only We Could Drive Like This Forever (1988)
Let Me Be the One (1996)
Excessive Joy Injures the Heart (2000)

POETRY

Fortress of Chairs (1992)
The Long Cold Green Evenings of Spring (1997)

ANTHOLOGIES

A Room at the Heart of Things (1998)

E X C E S S I V E
J O Y
I N J U R E S
T H E
H E A R T

E L I S A B E T H   H A R V O R

M&S

Canadian Cataloguing in Publication Data

Harvor, Elisabeth
    Excessive joy injures the heart

ISBN 0-7710-3963-8

I. Title.

PS8565.A69E92 2000   C813'.54   C00-931649-3
PR9199.3.H37E92 2000

We acknowledge the financial support of the Government of Canada
through the Book Publishing Industry Development Program for our
publishing activities. We further acknowledge the support of the
Canada Council for the Arts and the Ontario Arts Council for our
publishing program.

Excerpts from this novel appeared in quite different form in *The New Yorker*,
Event, *PRISM international*, and also in Elisabeth Harvor's collection *If Only
We Could Drive Like This Forever*.

Typeset in Centaur by M&S, Toronto
Printed and bound in Canada

McClelland & Stewart Ltd.
The Canadian Publishers
481 University Avenue
Toronto, Ontario
M5G 2E9
www.mcclelland.com

1   2   3   4   5   04   03   02   01   00

For W

EXCESSIVE
JOY
INJURES
THE
HEART

Because the storekeeper is wearing his white butcher's coat he makes her think of a movie she went to with her husband once — back in their married days — a movie in which a butcher (who was also a psychopath) courted a beautiful woman with fresh cuts of meat. He would appear outside the little school-house where the woman was giving lessons to her students, the newly sawed leg of some animal wrapped up in pink butcher paper, a florist's twist where its hoof would have been. The memory of the shock she'd felt when what she had taken to be a bouquet of flowers appeared, in the camera's close-up, to be a crude bouquet of blood-red leg of lamb or cow, makes her almost jump when Habib bows to present her with a bouquet of actual flowers.

"Thanks, Habib, but what's the occasion?"

"Spring is the occasion. And to celebrate this rare Canadian phenomenon we are making a small presentation of flowers. But only to our very best customers."

"In other words to all your customers."

"Yes," Habib tells her. "All."

~~~~
~~~~

Speared and furled in their greenish glass jug, the irises have a churchy but phallic look. She places the jug on the windowsill above the kitchen sink, then carries the tulips, in a clear glass pillar, to the room whose sofa looks out over the muddy back garden. But before she was awarded the flowers she was perched on another sofa – the sofa at the Fowler Institute – waiting to see which of the Institute's four doctors would turn out to be her doctor. The doctors at the Institute were medical doctors who no longer practised medicine. In fact the friend who'd recommended the Institute to her had referred to her own Institute doctor as a psychoanalyst who was also a gymnast. It was clear that these doctors weren't the sort of doctors who would attire themselves in the white lab coats of butchers or shopkeepers, they were the sort of doctors who attired themselves in the jeans and checked shirts of farm boys. One of them had come out of a consultation room to look for a chart. He was wearing a midnight-blue corduroy jacket along with his jeans. She had hoped he wouldn't turn out to be her doctor. He was attractive, certainly, but there was something really quite sad about his shoulders. He had also seemed to be somewhat shy. While he was sliding a chart into a wall of charts he had coughed briefly and she had imagined his skin: warm with fever.

When he'd said "I wouldn't dream of it," she had secretly studied him, uneasy and puzzled, from where she was lying on the treatment table, one arm bent under her head. With his long sideburns and his long-waisted blue corduroy jacket he'd made her think of a doctor from another century. But his voice came out of the modern world and was modernly hoarse. Well, naturally; he had a cold. She'd smiled up at him. "Why wouldn't you dream of it?" (She'd half-thought he would say "Because you are too intelligent.")

"Because you are living too much up in your head."

"I'm too skeptical to be hypnotized?"

The smile in his eyes gave her full marks for naïveté if she was naïve enough to suppose that he (or anyone) would be so naïve as to label her skeptical. "Skeptical is the *last* thing you are. But we'll have to talk more about this the next time I see you. Which won't be as soon as I would like" — not being in sight of a calendar, he raised a bare wrist to mimic a quick, pre-occupied glance at a watch — "because I'm very booked up at the moment. I think what we'll have to do right now is set up a few weekly appointments for you three or four weeks from now, after I've moved to my place out in the country."

Again she uneasily studied him. But this time she was sure her uneasiness was tipping over into skepticism. The sad thing was, he didn't see it. "I've had quite a lot of therapy already . . ."

There was a silence.

"Psychoanalysis," she said.

"That was for your head. This will be for your body."

"What about the insomnia?" She was at last driven to ask. It was why she had come to see him. "In the meantime, I mean?"

"I'll set up a few quick appointments for you here in town — for acupuncture treatments — and I'll also teach you a few breathing techniques that might be helpful."

She wondered why he had said she wouldn't be a good candidate for hypnosis. Didn't this mean she wouldn't be willing to give herself over to the experience utterly? Unless it meant the opposite: she would go into a trance and never come back.

When it was time for her to leave, he told her that he preferred to be called Declan, not Dr. Farrell, and he pulled a map of Ontario out of a drawer to show her where he lived from May till September, on the outskirts of a small town called Ottersee. He spread the map out on the treatment table and they looked down at it together.

So there it was: unwieldy Ontario. Antelope-coloured, immense as a continent.

"Ottersee," she said, liking the sound of it. "And so are there a lot of otters out there?"

"No sea and no otters. Or at least not any more."

"Is there a bus?"

"You don't own a car?"

"No."

"I think there might be a train."

To her surprise, she discovered that she liked standing beside him. He all at once seemed like a genuine person, democratic and tactful. There was nothing lush or overly ripe about him, he was too reserved, too thoughtfully formal. But did she really want to travel so far out into the country? At the mercy of trains?

He was printing CLAIRE VORNOFF on a clean page in his notebook. "You're Russian?"

"No, the Vornoff is from my husband. But we aren't living together any more." This was more information than he'd asked her for, and so she quickly said, "His great-grandparents came out here from Russia the year the *Titanic* went down."

He smiled.

"But they weren't on it."

When he smiled again she told him that even if she did own a car she wouldn't know how to drive it.

"Why is that?"

"I'm too much of a dreamer to ever drive a car . . ."

"So now you could learn."

Yes. As long as I don't kill someone, she thought.

But now he was asking her what kind of work she did.

She told him she was working for a doctor who practised family medicine. "Shrieking babies," she told him. "Bulimia and glaucoma." But she left out all those blank bits of the day in which for a minute or two she would daydream while waiting outside the examining room for patients to slip off belts, boots, earrings, stockings. Followed by the quick shy rustle of the paper gown, then a pause, then a sigh, then a tremulous voice calling out "Okay, nurse! I'm ready now!" She was not, however, a nurse. "What I do is more like being a hostess who knows how to take blood pressures and measure and weigh people." After she got married she was offered a job working as a receptionist for a gynecologist friend of her husband's. "And it just sort of went on from there." But what did she dream of, waiting for Dr. Tenniswood's patients to pull on their paper gowns? Only the usual: love, sex, tenderness, and the day she would prove to every-one who'd ever shown disdain for her that she was amazing. "But I'm hoping to better my lot in future. I'm working my way toward a degree so I can teach."

"Good," he said.

When she stepped out into the late afternoon, the day was cooler and clearer. A windblown jet trail was even hanging like a length of white fringe in the sky. But was that really true? That she was living too much up in her head? At twenty, on her honeymoon with Stefan in Europe, she had sat barefoot one cold May morning in Paris, shy and sex-obsessed and pretending to be demure as she'd begun to read Turgenev's *First Love* while a shoemaker was tapping new soles onto her sandals. But now and then she'd glanced up to discover that he was looking over at her. He'd had an emotional face and this had made it nearly impossible for her to concentrate. She'd felt she was on display and so must try to look sensual and poised and pure of heart all at the same moment. And then when the sandals were at last ready and he was buckling them on for her she'd asked him how much she owed him. "*Rien*," he'd said. And to her puzzled "But I must owe you *some*thing . . .," he had only smiled, shaking his head. And then when she'd stood, drawing the broad strap of her canvas bag up over a shoulder, he had also stood, just a little too close to her, somehow letting her know that what he wanted was to hold her. Hold her or kiss her. Or — and this was what it turned out to be — hold the weight of young foreign breasts in his hands. They didn't speak, and as he stood cupping her breasts his eyes filled. His tears seemed to her to be the sign that their weight was the right weight: a weight he remembered. It was over when he thanked her. Then she had dizzily stepped out into the bright light of the day feeling restored, feeling this is real life, this is my body.

Out-of-control birdsong and the cries of children down on the street were the first sounds Claire heard the next morning. She went over to her window to look out and saw that it was a rinsed, perfect morning. But it was also looking quite cold – brilliantly sunny and cold – and so she pulled on a heavy sweater for a trip out to the store.

She unlocked her bike in the clear leafless light, a night-glisten of ice bordering the edges of the puddles, biked out to Habib's. But as she was coasting back down her hill, she saw that the children who'd been playing on the sidewalk when she'd gone out to Bank Street were now squatting in a circle on the lawn close to the van der Meer front door.

She chained her bike to a tree, then walked up the path to her own narrow entrance, stopping for a moment to call over to them. "Is it a dead bird?"

Two of them stood up to call back in proud unison, "It's a *mouse!*"

She let herself quickly into the house before they could show it to her.

She was half undressed when her doorbell buzzed and so she grabbed up the sweater she'd just pulled off and pulled it on again on her way down the stairs. She was afraid it was the children, wanting to show her their mouse in its match-box coffin, having mistaken the smile she'd so unwisely smiled for curiosity about the small rodent corpse. A woman without children, she felt tender toward children, but she was definitely squeamish about the joy they so often appeared to feel about any small bird or animal that happened to be dead. She was never the undertaker for the bird or mouse funerals of her own childhood, she was always the priest or the florist.

And so she opened the door cautiously – braced to smile, not recoil – to discover that there was, after all, nobody there. "But I'm *sure* there was somebody *here*," she cried out in a stagy voice, aiming to please. She stepped out into the day to take a turn in the spotlight of sunlight and was rewarded by the sound of laughter from behind the hedge and one of the trees. Now that they'd witnessed her being tricked it should be enough for them, and so she quickly let herself back into the house and again ran up to her apartment.

The doorbell buzzed again almost immediately, nine or ten long flirty buzzes. The five little mourners. But she had to ignore them.

By the time she turned onto Wilbrod Street it was only ten minutes before Dr. Tenniswood's first appointment for the day and so she was startled to see him out at the front of his house, his back to her while he was forcing a gardening fork into the lawn next to the flower beds, then grunting at the placentas of roots whose pebbles of dirt he was shaking out as he wrestled bits of decaying tree trunk from his garden. He was wearing his grey flannels and a grey tweed jacket and he was looking so unusually massive, even out here in the diminishing sunshine, that he made her think of the part of southern Europe called the Massif Central. He's like a buffalo, she thought, but at the same time he's like the buffalos' plains. A body to graze on. But by now she was close enough to see that this morning his necktie had a marine motif: florid white conch shells, their slit-like apertures rosily flaring with pink.

She had just stopped to say hello when the front door clicked open and Zuzi Tenniswood, looking sleep-drugged and sour in a plaid halter and wrinkled pale shorts, came down the steps, her open palm held out as if testing the sunny morning for rain. With moody delicacy she stepped across a narrow strip of dewed lawn to her father. "Car keys," she said.

Dr. Tenniswood drew off his gardening gloves to fish a ring of keys out of a pocket. "Say hello to Claire."

The girl did not throw Claire even so much as a glance. She was seventeen, but a very young seventeen. She looked elsewhere to say "Hello to Claire."

Claire said hello, but immediately clenched a cold hand inside a pocket. The first summer she had worked for Dr. Tenniswood, eight summers ago, Zuzi had made a morning ritual of coming into the office to borrow one of the stethoscopes so she could check the heartbeats of a whole family of rubber dolls.

But now Dr. Tenniswood was smiling at Claire in helpless apology. "And so how's our timetable for today, Claire? Have we got a full house?"

They were scheduled for a morning of baby visits, and once it had begun, Claire held the babies to a shoulder, one hand capping their wobbling and warm little heads while Dr. Tenniswood crept up behind them with his injections of vaccine. There were days at work when she felt like an accomplice.

But by eleven already the sun had gone, leaving behind it a blowy morning, the trees bowing down in a rainy warm wind. Weather to go out for a walk in, but Claire couldn't, she had already been invited out for lunch by Lisa Pitt, the friend from her British novel class who'd been the one to recommend the doctors at the Institute to her for her bouts of insomnia.

Once the babies were immunized, Claire, sitting at her desk, went travelling. She went to a lake, went swimming, then she was hoisting herself up onto the soothing heave and bob of a float pontooned on old barrels while a man came swimming darkly toward her in bright sunlight, his head a dunked and gleaming helmet of wet hair, the hot sun making her want to slightly part her warm thighs, then he was heaving himself up onto the rocking float with such a panting scatter of droplets that she'd be wanting to tell him that he must have swallowed at least half the lake. Other times she was lying belly down on a float (and it was even the same float) but this time she was peacefully alone and reading book after book, inhaling the smell of wet swimsuit while doing a crash course in the inner life. Wanting to educate herself in the sunlight.

But at last the morning was winding down, and by

twelve-thirty there was only one more patient, a schoolgirl carefully hanging a shining black plastic raincoat up on a peg out in the hallway.

Nervous in her school uniform she came over to Claire's window, and in a voice low with apprehension told her her name – Amanda – and that she had skipped two periods. And because she was still so young, and also because she was so clearly a student (and in all likelihood a student at the convent school over on Friel Street) Claire for just a moment understood her to mean that she'd skipped two periods at school – math, history – not, or at least not immediately, thinking of blood. A school smell even floated down to her at her desk: a mix of cigarettes and chalk and Trident gum and the bruised-leather smell of the girl's school satchel.

Claire sent her down the hallway to one of the examining rooms, then made a quick phone call about a changed appointment before going down to talk to her. But when she came into the room she could see that the girl was on the point of crying. She sat down beside her. "How many weeks has it been then?"

"Eleven." (A very small whisper.)

But how brave she was, this fat-thighed little Amanda, to stop in at an unknown doctor's clinic on her way home for lunch, to climb the unknown steps up to the clinic carrying her school bag. She had chosen Dr. Tenniswood over the kind nun (if there *was* a kind nun) in the convent infirmary; she had chosen him over her parents (but of course) and over the priest at confession (but of course times ten). "Everything's going to be all right, Amanda. A lot of girls your age come into this office with exactly this problem. And we're always able to help them . . ." But was this really true? Pregnant girls did come in, but only now and then. "And what about sleeping? Are you able to sleep?"

Amanda could not look up, but she did shake her head.

"It could still be a false alarm," said Claire. But she doubted it. "I'm not all that sure the doctor will be able to see you today though, it might have to be tomorrow, I'm just going to go have a quick word with him now."

Dr. Tenniswood was in his office, pulling on his jacket, he had to run off to a medical meeting.

"Jack, there's a fifteen-year-old girl in Room Three who's afraid she might be pregnant."

"You'll have to get her to come back tomorrow then, Claire, I can't see her now. I'll examine her tomorrow and we can talk then about a referral." His dull grey hair stood up; it was dully healthy and woolly. A whitening woolly grey crop: he would never go bald. But he was looking short of breath, distracted, he was patting his jacket pockets, missing something.

"What," she said, like a wife. "Reading glasses? Memo pad?"

"Memo pad." And he raised a foot onto his chair, then plucked back the crease of his pant leg because one of his shoelaces was undone.

She sifted through the papers on his desk until she found the memo pad, then fitted it into his shirt pocket while he was breathily tying his shoe.

Two summers ago she'd started calling him Jack, but behind his back she still always called him Dr. Tenniswood, a name that made her think of the names of the characters in *Decline and Fall*. On the days when there were only two or three patients waiting to see him she could usually get a laugh the times she jutted out a hip to ask in an arch voice, "Dr. Tenniswood, anyone?" But she had to go back to see Amanda again. "She's also not sleeping, Jack."

"Get her a Valium then. But only one, and only half a milligram, just for tonight."

Not long after he'd hurried off to his meeting and Amanda had gone back to her school with a pill in a pocket, Lisa Pitt came up the steps in the company of a friend who'd just come back east after a week of skiing at Whistler. This friend seemed still to be smelling of sunlight and snow and lanolin; it was as if she'd rubbed lanolin into her skin and her frizzy fair hair and her heavy boots. Perhaps this was what gave her such a dreamy self-absorption, but there was something open and healthy about her too, as if every morning she drank down a tall glass of sunshine with her handful of vitamins. Claire (with a kind of wistful envy) pictured her life in the mountains: the sideways sprays of skidded snow, the falling showers of freezing sparkle. All that pleasure and clean light so far far away. But now here they all were, down here in the fogbound East, and the rain had stopped and so they walked together down Nicholas Street. The sun was even starting to come weakly through the rain-haze and as they were walking, the friend (Hartley Lear) didn't converse, she extolled. She kept praising people and seemed to want to be praised for praising them. "Aren't women *wonderful!*" she cried. "The way they move so many body parts as they walk!"

Claire glanced coolly over at her, then looked quickly away. But now they were already coming up to the intersection to stand behind a delicate young Chinese mother in a quilted silver jacket and slim black silk dress who was carrying her young daughter held to her abdomen, the girl's long legs straddling the mother's narrow Oriental hips. "Isn't she a *darling*?" Hartley Lear cried to Lisa Pitt and Claire, her voice insistent, unhappily sweet.

Lisa Pitt and Claire looked over at Hartley Lear in unison, their half-smiles cynically maternal, half-smiles that said, "Since we are women ourselves, we not only move so many body parts as we walk, we can also see through you . . ." Or so thought Claire, and so she also thought Lisa Pitt was thinking. But now Lisa Pitt was asking her if the Institute doctors had been able to help her at all with her insomnia.

Claire was afraid that the more she talked about not sleeping, the more it would go on, and so she only said, "I don't know yet, I've only been there for one appointment."

"So who did you see?"

"Declan Farrell."

But Hartley Lear was the one who said, "You were lucky then. Because that man is an artist, he's just *so* intuitive." She glanced sideways at Claire with a punitive, inhaling look. "Weren't you in awe of him?"

"He seemed like a fine person," said Claire. "But I still think I might want to look around a bit more, try to find out who I'd really like to see —"

The restaurant turned out to be unexpectedly swish: pink linen tablecloths on two tiers of tables at the bottom of an old brick house whose lower level was protected by a sort of greenhouse that looked like an igloo of glass. But the doors to the igloo's glass tunnel had been thrown open to the street, allowing exhaust fumes to float in over the salads. Claire wanted to leave, go to another restaurant, but she didn't want to fuss. And by now Lisa Pitt and Hartley Lear were already fitting their jackets onto the backs of the chairs at a table in the far room, then they were all going down the shallow steps to the aspics and pasta salads and big bowls of hot food.

By the time they'd all got settled back at their table again the exhaust fumes had drifted away and it was possible to take in the much more elegant sights and smells of privilege: the cool smell of linen, the effervescent decay of the wine, the raked pats of cold butter. They talked about movies all through their calamari salads, then went back to the buffet for thin pancakes separated by a silt of chocolate paste that tasted as if it had been steeped overnight in vanilla and rum.

While they were drinking the last of their coffee, Lisa Pitt told Claire and Hartley Lear about an affair she'd with her yoga teacher and about how after it was over she'd contracted a urinary tract infection and had to wear a catheter inserted up inside her for two months and of how she had eventually gone – in a horrible depression – to see a Jungian analyst, who'd told her "But you must see what you're doing: you've even arranged to pee standing up." No sooner had this been said than she knew it to be utterly true – "A eureka experience!" – she'd even hurried home from the doctor's office to pull out the catheter and jump into the bath.

They all laughed at this story, even Hartley, who also spoke of a eureka experience as they were all walking back to the clinic. It was an experience she'd had back in the days when she was a client of Declan Farrell's. "He works only with cases that really intrigue him, and so if he agrees to work with you it's an honour . . ."

But as they were saying goodbye she gazed at Claire for a long moment, her eyes diagnostic, coldly pensive. "Take care," she said. "Take care and good luck."

Back at work again for the afternoon rush of the usual maladies — fungal infections, broken bones, parasites, broken hearts — Claire couldn't account for her wistfulness, unless it came from the morning of baby visits. Her arms were still carrying a memory of baby skin, the sweet ache of baby weight, her breasts were still so alive from the memory of baby mouths hungrily brushing back and forth over the front of her lab coat, trying to find a nipple among all her clinical buttons.

Saturday morning was cold and grey with the taint of the weekend on it: the yells and commotion of the neighbourhood children playing down on the street, and after Claire had sat at the breakfast table going over her notes she pulled on her jacket and ran down into the day. There was such a musky, grassy smell in the air, such a smell of swamp in the city, that she wished she could go for a bike ride on one of the bicycle paths instead of biking to Carleton for her exam on the nineteenth-century novel. But as she was unlocking her bike she saw that its front tire had a flat and so she had to walk fast through the little park behind her street, then hurry across the football field to Bronson and the campus.

The first question on the exam was a "discuss" question: "What did Tolstoy mean by Anna Karenina's suicide? Discuss in either psychological, philosophical, theological or societal terms." There were also several questions about the novels of Flaubert, Gogol, and the Brontës. Claire wrote quickly, somehow contriving to give the answers she'd planned to give, even though she hadn't been asked the right questions.

When she got home she wrote out her rent cheque, then went down the stairs to knock on the van der Meers' door.

Judy van der Meer opened it. Her face had a scrubbed look, her eyes so blue and bright that Claire wondered if she'd been crying.

"Come in for a coffee."

The interior of the van der Meer house was always profoundly relieving to Claire; it was so much more untidy even than her own untidy apartment. Everything in it looked so chewed and awry, as if only dogs lived in the kitchen, in the parlour. And of course there were actual dogs too, dogs who wallowed all the places dogs like to wallow, turning the whole house into a kind of musty lair lined with silver and white dog hair.

Out in the kitchen, Judy filled a pink mug with coffee and slid it across the table to Claire.

Claire sipped at it, but found it too cool and bitter. "So how are things?"

"Dirk came home last night."

"How's that been, then?"

"It's been difficult for Lynnie. He wasn't home for ten minutes before they had one of their really awful major fights. But for *me*" — and it was at this point that Claire understood that her scrubbed look was not coming from tears but from her looking so pink and guilty, sexually consoled — "it hasn't been difficult at *all*, really —" But she couldn't say more because someone was now coming down the stairs.

Claire hiked her chair closer to the table, pushed up the sleeves of her sweater. Dirk was magnetic, although the night she'd first met him he'd seemed a bit greenish and mean. But now she could hear an excited scuffling as well, then the sound of the front door being opened to let the scuffles out, then human steps were coming toward the kitchen, and now here he was, his bare feet in thongs, and above the thongs nothing at all but a pair of tired grey shorts. She wondered if he'd been sleeping, he was looking so drugged and flushed, but at the same time he seemed to be giving off a kind of decayed sexual heat. He even seemed a bit bashful as he planed back his hair to aim a sleepy smile her way. But his eyes were holding their real sexual challenge out to Judy. "Gossiping?" he asked them.

~~~~~
~~~~~

Severe muscle cramps in her legs jolted Claire awake the following sunny Monday morning. She couldn't even walk as far as the shower until she'd massaged them for four or five minutes with Tiger Balm, the whole time whimpering in surprised pain while she kept trying to remember what Dr. Tenniswood prescribed for his patients with muscle cramps. Was it quinine? But wasn't quinine what doctors gave to patients with malaria? It did make sense though, that there would be muscle cramps with malaria, that the body would perspire so much it would lose salt, and that this salt loss could lead to leg cramps – wasn't salt loss the reason athletes got leg cramps? especially runners? – but where in the world would she ever find quinine? She didn't want to ask Dr. Tenniswood for a prescription, she wanted him to think she was at all times coolly in control of her life, but then it occurred to her that tonic water had quinine in it, and so after a hot shower she opened an old bottle of tonic water that had been shoved to the back of her fridge and poured herself a stale glassful of it to drink with her scrambled eggs and toast. Magnesium, she needed that too, she'd read somewhere that magnesium was supposed to be good for leg and foot cramps, and when she had to get up twice the following night to take hot showers and drink even more tonic water, she tried to decide what would be best to do: try to get Declan Farrell to give her an earlier appointment, or – and this would be so much more convenient – stop in for a reflexology treatment at the Muscle Therapy Clinic she passed every morning on her way to work.

~~~~

Gary Ekstrand, the reflexologist, was rangy but dyspeptic, and as he was beginning to work on her feet he told her that he was a Mormon who'd grown up in the foothills of Alberta.

"A Mormon preacher?"

"An elder in the Mormon church, yes."

"And so did you roam the foothills trying to convert people?"

Could eyes be both canny and puzzled? His were. "All Mormon men," he told her, "bring the ministry where it is needed when they are young . . ."

She felt a little ashamed of herself for trying to tease him. He was not a man, she saw, who could take pleasure in being teased. And so she told him that she was a Westerner too and, like him, had grown up out in the hinterland. Mormon boys had sometimes come through St. Walburg and stayed the night with her parents. Or at least stayed for dinner.

Ekstrand frowned at this but didn't respond to it; he instead kept breaking up what he called "the crystals." As he pressed his thumb higher up, making a bracelet of dents all around each of her ankles, deeper dents up her legs, the pain was at times extraordinary, electric. "You have inflammation, I can feel it, a layer of it above your muscles."

"I think it's just in the legs though —"

He rubbed a small steel ball back and forth along the instep of each of her feet. "It's everywhere. Everywhere that I've felt so far. If I'm to do you any good, I'll need to see you at least twice a week."

"I could probably come after work on Monday afternoon."

But this wasn't possible, he was at another clinic on Mondays. "But listen, I'm mobile in the evenings, I could drop by at your place."

"Oh no," she said. But this sounded too unfriendly and so she decided to say, "It's much too untidy."

"Then you could come to my place. Which is a madhouse, of course, with three daughters . . ."

This was so proudly said that she felt reassured. And so, late on Friday afternoon, she found herself walking along suppertime Daly Avenue, then up the walk to a bonnet-roofed house with a pebbled foundation and a bike chained to a concrete hitching post. She rang the bell and almost at once Ekstrand (looking showered and fresh in a brilliant white shirt) came to open the door. She followed him through an askew living room and a cluttered kitchen — but where were the three daughters? There was no sign of them, there was only the faint sound of music drifting down from upstairs. "My treatment room is down here . . .," he was telling her, then it was down a dim set of stairs into the disarray of a basement, past vinyl sofas with slits and abrasions, past old paint cans and wrecked machines, beaded curtains leading into a room with a high hard bed, almost a royal bed, almost Egyptian, the cover tucked around it smelling of ancient damp, at its head a hard pillow covered with a stiff pillowslip that was a dirty gold taffeta, behind it a poster with a picture of two feet turned away from each other, each foot a Europe of the foot, like those cross-sections of beef cattle that used to hang on a wall of her schoolroom — the organs turned into maps that were always in the same three colours: clear red, tan, and sky blue — but now he was handing her a maroon nylon hospital gown and she was asking him if she could change in the washroom, he said it was to her left, but there was a piercing grit under her feet as she walked, a kind of painful glitter, what could it be, she called back over a shoulder to ask how much she should take off, then heard his voice: "Just whatever you're comfortable with! But the more the better! The better to work with you . . .!"

God, she should have eaten something, even if only a banana, her blood sugar was too low, this must be why she was feeling so dizzy, the washroom was awful too, like a toilet in a bus terminal. Then she was back in the room again, carrying her clothes with her, and after she'd hung them over the back of a chair and climbed up onto the hard bed Ekstrand said, "Hopefully you'll be feeling a lot better real soon," then he was rubbing what smelled like a blend of lavender oil and lanolin into her hair and she remembered that lavender was a sedative or at the very least a relaxant and she warned herself to keep alert, but now she could already feel him drawing her hair up into oiled peaks, then she could feel his hands moving down the length of her back while his voice was asking her if she had any friends at all here, people she could talk to if they got into emotional material that was too "heavy," and she said, "Yes, a few." But now she was beginning to feel drowsy, her thoughts came and went, disconnected, she wondered if she should buy carrots on the way home, but not from the health-food store because half the time the health-food-store carrots tasted as if they'd been peed on, there must be mice down with all the sacks of rice and nuts in the basement, but then she had to remind herself that she too was down in a basement, and no one (not Dr. Tenniswood, not her best friend Libi, not *anyone*) knew she was here, and where *were* the three daughters, did they even exist, then she was half-dreaming again, thinking of Mormons and were they still polygamous, at least were they polygamous when they lived far out in back country, and she thought of the Hutterites too, the stories she'd heard about young Hutterite men going into bars in Saskatoon and picking out good-looking college boys and offering them money to come out to their farms and have sex with their women, all with the aim of bringing variety to the Hutterite gene pool. But now Ekstrand's voice was dropping to an experimental low sing-song, the voice of someone reading out of a textbook: "You are a precious person. You are precious to me . . .," and so this was not going to be a person she could trust, but she must take care not to let him know it, just let him finish the treatment and let her not seem to be distrustful, the minute it was over she'd look at her watch, say she'd have to run. No, that carefree little word wouldn't sound carefree, not under the circum-stances, it would be so much better to say, "Look, I should be on my way . . ." But now she could hear his sing-song voice swinging out with more words, his voice sounding hypnotized, even more false: "I have a wonderful wife . . . she's a wonderful mother and a wonderful cook and wonderful at playing the piano and a wonderful housekeeper . . ." and to her continued silence he finally said, "Well, not down *here*, of course, this is *my* territory . . ." then there was more massaging and as he was moving lower down he was asking her how long she was married, and now his voice was sounding voyeuristic and cold, but still she responded (as if under oath): "A long time. I got married when I was twenty and the marriage lasted fifteen years," while at the same time she was wondering why she always felt obliged to tell people the truth, why couldn't she just lie a little? What would of course be useful would be to know why he was asking, still he'd been helpful to her, at least so far, her leg cramps were better, but now something else must be happening, she felt his hands stop, heard him say in the stagy, eyelash-batting voice of an adult addressing a very young child, "Did I hear a knock? *Did* I?", then there was a whiff of cold air, the sound of clicking beads being parted, then lazily swinging to click back, then a barrage of intense whispering (Ekstrand's and a child's), then Ekstrand's voice was coming back again to tell her, "What all that was about is that one of my daughters is planting some tulips in the back garden . . ." and so there *were* daughters then, or at least there was one daughter, or was it a little boy, then there was the muffled ringing of a phone – a muted sting of sound – at first Ekstrand ignored it, but it kept ringing until with a grunt he squatted to rummage through a pile of old sweaters and beach towels to fish it out, this distraction allowing her to seize the few moments while he was occupied to dizzily sit up and haul on her sweater and trousers, then as he was setting down the phone she slid down from the table and quickly said "I have to go now, I need to call a cab . . ."

Ekstrand cast a bleak look back at her over a shoulder. "A cab?"

"I have to get to my local food store before it closes at seven."

"The appointment we made was to last a full hour."

"I'm sorry, but I really do have to go."

"But we still have work to do, we've only just begun . . ."

She dug into her money belt, read out a number so sternly that he dialled it while she was trying not to look at her face in the mirror, she was sure it would be too much the face of a worried clown, her eyes round and alarmed, her nose shiny and red in the upset white dab of her face, her hair peaked up into greased tufts, how easy it is to lose everything, she thought, but he was letting her go, she could hear his footsteps coming up close behind her as she was walking up the stairs. Then he was following her to the front door, she could hear his voice say, "Call me tomorrow to let me know what times you'll be free to see me next week . . ."

She said yes without looking back, feeling unsteady as she was walking down the porch steps and out to the cab thinking how feeble and destroyed she must look, but the driver didn't seem to notice, and in fact didn't glance back even once at her greased and spiked hair, he was a Westerner and lamenting his move to the godforsaken East, and after he'd let her out on the corner of Hopewell and Bank she walked back to Habib's but he was already closed, then she walked to the convenience store up at the top of the hill.

And then the next morning she didn't even want to call Ekstrand to say she wouldn't be coming back — there was no law that said she had to — she wanted to forget all about him, her early-morning dreams had been populated by soundproof rooms and heavy cold doors, the whole careless family life on Daly Avenue going on up above her — she even walked to work by a different route, not wanting to run into him — but when she got home at six, the message light on her phone was flashing and when she punched in her code she heard a click on the line. The following night while she was shaking a bouquet of parsley under cold water she turned off the tap to hear the phone ringing. This time it was a sweet-voiced child, and when she said to her, "Who *is* this?" the child said, "Sorry, I must have the wrong number." There were two more clicks the next night, and the following morning, just as she was leaving for work, there was another call. She picked it up to hear the voice of the child from the call yesterday: "Is Dorothy there?" This seemed to her to be the worst thing of all, Ekstrand using his children to make his calls to her, she could feel the wary weight of Ekstrand's listening on another phone, and at the end of the evening when she came out of the shower to see that the red light was again flashing she punched in her code to hear his voice stiffly saying, "Hey Claire, I'm just calling to confirm our appointment for tomorrow. I have you written down for 5:10, please give me a call if there's anything that's going to stop this from happening . . ." She took the phone off the hook overnight, and even slept well, and the next morning she left a message for him with his receptionist to let him know she was going through financial difficulties and wouldn't be able to come back.

That night when she got home the red light was already flashing and then there was Ekstrand's voice again, this time sounding rehearsed, emotional: "Sorry to hear your decision. I was planning to give you a free treatment today since I kept you overtime last time and it was probably hard on your budget. Hopefully we can resolve this somehow. I was looking forward to seeing your progress . . ." a long pause here, and when he spoke again he sounded almost as if he'd been crying ". . . and seeing your growth." Then, after another pause: "It's not the money that matters, it's the interest in you that I was concerned about. Seeing the changes. Hopefully I didn't do anything that displeased you" – here his voice sounded desperate but prissy, breathless again – "and hopefully we can get you going again and finish what we got started. So. Give me a call back please, Claire. . . . Bye for now."

While she was drinking her breakfast tea the next morning, the phone rang again. She stood alerted, let it go to the tape. Another click. But that night when she got home there was no red light flashing to warn her that she had not yet been forgotten.

The wind was wild off and on all the following weekend. It came in great gusts. Swooping in to push at the storm door of the kitchen, it made the glass in its windows squeak. But after lunch the day turned into a bright and unusually hot Saturday afternoon for May, and a little after two, Claire took a bus out to Earlton, then walked toward the field of white tents just beyond the east end of the town. She could see a long line of cars parked at the edge of a sunlit irrigation ditch and on the far side of a wooden bridge, arched as a bridge in China, she could see Declan Farrell standing talking to two men wearing cameras slung over their shoulders. There was something bashful about him as he stood and talked to these men, something boyish and eager to please. An eager boy trying to impress, with a shy boyish bravado, two man-of-the-world fathers.

She cut off to the left to steer clear of his little group, then detoured over to the Acupuncture Tent where a tiny Chinese doctor had rolled a chart down from a bit of temporary scaffolding and was using a bamboo stick to tap at acupuncture points on an enlarged and densely numbered human ear. The little doctor was dressed in black cotton trousers and a white cotton jacket that gave him the look of one of the waiters at the Ho Ho Café, and because of this she at first found it difficult to concentrate on what he was saying. The problem, too, after he'd rolled up the pink ear, was that he was speaking so poetically that she was seduced to the point where her mind, caught up in the beauty of the words, was too often tempted to wander. He quoted something (or someone) called the Nei Jing. He said, "The Nei Jing say, 'Man possesses four seas and twelve meridians, which are like rivers that flow into the sea.'" And then he named, as if they were soups on a menu, the four seas:

The sea of nourishment
The sea of blood
The sea of energy
The sea of the bone marrow . . .

Then he was speaking of the pulse again, quoting some ancient Oriental authority on the body: "On a spring day the pulse is floating, like a fish swimming on the waves; on a summer day it is superficial, in the skin —"

At this point Claire noticed one of the men she had seen talking to Declan Farrell taking the pulse of the woman beside him and smiling down at her. But where was Declan Farrell? She looked all around her but couldn't see him, and she again tried to pay attention to the words of the Chinese doctor as he was saying, "On an autumn day it is below the skin, like an insect creeping into its winter shelter; on a winter day it is in the bone, hidden like an insect asleep for the winter . . ." And while the doctor was listing the Seven Emotions – anger, anxiety, concentration, joy, grief, fear, and fright – and was saying, "Excessive anger injures the liver, excessive anxiety injures the lungs, excessive concentration injures the spleen, excessive joy injures the heart . . ." words bobbed around in her head, words like *field* and *force field*, and she wondered if he was meaning a kind of scattering of the heart energy, Oriental medicine being so obsessed with contraction and scatter. And it was at this same moment that she looked up to see Declan Farrell standing three people to the left of one of the men with the cameras, beside him a petitely gleaming woman, her brown bell of hair shining in the Earlton sunlight.

After the numbered pink ear was rolled up, a daffily hopeful-looking man in a paper party hat climbed up on a tree stump to announce a talk on bioenergetic theory by Dr. Declan Farrell, and as he was speaking, people began to move in the direction of a grove of trees at the western end of the field. But by the time they'd all arrived and were milling about under the beech trees, Declan Farrell seemed in doubt about where he would stand. He stood in the shade of the tallest of the trees, but then walked out into the bright sunlight in the middle of the clearing. People began to drop their jackets and sweaters and then to sit down on them on the hard ground. But now Declan was changing his mind again and seemed so indecisive that people began to get up, wander off. Claire heard a sunburned man whose sunhat looked like a pith helmet call out to two girls who were walking by, "When the hell is this show going to get off the ground?" and she worried that Declan Farrell would be left without an audience, that he would be left with no one, that he would be publicly obliged to stand talking to only two or three people (she being one of the two or three) and she couldn't bear it for him, the prospect of any kind of public shame, as she dropped her jacket on the ground and sat down next to the man with the pith helmet. Who then cynically smiled and said to her, "So who is this guy anyway?"

"He's a medical doctor, but he's given all of that up."

"So is he a Reichian or what?"

"I think he might be a little bit Reichian," she said, not planning to let on that she actually knew him.

"An orgasm a day keeps the doctor away?"

She smiled.

The man in the pith helmet took his pith helmet off, and turned to Claire. "My name is Mitchell."

"Claire," said Claire. Then after the slightly disorienting silence that so often follows the exchange of names she said, "The way he sees it, every single important emotional event that happens to a person is laid down in the body."

Mitchell said he knew the type. He fitted his sun helmet back on again, using a primping hand at the front and another at the back to get the right tilt for parody. "Za body iss a clue," he said. "And iss also a map and a history book . . ." But Claire's eyes were on Declan Farrell again, who at last seemed to have found himself a spot that would do, under the largest of the trees. By now only two other people were sitting waiting. Still, he seemed calm as he stood in apparent comfort to begin his introduction. And within three minutes he had an audience. Where had they come from? Up out of the ground? They had come from all over, he was the Pied Piper of Earlton, there really is something almost shamanistic about him, thought

Claire, mesmerized, as she sat watching him move in the windy
and shady light, demonstrating certain useful techniques to help
people breathe better, teaching people how to let their feet feel
true contact with the ground.

When his talk was over, a group of women admirers gathered with tight love around him. Many of them were in their
late forties, early fifties — vibrant older women who seemed
affectionate toward him, jokingly maternal. They spoke easily
with him as if they knew him well. It was his birthday, they
were taking turns hugging him and calling him the birthday
boy, but then there was a little tremor in the group as people
turned to look eastward to watch nine or ten women come
walking toward them across the parched open field. The woman
at the head of this procession, picking her delicate way over
twigs and stubble, was the woman who had come to the fair
with Declan Farrell.

Who was now calling out to her, "Hello, love!"

She came up to him for an embrace, and as the group
around him parted to make way for her, she said in a voice
that was either babyish or Southern, "I walked all the way over
here in my *bare* feet." And the circle of older women, bright-
bloused and bright-eyed, all smiled down at her with a terrible
predatory affection.

At the Institute the following Monday afternoon, Claire spoke to Declan Farrell about her tendency to become "just a little bit obsessive."

"Just a little bit obsessive," he said, and she could hear that his voice had a smile in it. And so she quickly corrected herself: "I *know*, you can't say just a little bit, can you? About obsession? It's always a whole lot more than just a little bit . . ."

"But a tendency to become obsessive is something we can definitely work on by doing work with the body."

"What I've been thinking though" — she was speaking quickly, in an apprehensive rush, as she was taking her leave of him — "is that if I'm going to be getting into something fairly long-term here, then I should probably look around for a bit, decide what sort of treatment I really want to pursue . . ."

Did he mind? Hard to tell. But he gave her a name: Dr. Alan Breit.

She called Alan Breit the following morning to see if he could give her an appointment on her next day off. His voice was intelligent, British, and (in the manner of the best British voices) sexually wistful. He said, "I could fit you in, I think, on Thursday morning . . ."

~~~~
~~~~

Just before midnight on Wednesday night it started to rain, and the sound of it moving over the roof made Claire feel less alone as she drank a cup of camomile tea (strong, with two tea bags in it) before turning off her light. Then she lay in the dark listening to the multiplying ticks of the rain, the tiny ticks on the leaves, until she at last fell asleep, dreaming that she couldn't sleep, but finally understanding that she must have dozed at least because a sound of banging startled her awake sometime toward morning. She sat up, then decided it was nothing, only the wind slamming a door shut, somewhere farther down the street. The rain was by now heavier too: dense, sedative. She got up to pee and on her way back to bed remembered a dream she'd been having about Steff. He was telling her that he'd been diagnosed with a disease called anti-macassar and he needed her to come with him to a Special Treatment clinic over in Sandy Hill so he could get an injection. Words bobbed in her head — injection, erection, little games of the unconscious — but once she'd crawled back into bed the rain almost instantly put her to sleep again.

The wind blew her up Dr. Breit's red brick walk in the rain. But the house startled her, it looked so abandoned, closed up for the season. But what season? It wasn't even winter. White blinds were pulled all the way down in all of its windows. Had the man with the sexually wistful voice forgotten all about her? She found the thought unbearable. To be forgotten by a therapist! She also found mail wedged between the two doors, another bad sign — two airmail letters from England, a rained-on copy of a magazine called *Motorcycle News* — and after ringing the bell, dipped her knees to pick up the letters and so was nearly toppled sideways into the hallway when the door was pulled back to let her come in.

She stood to present the man who'd opened the door to her with his damp correspondence.

But he didn't at all look as she had imagined he would look. He instead seemed almost pathologically indolent. He was even looking as if he had spent his entire life up till now doing nothing more arduous than lapping up the contents of giant saucers of cream.

He also looked familiar.

But he seemed to be concluding that she looked familiar as well. "I have a feeling we've met." He relieved her of her soaked raincoat, fitted it neatly into a cramped closet that gave off a faint odour of straw hats, abandoned rubber. "I do know that I know you from somewhere . . ."

She followed him down a long hallway hung with ornate wall-rugs that had round little mirrors the size of dental mirrors stitched into them. But the rest of his house was extremely cold and smelled unpleasantly of newly stripped and polyurethaned floors, new paint. He led her into a room with a pale-pink futon on the floor. There were also several large pale paisley cushions scattered about. In terracottas, pale pinks. He offered her coffee, then took off for a darker part of the house to prepare it, calling out to her to find herself a chair, make herself right at home.

But there were no chairs there.

"Cream?" he called out to her.

From his giant saucer?

"Just black, thanks!"

He came back into the freezing room bearing a black lacquer tray with two grey pottery mugs on it, set it down on the floor, then settled himself down behind it. She followed his example and sat down across from him. Out in the kitchen he'd remembered where they had met — at a party at the home of an architect friend of Steff's.

"Yes," she said. "I remember that too." She had the feeling she would find him easy to talk to. It was the kind of morning it was too, so windy and dark, a morning made for revelations and gossip.

She asked him what she would wear for their sessions.

"A bathing suit," he told her. "Or shorts and a top. The sort of thing you'd wear for a gym class. Or anything, really, that won't restrict your freedom of movement." He took a little sip of his coffee. "You do look most awfully well, I must say. Much better than you looked the last time I saw you. You've lost weight, I think."

"A bit." She could feel a reluctance in his eyes to take leave of her breasts, and she was all at once aware of beginning to feel a little uneasy in his presence, even though she didn't feel he was all that attracted to her, not really. She decided she should establish the fact that she was still looking around, that she hadn't had time to make up her mind yet. But instead she found herself telling him about her meeting with Declan Farrell. She told him that Declan Farrell had said she was living too much up in her head.

He gave her body a rather prolonged diagnostic look, then gave her his conclusion: *"That's* a bit glib."

This should have pleased her but did not. She apparently did not want to hear Declan being called glib, even though she was the one who had arranged for him to be called it. She felt a childish desire to say: He didn't say a word against you, you shouldn't say a word against him. But now he was only asking her what sorts of things made her angry.

All she wanted was to learn how to sleep. But would it be accurate to say that not having learned it made her angry? She didn't know. If she really thought about it there was hardly anything that didn't make her angry. It was just that being asked to list her angers made her forget what they were.

But had *he* fallen asleep? The sight of his closed eyes filled her with a dread close to terror. Caught in the grip of it, she quickly came up with ways to excuse his nodding off. The moment he flinched awake, embarrassed, she was primed to cry out, "Don't apologize! Please! The rain always makes me feel incredibly sleepy too. And it's so dark out!"

Sleepily, a man drugged by the rain, he half-opened an eye. "So what about you, then? Where do you fit into the hierarchy of your family of origin? Not the baby, I take it?"

They shared a small laugh over that, at least until he made the decision to speculate. "If there were three children, you were the middle one. If there were five children, you were still the middle one. If there were four children you were the second oldest one. You were the mediator, you were the guilty one."

"The third child of seven." Then, not to be too much the mediator, the guilty one, she asked him how much his fee would be.

A pale man, he seemed to grow paler. He said he thought he could give her a reduced rate.

She thanked him for his kindness, then asked him how, exactly, they would work together.

He glanced at her knees, then looked quickly away. He indicated the futon. "You'd lie here, on the futon . . ."

In my little bathing suit . . .

". . . and I'd be working on breathing with you. Breaking up your energy blocks. . . ." He squeezed up a doughy fistful of flesh from his own belly. She imagined him breathily leaning over her, squeezing her breasts. She pictured herself being so alarmed that she wouldn't be able to distinguish between what was lechery and what was therapeutic. What if she was too anxious to speak, too anxious even to ask him to turn the thermostat up?

Out in the chilled hallway, drawing on her damp raincoat, she worried that she'd feel obligated to see him again, now that he'd offered her a reduction in fee. She felt burdened by gratitude and, because of it, suspicious. Why didn't he have any other patients waiting? Did he even *have* other patients? She told him she would have to call him to set up another appointment, her schedule was a little uncertain just now.

He said, "Fine." Then he said it again, which meant that it wasn't.

She would write to him, she would write and tell him no, but she felt terribly anxious while she was thinking this, they were practically shoved up against each other in the narrow hallway. She was afraid to look into his eyes, she was too afraid she would find something desolate and even destroyed there.

But when she stepped out into the wind she felt wild with relief in the rainy morning. She walked and walked, too excited by relief to look for a bus. By the time she reached Echo Drive the rain had stopped and the wind was just blowing the fog around, and now and then there was a lone raindrop in it. But the wind in the treetops was surfy, huge, and there was even a small windstorm as she turned onto Hopewell, one of those yellow windstorms of late spring that make pollen rain down on the world to lie in a fleecy yellow snow on the hoods of cars, on pavements.

The Polish émigré who always made her think of a wood-cutter came walking toward her on the pollen-slippery side-walk as she was turning the corner to her own street, a man who was so extraordinarily handsome that nothing could undermine his eerie glamour, not even the fact that the sleeves of his navy coat were as short as a boy's and looked as if they'd been dipped into a broth of splinters. Years of sun and wind had baked or blown age either to or from him so that he was either young and looked old, or old and looked young. He was also carrying his pink plastic radio high up on one shoulder. Could a smile be both mocking and consoling? His was. It made her wonder: Is he wise or is he a madman? His radio was (as always) tuned to a classical-music station, this time playing Handel. But she was always filled with fear whenever she saw him. Not of him personally, but of what he might stand for (her future).

"*Dzien dobry,*" he said.

She could already hear the phone up in her apartment ringing as she was pushing open the street door. She stormed the stairs to savagely unlock her own door, then pounced on the phone to cut it off mid-ring. But it only turned out to be her mother, calling from Saskatchewan. And so she braced herself for the inevitable question: "Do you have any new men in your life at the moment, darling?" (Yes, darling Mother, it just so happens that I've spent this very morning with a new man. We sat on the floor of his ice-cold front room and he's incredibly fat, which is really not all that surprising when you consider that he lives on nothing but saucers of cream.) But this time there was no dutiful small talk, no preamble to "Your daddy had a fatal heart attack this morning just after breakfast, can you come home for the funeral?"

After she'd put down the phone, Claire stood beside it for a timeless small time. She felt shaken but calm, almost elated. And she even knew why: because her father was free now. She also had calls to make. To Dr. Tenniswood. To Megan Battle, her replacement. To Air Canada. On compassionate grounds, she was given a late-afternoon flight to Saskatoon. She went into the kitchen and looked out the window. The rain had stopped, but towering dark clouds were slowly moving in again, it was such a drenched and windy green day. She made herself a thick potato and mayonnaise sandwich, then got a tin of Portuguese sardines out of a cupboard (so much pinker and more delicious than Canadian sardines) and carried it, along with a package of crackers and several packets of tea (camomile tea, Think-O$_2$ tea) into her bedroom to be fitted into her flight bag along with her toothbrush and nightgown, then dug a pair of low-heeled black pumps out of her closet. She wanted to travel in comfort, but when she shoved back her row of brown and burgundy corduroy trousers she decided it would be best to wear a black skirt that could also do for the funeral. She didn't even own a black dress. All her clothes were the kind of clothes she could wear under a lab coat. She dropped three Valium pills into a bottle of magnesium oxide tablets (good to bring in case she got leg cramps) because there was absolutely no point in kidding herself: the nights she was in the magnetic range of her mother she would, without pills, find sleep to be totally out of the question.

Although out in the world it was already spring, the plane flew into a mild sunny day in the winter, flew above clouds turned into a field of snow that looked as if cross-country skiers had endlessly criss-crossed it all one of those mild afternoons in late winter, the snow having already started to die. But at Winnipeg, where Claire changed planes, the day was hot and clear, and once she was airborne again she could look down on real fields, tiny rivers.

The plane landed in Saskatoon three hot hours before sundown and she walked fast across the tarmac with the other passengers, as if the city would fly away if they didn't all race to catch up with it. Inside the terminal she went to look for a *StarPhoenix*, even though it was too soon for her father's death to be in it. But she wanted it to be, she wanted him to be praised. Then into a taxi, the leisurely sweep into town. She looked and looked, to both left and right. She had forgotten that there was so much green in the city, that the trees could be so soft and green in the overheated twilight, that they could speak so of younger memories in which – at nineteen – she had dreamed of the whole sweet life of the future.

One of her brothers had made a reservation for her at a downtown highrise on Fifth Avenue, in one of the tower's hotel suites. Fifth Avenue: she had forgotten that. Small-town streets named after the streets of New York. There was even a Broadway. And the Broadway Bridge. How American the West was. In the East you would never find a street called Broadway, streets in the East were named after the kings and queens of England.

A turquoise glass canopy on four steel poles sheltered the brick path that led into the tower and there was a glass elevator on one side of it. As she was paying her driver, she could see it rise up, its lighted interior going up empty.

There was no desk, and no one to greet her, but over the phone her oldest brother had given her the code for the lock box in the lobby. She punched in the numbers, and both the metal door of the box and the key for her hotel room fell onto the floor.

When she got off the elevator on 21 she went over to the windows to look down over the South Saskatchewan River and its Roman bridges. Didn't Saskatoon have seven bridges? Just as Rome had seven hills? One cold November Sunday when she was seven or eight she had walked with her father along the embankment and looked out at the giant lily pads of glittering ice being borne swiftly by on the river. And the little red brick church was still down there too, on its green apron of lawn, although she had never before seen it from so great a height, its black steeple just high enough to still be in the sun. Below it the green park, its tallest trees tall enough to be in the last light. Everything seemed clearer, more memorable, because her

father had died. There was still sun on the highest hills beyond
the embankment on the other side of the water.

But during the minute it took her to walk down the length
of the corridor the day turned into night, and when she
opened the door to her room on the opposite side of the
hallway the view, through a wall of windows, was of a great
city at night, a city that was so flat and far-flung that its lights
seemed to stretch out forever across the Saskatchewan plain.
And towering over that prairie world, the Sturdy Stone
Building, a kind of monstrous Aztec Eiffel Tower dominat-
ing the miles and miles of bright lights. It was so out of scale
that it made flat-topped Saskatoon look like a city in Mexico.
Or a city in Arizona. Saskatoon-Phoenix.

The hotel suite must have recently been renovated, it was fur-
nished with low glass tables and sofas upholstered in a new-
looking cream fabric patterned with silver leaves. She went into
the bedroom to find a wide double bed and, hanging above it, a
print of a Victorian woman in a long white dress wading down
a dim weedy field given life here and there by torn splotches of
red meant to represent poppies. She took off her perspired-in
jacket and hung it in the closet, then went out to the kitchen and
opened her sardines and crackers. Once she had finished eating
— it was, after all, two hours earlier here than it was at home —
she again went out to the elevator and sank down to the city.

Which she now saw as a surreal city, the Yellowhead
Highway vs. the Yellow Brick Road, Saskatchewan the Canadian
version of Kansas, and then here it was again, that great and
weirdly comical concrete monolith, the Sturdy Stone Building,
a splay-legged stone giant towering over the flat little metrop-
olis and, just beyond it, an automated primeval chirping at the

intersections of the streets close to City Hall. But what is all this chirping *for*, she wondered, then it occurred to her that it must be for blind people, they would need to have some kind of instructions on how to hurry across the street, Western drivers were such cowboys, but when she turned back toward the park (not feeling quite safe on this street after all) she saw the way the bellhops carrying suitcases into the hotel across the street from the Bessborough were dressed like Hitler Jugend, and it was at this point that she considered crossing over to the Bessborough for coffee in the little café up on the mezzanine – what was it called, Tree Tops? – so she could sit at one of the window tables and look out over the floodlit lawn at the back. But she wanted to be out in the city even more, it was a Thursday night and people were still out on the street, she wanted to be walking among them. Which had to be wrong, on the day her father had died. Even if she was continuing to feel absolute relief for him. She also couldn't stop hearing the lines from "Chelsea Hotel" that kept repeating themselves in her head. But wasn't that a song about suicide? Well, so it was then, what of it?

A cowboy wearing a white Stetson was coming toward her as she was walking in the direction of the Midtown Plaza. She decided that he must be from somewhere even farther west because except for the Hutterite cowboys dressed all in black and wearing black Stetsons, Saskatoon wasn't really all that much of a cowboy town. "Hey!" he called out to her. "Hey. You look lost."

"I'm not lost," she told him. "How can I be lost? This is almost my hometown."

"Almost! So what *happened*? Didn't we make the *grade*?" Dancing backwards, or at least dancing as much backwards as his drunkenness would allow. Really, it was an attempt at dancing backwards that was more like stumbling sideways to the music of a joke only he could hear.

But then she saw that he wasn't really all that drunk after all; his eyes were undrunk as he asked her if she would care to join him for a drink at the Senator Hotel.

She said, "I can't, I'm too tired, I have to get up early tomorrow morning for an appointment." She noticed that she was unable to say that her father had died, it was news that she couldn't bring herself to give to a stranger. And yet she wanted to. Wanted to say, This is the real world, this is real life, this is what happened: my father died.

"An appointment," he said in a marvelling voice.

"Yes."

"How dull."

"Not really."

"Not really," he mimicked her.

"And so I have to go now."

"So go then. Am I stopping you?"

No one was in the lobby when she stepped into the glass elevator, and her relief at being alone was so extreme that she almost mistook it for happiness as she looked out at the lights on the far side of the dark water.

Once she got back to her room she made herself a cup of Think-O_2 tea and then stood at the big windows drinking it while she looked out at the lights. It still amazed her that at nine o'clock this morning she'd had no idea at all that by sundown she'd be so many hundreds — or wasn't it even thousands? — of miles from home. She looked out at the Sturdy Stone Building in the eerie hot blue of the prairie night and remembered her father reading her the story about the houses of the three little pigs: the house made out of straw, the house made out of bricks, the house made of something else, she thought it was sticks. But there could also have been a fourth building, a sturdy stone building, or at least this was how she'd thought of it when she was a child, but at some point someone must have explained to her that the sturdy stone building was only called the sturdy stone building because it was named after two Saskatoon politicians, a Mr. Sturdy and a Mr. Stone. Wasn't her father the one who'd taken the time to tell her this? She remembered him reading aloud to her at bedtime. The story about the Snow Queen, and *The Wind in the Willows*, his voice in such a familiar and soothing monotone (from exhaustion, she now understood, although at the time it had just seemed to be the voice he used to read aloud to his children).

At ten the next morning, an uncle of her mother's came to pick her up for the drive north. She sat beside him in a car that smelled offensively new, her chilled feet in the ballet slippers she'd brought along on the plane to use as actual slippers. She was so longing for him to drive faster that she kept tensing her feet to urge him over the speed limit. She knew that her father was dead, but she wanted to get to him in time to say goodbye to him before he died. This didn't make any sense, even to her, but her feet believed it.

She was also afraid that her mother would be angry with her because she hadn't brought the right clothes for the funeral, she only had her black skirt and her grey silk shirt, her grey jacket. Not that her father would have given a damn, he would have just wanted beautiful music and people wearing whatever they happened to be wearing when they heard he was dead, he

wouldn't want people dressed for grief and getting all miffed
behind spooky black veils, he'd hate all that, he really would,
and she began to see herself as the ambassador for her father,
as the one who must stand up for his rights, what he would
want, against the self-serving demands of the living, and she
looked out at the prairie and saw herself at his funeral, heard
voices behind her here and there: the only daughter, his
favourite, she was always such a beautiful girl, she'll miss him.
She felt deeply ashamed of herself, using her sorrow as a platform on which she was the star, but it did seem to help her.

But now they were already driving through Turtleford,
then beyond it, driving west to St. Walburg, stomach-
dropping country, home, almost home, then there was the
house, set far back from the highway and still painted a sodden
Italian mustard, a Tuscan villa on the Saskatchewan plain, and
as they were slowly proceeding up the long drive she remembered being drunk at a party one night last summer and telling
people that when she was a child her mother brought so many
cushions and fabrics home from Ikea that she thought Ikea
must be a country in Africa. A fabrication, of course, but now
they were already here and walking across gravel to find the
house crowded with brothers and wives and girlfriends and
nephews and neighbours, her mother somehow fiercely vague
– could someone be that? – in tan slacks and a black sweatshirt, glancing over at her to say, "Oh *there* you are, why don't
you come with me to the funeral parlour and we'll pick out a
casket for Daddy . . ."

"But didn't Daddy always say he wanted to be cremated?"

It was as if she had just said something in extremely bad
taste, for her mother's look was now the look of the other

mother. Not the mother who wrote on mauve notepaper "Much much love and kiss-kiss," but the mother who stared at her children coldly, her fixed gaze inspecting, unkind. "Please don't start making complications, it's too difficult —"

And so before she had time to say hello to any of her brothers or her little nephews she was already off again, climbing up into the cab of the truck with her mother, then they were bumping out to the highway, fields coming at them backwards, fields spinning around them — I'm going to be sick, she thought, I'm going to throw up if I don't get some air — and she tried to roll down the window although it felt sealed, the air airless, but at last she was able to squeakily roll it part of the way down, the hot wind coming into the truck as they were rattling toward North Battleford.

I've forgotten all of it, she thought, but it wasn't true, it was all here, she remembered everything, then she was asking her mother about the brother in Tanzania and the two brothers in London and her mother was telling her that they wouldn't be able to get home for the funeral, but now she was also noticing something she really *had* forgotten: that her mother's way of announcing her virtues was to apologize for them. "I apologize for all the commotion back at the house," her mother was saying — her mother! who never apologized! — "but I *did* want to invite everyone to sleep over who needs to sleep over. I'm just not a selfish person. I wish that I could be, it would make things so much easier. But I'm not, it can't be helped, I've always been generous. So be it."

The funeral parlour, a small white colonial mansion — could a mansion be small? — had a black door with a brass knocker on it. But there was also a bell. Claire's mother, pressing it, whispered to her, "You wait in the reception room while I deal with the undertaker."

Claire stood in a formal room whose wallpaper was silver with tiny white ferns on it. She still hadn't cried, there was only a high nervy ticking up on the right side of her forehead, not quite a headache, she rubbed at it with her fingers while she tried to identify a clop-clopping from farther down the street. It kept getting louder until a polished brown horse went smartly by, pulling a black carriage, a man in a black coat and top hat up in the driver's seat, a cargo of women in sunglasses and cardigans in the back. Were they tourists? In North Battleford? But where was her father? Was he shelved away in cold storage in some room at the back?

She had to find herself something to read, if she didn't distract herself she was going to go mad. She went over to a small magazine stand and picked up a copy of *National Geographic*, then sat down and flipped through it. But she wasn't able to take any of it in.

Then home again: her nephews running to her to show her their new yellow kites, each kite with a big blue fish on it, wanting her to watch as they made them fly, and she did watch for ten minutes or so, then walked around to the front of the house to look for her brothers. She found them talking in a conspiratorial little group down on the front lawn, all of them barefoot in the hot spring afternoon and all of them smoking. They were country boys and they were all still smokers. She accepted a cigarette when Felix, her youngest brother (looking impenetrable in black jeans and dark glasses) offered it to her, in memory of their father.

The screen door slammed a few moments later, and their mother, who'd now changed into black nylons and a black dress, came out and stood on the verandah to watch for the hearse. And here it already was, winking in the bright sunlight as it turned onto their laneway, then making its way up their drive. It came to a dignified stop to the left of the verandah and four undertakers (four farm boys) in navy-blue suits got out of it. They carefully eased the grey coffin out of its back end, then carried it up the verandah stairs and into the house. Claire and her brothers watched as it was carried up the steps, and they were still watching when the four undertakers came back out again. They all watched as the four of them got into their deluxe black panel truck and drove sedately away.

"The fab four," said Max, and they all smiled with a certain impressed sadness at that. But Max was the most formally dressed of all Claire's brothers, in a white shirt and black dress pants, his hair combed back into a ponytail of fair quills and held in a circlet of berry-red beads and black twine.

But now Helmut, their oldest brother, was narrowing his eyes at Claire. "So you're a college girl now."

"After a fashion."

"How long has *this* been going on?"

"For three years," she told him. "As a matter of fact."

"Then what?"

"Then I'll have to do a graduate degree, then my doctorate, so I can teach." But she was thinking, with a kind of despair, of the long years ahead of her.

"Claire as a professor."

"The thought amuses you?"

"Just a bit."

"It frightens me."

"Why do it then?"

"Because the one thing I've learned from all these years of being your sister is that terror is thrilling."

Her other brothers laughed, and Helmut even laughed too, but then he couldn't control himself, he had to reach over to shove her dark glasses back up on her nose. She was surprised, but only batted him away. "My brother, El Mosquito." He had always been her most bossy brother. He was called Uncle Hell by his two little nephews, and whenever he sent Claire a Christmas card he always wrote inside it in green ink, "A very happy Christmas from all of us here." And then, in parentheses, "Uncle Hell and family." But at this point Max, her sweetest brother, offered her another cigarette, then pulled a lighter out of his pocket and held the flame out to her. "Here, Claire. Let me light that for you."

Helmut said, "This is the brand Dad smoked."

Felix looked over at him. "The brand that killed him."

"Overwork killed him," said Helmut.

"That too," said Max.

The phone ringing in the middle of the night was what Claire remembered most, her father's footsteps running down the stairs in the dark, her own quick run over to her bedroom window just in time to see him, his overshoes still unbuckled, wading through the blown snow out to his truck with his canvas veterinarian's bag and then using his right arm as a giant windshield wiper to wipe the left-hand side of the windshield clear of snow.

"Anyway, last year, just after New Year's," said Max, "he switched to a pipe."

"*Did* he!" said Claire and she was almost ashamed of how animated and social her voice sounded. "You know, I can *see* that! He was more of a pipe type!"

Her brothers all laughed at this, and their laughter must have been what their mother heard when she came back out onto the verandah. She looked down on them all as if her low opinion of them saddened her. Then she called to them to come up on the verandah and help her with the flowers, she wanted the flowers to be carried into the parlour.

When she followed her brothers into the cool of the shaded parlour with the flowers, Claire was relieved that the coffin was still closed. It was a grey coffin and its lid had a streamlined long lip like a dolphin's. It was a relief to have something to do, to be able to get away from it, to have to go back out to the verandah for more flowers. And so back and forth she went, among her brothers. But as they were fetching and carrying she was overwhelmed by a longing to see her father again, although only if he could still be alive. She felt a fear of seeing him dead.

The coffin looked too light to contain him and feeling a need to get away from it — its greyness (its greyness, Your Highness) — and away too from the chilled fragrance of the banks of carnations and lilies, and above all away from her mother, rearranging the flowers around it as if she considered it an elegant but slightly problematic addition to the decor, Claire went down the steps to the sunnier living room with its sun-blocked Peruvian rugs and Mexican baskets and all its little chests and commodes in faded black, faded coral, and the house became (or had never stopped being) the house she had known at sixteen, seventeen, a house that was an endless credential, all the darker emotions held at bay by great paintings and a great distribution of light. But at the same time she loved it and felt convinced she would have sold her soul to live in a house with just these rugs and this view: the bleached fields and the wind-break of cyprus trees in the distance, the trees looking too eccentric to be mourners, too like upright Victorians in dark coats who belonged to some sort of stern worthy sect. And then there were all the visual pranks and odd conjunctions: her mother's wedding bouquet dismantled and its parts mounted behind glass like a series of botanical specimens; a black whale Helmut had painted on the white piano; an unframed canvas of a small white arm boldly thrust out, a bouquet of blue flowers in its fist, the arm jubilant, disembodied, a brave little arm that made her eyes fill with tears for her father.

~~~~

Later in the afternoon, while her brothers' wives and girlfriends were out in the big kitchen making the supper, Claire sat with her two little nephews on the sofa in the parlour to read one of their storybooks to them. She breathed in the smell of their hair as she was turning the pages, a mucky toffee-and-dirt smell, and as she was reading them the story of a little boy pulling his sled through a blizzard she recalled a visit they'd made to her at Christmas and the way they had flung themselves at her, catching her thighs in tight thigh-locks and impeding her walking anywhere, and the way they had also charged at her in their Scandinavian sweaters and little red leggings, the ones that made them look so bow-legged and comical in their tiny old men's maroon leather slippers, their paintings flopping and dripping with paint, damp heavy paintings in the browny blues and muddy reds the paints would turn into the times they'd used them to paint (with the help of their spilled pineapple juice) the damp sun or pond in the middle of a landscape. "Now let's look at *this* book of pictures," she said, and she opened a book of reproductions of twentieth-century North American paintings, each waxy page announcing a print: the totem-pole paintings all luridly oiled and streamlined, the more impressionistic ones of women sitting at tables or walking in leafy gardens all blurry and swift.

Today was also the birthday of the littlest nephew, and while a chocolate cake was waiting at the end of the long table in the kitchen – three yellow baby candles stuck into it – and they were all (except for their mother, who was upstairs, lying down) just about to pull out their chairs so they could sit down to eat, the older nephew careened past it with a roar and a tilting low-flying wing, swiping the candles and the whole moist chocolate roof off the top of it while at the same time extinguishing the tiny fires and conveniently bearding his sleeve and even one of his armpits with peaks of wet chocolate, which led to his being smacked on the bottom, then banished (with a howl) up the stairs to his room. Three new little yellow candles were then poked into the cake and a new match was struck to light the tiny new fires (the cake looking scorched without its chocolate coat), and as the supper slowly and awkwardly progressed in the non-birthday boy's absence (mashed turnips and overcooked green beans and very pink ham and sweet yams) and progressed too, through a constrained silence, a child-has-been-punished silence, somehow presided over by an air of unexchanged glances having to wait until after the meal was over to meet other unexchanged glances, Claire found herself longing to go up to visit the young offender, the little criminal, longing to bring him back downstairs to have real food to eat, or at the very least she wished she could bring a plate of the birthday cake up to him, but she couldn't very well undermine the authority of his parents, and so she had to take consolation in picturing him squatting up in a corner of his room, triumphantly sucking at the sweetened wool of his sleeve.

〰〰〰

Claire stayed up late, talking to Max and Felix and Helmut until almost three. But as they were talking about their father and about local politics and also finishing off the leftover wine, Claire would now and then picture the Valium waiting upstairs for her in her flight bag like a promise that could never be broken.

At last she said goodnight to her brothers, then carried her wine upstairs with her to swallow down her pill. It was not the most brilliant idea to swallow it with wine, but it was only half a milligram and she wanted to be knocked out. She set her wine glass down on a chest carved by her father and after she got undressed drank the wine down like medicine to toss back the tiny white pill.

After she got into bed she fell asleep at once, immediately making her way through a long series of confused dreams until she found herself sitting next to a woman who was reading a book by a woman writer. The woman asked her if she'd ever heard of the book, but before Claire could see what it was called, the woman lowered a little brown velvet curtain over the title. A hard flurry of knocks came next, and she thought it was the same woman, but it was already morning, it was her mother, her greyly fair hair tied back with a narrow black velvet ribbon, then she was already sitting down on the end of the bed, depressing its mattress and making Claire's legs sink. Dressed in black slacks this morning, along with a black workshirt, she had already somehow managed to acquire a tan. But didn't she have a tan yesterday? She must have, and yet Claire's memory of her was that she'd been pale. She was also getting a bit of a moustache (bleached) and her eyes were making Claire feel sickly alert. "I've just been downstairs talking to Daddy."

"What do you mean?" whispered Claire, raising herself up on an elbow with such startled quickness that one of the lace straps of her nightgown fell halfway down her arm.

"I've just been sitting downstairs with him, down beside his coffin, talking to him."

After her mother had gone down to the kitchen, Claire picked up her watch and saw, with a moan of sleepy fury, that it was only ten after six. Childhood mornings that she hadn't been allowed to sleep in came back to her, early mornings when her mother simply could not bear to be the only one awake. This was when it had all begun, the accounting, the bitter arithmetic that was a half-awake attempt to add up how many hours of sleep she'd managed to extract from the night, although she couldn't honestly say that when she was a child she had minded being pulled out of sleep. Being awake was even almost always more fun than being asleep. And often there were treats: hot muffins with strawberry jam or a fast trip into North Battleford before breakfast to buy apple cider or hot cornbread. But now all she could think was: When is Mother ever going to learn that not letting sleeping people sleep is a criminal act? If *I* had a child, that would be rule number one: Let the sleeping child sleep. There was no point in trying to go back to sleep either, and sitting up to dully pull on her leg-fattened black pantyhose she remembered Donna, a friend of hers from school, asking her one afternoon when they were both in grade ten, "Does your mother ever look at you as if you're something she'd just like to *squish*?"

Oh yes, Donna, yes.

~~~~

Packed tightly between brothers solemnly singing all around her, Claire tried to concentrate on correctly singing the words of the hymns – the hymns, the massed force of them, somehow holding her up – but all she could think of was the way her father had never once made her feel ashamed to be herself. How many women could say the same of a father? But how unfair life was. And death. If only her mother could have been the one to die! She bowed her head as she was following her brothers out of the cathedral. Go in peace, darling Papa.

But on the way down the stone steps into the sunshine her right leg gave out on her, and if Max hadn't been beside her she would have fallen. Just for a moment it was as if there was only air, there was no leg there. "Hey," he said. "You okay?" She said she was, and in fact she seemed to be, but he kept his arm squeezed around her shoulders to support her as they were walking through the gate to the cemetery, and she held an arm around him too, feeling the sweet consolation of his male midriff, but too soon there was the odour of deep earth, shovelled up, the smell of the deep ditch for the coffin. Followed too soon by the fragrance of the healthy green grass that kept on being sunk into, by flocks of highly polished high-fashion black heels, on the way to the cars.

Back at the crowded house again Claire kept half-expecting her father to come into the big front room any minute. She thought, You should really *be* here, Dad, so many of the people who are here think really, really highly of you. Every time the front doorbell rang, she was the one who hurried to open it. And then, greeting whoever stood out on the doorstep, she could barely contain her disappointment. After she'd passed around trays of teacups and poured tea and over and over again said yes and yes we will and thank you, she slipped upstairs to look at the photo albums. She wanted to find a photograph of her father when he was four years old, and after leafing through only two of the albums she found him standing posed against a photographer's backdrop of a park in winter in either Berlin or Toronto. How very small he was, in his miniature boots and tiny belted coat. She worked the photograph out of the album and slid it into an envelope, sealed it, then hid it inside the deepest pocket of her jacket. A necessary precaution since her mother couldn't bear to see any of her possessions leave her house. Then she looked for photos of herself when she was in high school, but was able to find only one that conveyed any kind of thoughtful adolescent sadness, her hair brushed back and her eyes gone astoundingly dark, her pupils were so dilated. Which was when she was able to remember occasionally feeling pity for others. Pity for the few people her own age who were, thank God, even more inept and lonely than she was.

But now footsteps (her mother's!) were quickly coming up the stairs. She grabbed up her hairbrush and began to take quick swipes at her hair, she was always so afraid her mother was going to accuse her of something.

"What have you been doing up here all of this time? Everyone else is downstairs having tea . . ."

Claire's heart was beating wildly, she was so intensely aware of the light but illicit weight of the photograph in her left pocket. "I've just been looking at the photo albums. Pictures of Maxie and me when we were in high school. I just can't seem to stop looking at them."

"But how strange."

"You find it strange?"

"Yes, I do."

"But why?"

"Because it's only the past."

～～～～
～～～

Max was the one who offered to drive her to the Saskatoon airport on Sunday afternoon. Another desolate afternoon of prairie wind, perfect sun. They talked about their mother, her theatrical refusal to be consoled. They talked about their father too, a little. They'd always called him Dad, or sometimes (in Claire's case) Papa. Their mother they had always called Mother. Wouldn't *that* tell a stranger something? Wouldn't that even tell a stranger everything?

Beyond the windshield the plains passed by them slowly, endlessly. Max hung an arm out his window. "Good old

Prairies . . ." he said. Then he glanced over at Claire, raised his eyebrows at her. "Hypnotic, right?"

They laughed. "Right," said Claire, for she too found it next to impossible to stop watching the fields repeating themselves over and over. She wanted never to come back. The plains, the vast distances, all of it filled her with too much emotion. She worked her feet out of her pumps and drew them up on the car seat so that she could sit mermaid-style next to Max to say in a lighter voice, "Do people still call Saskatoon the Paris of the West?"

"Still! Did they *ever*?"

"They did sometimes when I was in high school."

"Meanwhile, back here in the Parisian hinterland . . ." said Max.

Claire smiled over at him with affection. "What do you think Mother will do now?"

"Get married again."

"Do you really think so?"

"Don't you?"

"Wouldn't any intelligent man be able to see through her?"

"Dad didn't."

True, but it seemed to Claire that Max was a little bit sad, with a sadness that must have settled into him months (or years, even) before their father's death. She had to control a desire to ask him if everything was all right. To ask: "Are you happy?" But she couldn't allow herself to ask it because it was a question she could not bear to be asked herself. And above all she could not bear to be asked it by the wrong person (by which she meant a kind person, a person like Max).

~~~~
~~~~

It was real night by the time the plane began its descent into Ottawa, and the city's fields of lights tilted to the left, to the right. Claire was gathering up her belongings, pulling the zipper across her flight bag, when she at last understood: she would never see her father again. She wanted not to get off the plane then, she wanted to fly back, she wished that on the way to the airport she had asked Max to drive her to the churchyard so that she could at least have sat with her father for ten minutes or so. This, she saw, would always be her regret, that she didn't go alone to his grave and sit beside it and try to be heard by him. Her throat hurt her and she had to turn her head away from the man sitting next to her to hold an arm over her eyes so that her seatmate (if he bothered to look) would decide that she was just trying to catch a few last stolen moments of sleep.

But as the plane taxied to a stop at the back of the terminal and people were sleepily standing to tip their luggage down from the storage compartments, a male elbow dug into one of her breasts, and this unexpected contact with softness so startled its owner that he turned to cast a frightened glance back at her. "Hey, sorry," he said. "Listen, I'm really, really sorry."

"That's all right, no problem. Really." But lately she too had been saying she was sorry too much. She said "Sorry" when people bumped into her or stepped on her toes; sometimes she even said "Sorry" in a sickeningly pleading little voice to herself. Sometimes she even wrote PLEASE NOTE on little cards she taped to the fridge, as if she felt she had to be eternally polite to the whole world, even to herself. Which was not at all like writing PLEASE REMEMBER, YOU IDIOT, TO BUY TOOTHPASTE AND

ONIONS, and then harshly underlining the PLEASE at least three times in irony and fury. She was not a Catholic, but walking into the terminal it occurred to her that she would have made a marvellous Catholic: weren't Catholics more or less honour-bound to apologize to each other and to God every other minute?

Waiting for her taxi, she analyzed her psychoanalysis with Dr. Gleidman. The first two years they had devoted to talking about her mother. The third year they had devoted to talking about books. She would bring novels to Gleidman and he would read them and after he'd read them they would have their own little Great Books discussion group. But one day toward the end of Year Three he'd tossed the envelope with her cheque in it onto his desk, and during the session that followed, his interpretation of her dreams was innovative in a way that had seemed engineered to make her appear infantile. When the hour was up, she sank down in the elevator to the lobby and because she was crying she didn't at first understand that it was raining out in the world. She was walking along Somerset Street when someone hurrying just behind her snapped open an umbrella and a male voice blew down to her: "Let me protect you." She'd looked up to see that its owner looked to be nine or ten years younger than she was — twenty-five, twenty-six — but there was also something of the favourite uncle about him. "But why are you crying?" (Smiling down at her peeringly.) "I've just come from seeing my psychiatrist." At this he had smiled an even more entertained smile: "Then I think what I'm going to pre-scribe for you is a new psychiatrist." Which had signalled the beginning of the end for Dr. Gleidman. The stranger with the umbrella had, after all, only expressed what she had begun to be convinced of herself. But she hadn't been willing to warn Gleidman she was leaving, she had instead made arrangements to give him the slip. At a time when she'd known he was in consultation with one of his other patients, she had tiptoed into his waiting room with a note that said thanks for everything and that she wouldn't be back. And along with the note a book of travel essays wrapped up in pink metallic paper with a pattern of silver forest fires burning on it.

His tray of needles in one hand, Declan led Claire into a formal grey room. Leaves from the lilac bushes in the Institute garden were brushing against the windows and when the wind moved roughly through them they set up a trembling of leaf-shadows on the glass that protected medical diplomas and a photograph of snow falling into a dark pond. Claire stretched herself out on the high table to wait for the miniature needles that looked even more frail than pins, and as she felt the prick, then the wiggled electric jolt of each needle, Declan named the part of the body it was meant to help. "Liver," he said.

And a few moments later: "Heart."

The touch of his fingers, resting lightly on her left arm, felt intelligent and kind. She looked up at him. "But why all this trouble with my skin? Why all the spots?"

"Weakness in the lungs."

She was trying to remember what the little Chinese doctor had said about the lungs. Excessive something injured them, but she couldn't remember what. "What injures them?"

After a slight pause he said, "Grief."

But now he was leaving her. He looked back over a shoulder at her when he got to the door. "Do you want the lights high or low?"

"Low."

"Do you want music?"

"Yes," she whispered. "Thank you."

He pressed a button and a Vivaldi concerto bubbled – percolated, almost – into the dim windy room.

When he came back with his tray again, to take out the needles, he said, "And so what's been happening with you, Claire? Since we last saw one another?"

She told him about her visit with Alan Breit. "And so then after that I made a definite decision to come back and see you."

He had nothing to say to this, he even seemed a little humble and shy.

But then she hadn't called right away because there was a death in her family.

"Who died?"

"My father." And although she hadn't at all expected to, she turned her face away from him and began to cry. A painful crying without tears that was really a series of breathless little squeaks. And as she cried, Declan stood with a hand on one of her shoulders, in his astringently formal way giving her comfort.

The following week when she saw him again he worked at the knotted muscles in her aching back, tight little nuts of enduring pain, each little nut representing some despicable emotion. Like what? Like bitter indignation. Lying on her belly on the treatment table, she winged her arms back to undo her bra hooks so that he could make his way farther down her back. Her breasts plumply pancaked beneath her, she almost dozed off, safe in her conviction of how absolutely correct it all was, Declan's clinical fingers moving methodically down each side of the spine of her sore back, colonizing her resentments.

On her way back to work after her appointment she even surprised herself by experiencing euphoria. And no pain. She floated across Bank Street with its exhaust fumes, mixed in as they were with the hazily fragrant air of the spring afternoon.

There was a train to Ottersee but it was an evening train. It left Ottawa at five and reached Ottersee two hours later. And the return train didn't come back through the town until midnight. With the bus it was the same story but at the opposite end of the day: the only bus reached the town before breakfast, then left again twenty minutes later, not to return until the following morning.

Claire signed up for classes with a driving school even though she didn't own a car. She planned to rent one, one day a week, when the time came. And so this became her social life, all through the weirdly hot nights of early May, a driving lesson three evenings a week with a man named Gordon Stahl, evenings that in her fantasies would turn into marvellous drives through leafy Rockcliffe or confident sweeps up the cliff road that ran past the Shinto shrine lookout on the way to the Rockeries. But the night of her first lesson, Gordon drove her to an old airfield on the outskirts of the city. She tried not to glance down at the triangle of air that he was making narrower and then less narrow by the nervous wince of his thighs, and when they got to their teaching tarmac and he quickly got out of the car to wade through the weedy grasses around to her side — he, the instructor, had parked too close to the field! — she obediently slid over under the wheel. For the first few minutes of her lesson she felt stiff, apprehensive, but soon she was as drunk with shy happiness as a baby learning to dance. And when she was at last permitted to drive out on real streets — and even though she wasn't ever able to entirely lose her fear that she would make a wrong turn and kill someone — she also began to be bewitched by the sedate feeling of power, and bewitched, too, by the heady mix of spring and twilight, and by the terrific feel, on the homeward drive, of the warm night wind on her skin.

The night of her fourth lesson, Gordon came to pick her up in a car with a stick shift, having decided to devote the evening to teaching her how to shift gears. Following his directions, she turned off Eastbourne Avenue and drove up the slope of a cul-de-sac where seven or eight boys were out in the twilight playing street hockey.

Gordon placed his hand firmly over hers on the stick shift. "Good," he said, "now shift into low."

She shifted into low and flooded the engine.

"Turn off the ignition, then turn it on again, then back the car down the hill, we're going to keep doing this until you get it right."

She did it again, aware of the boys watching her, waiting for her to make another mistake. But this time, shifting gears halfway up the hill, she was successful.

They hooted and cheered.

"Good," said Gordon briskly. "Now we'll do parallel parking."

"*Here?*" Plaintively scandalized.

"Of course here. Why *not* here?"

As if they'd overheard him, the hockey boys were now mockingly orchestrating her every move while she was trying to park, using their hockey sticks as batons, but after several attempts Gordon pronounced himself satisfied and gave her his permission to turn down the hill and start out for home.

But then on their way across town another crowd of boys all at once appeared on her left, cruising up close to her left elbow, as she was driving along Wellington Street. "Step on the *gas*, you dumb slut!" one of them – a polite-looking boy in a short-sleeved grey shirt – yelled to her over the rockabilly music they'd turned way up high, while one of the other boys yelled, "Where's the *fire*, baby?" She was jolted, even though she knew there was no point in being hurt. Besides, it was really only a kind of flirting, so much of what happened in cars or between drivers was really a kind of flirting anyway, even the things that weren't, Gordon Stahl instructively capping her hand with his hand when she was learning to shift gears, in a way that made her imagine his hand capping one of her knees or cupping a breast, the real truth of the matter being that these boys not only didn't ruffle her unduly, they even made her want to smile, she was just so happy to be learning to drive.

~~~~
~~~~

The morning she was to take her driving test was a chilly clear morning violent with birdsong. She hurried over to the front windows to watch for Gordon, and while she was holding her turned-up wrist pressed to a breast to fasten her watch, she looked down to see him, his windbreaker hooked over his shoulder, crossing the van der Meer lawn to ring the lower doorbell.

He spoke soothingly to her as she drove, going over the questions the examiner would be most likely to ask. But the beauty of the morning was making her even more tense than a rainy or grey morning would have done. She was also feeling hypoglycemic, as if the bright light might make her faint, and every time she braked for an intersection, especially near the canal, there was a cool morning sweetness in the air along with all the delirious bird-tumult. But now the Pretoria Bridge was already swinging into view, the spooky musical-comedy bridge, its miniature grey feudal castles guarding its stone walls, the brilliant light turning it into a picture in a surreal children's book. She could also feel Gordon watching her and wished that he wouldn't, then she could hear his voice say, "What will you do with the licence once you get it?"

"Rent a car so I can drive out into the country once a week."

When he didn't respond she felt she ought to elaborate. "On a sort of medical project."

"Doing what?"

"It's a bit hush-hush at the moment."

"Hush-hush." This seemed to amuse him.

But then (so soon!) she heard him say, "Wonder of wonders, we're in luck. This boy can be a bit iffy, but he's not *half* as bad as some I could name —"

And so here he was then, her examiner, a sour man holding a clipboard. He looked precise, he looked fastidious, he looked like a man it would not be easy to fool.

After she'd brought the car to a careful stop, she queasily listened to the two men talk about the weather, then she could feel Gordon climbing into the back seat to sit directly behind her. All the way through her ordeal she was going to be able to feel his breath on the back of her neck, urging her to do well.

The examiner, on the other hand, leaned back at his ease, but spoke in such a low voice that she had to squint to hear him. "Turn right, then turn left . . ."

She drove slowly out into the paranormal sunlight, then under the trees.

In the small park behind the van der Meers' house there were the smells of uncollected garbage, the sour smell of blossoming chokecherry trees. And every blossoming tree and bush against an inhuman blue sky. It was the morning of Claire's first trip out to Ottersee, a clear day the second week of June. Declan had told her that his place out in the country was a former Anglican rectory and that he'd be sharing it for the summer with the family of a biologist friend of his. He'd told her they made quite a tribe. Two husbands and two wives and nine children.

At the car-rental hut she was given the keys to a blue car, but just after she'd ducked into it and breathed in a nauseating whiff of its upholstery with the hot morning sun on it she was gripped by stage fright. It was her first time alone in a car and her problem was serious: she couldn't remember how to proceed. She looked toward the office to check if the two rental men were watching her (they were) then with quick guilt she played for time by pretending to primp in the rear-view mirror.

The one with the dry little moustache doesn't like me, she thought. Unless he really *does*, maybe that's why he looked so grim when he shoved me the keys. But then everything did flood back to her and she was able to swing with an almost delirious verve out into the post-breakfast traffic.

For a long time after this, as she changed gears, as she signalled, as she changed lanes, as she played with the radio (changing stations), as she flew through more open country, she felt weak with cleverness and relief, and when she finally pulled over onto a marshy shoulder of the highway to study her map, the sound of the forest's front line of breeze-rattled poplars moved up her body the way she imagined the sound of applause would move up the willowy limbs of a sexually shuffling dancer. How could she have forgotten that this amazing world existed? With its balmy country air and its busy northern leaves and all of its forest-parts so shiveringly rustling? She felt an absolute longing to come and live out here, to come out here and live in the breezy free country.

Declan's rectory was on the far side of Ottersee, on the road to New Dublin. Claire drove past an auto-body shop with a billboard mounted up on its roof, then past an ice-cream van, then past the town's two gas stations, facing each other across the highway like the gates to a mansion, then past a scattering of low houses painted in dead pinks, pale greens. Small-town bungalows on their careful small lawns.

But now here it was, off to her left and a little remote from the life of the town, up on a knoll at the end of a very long driveway, a handsome old fieldstone house with a fanlight over its wide white front door. And in the field next to it there was even a black-faced white sheep standing under a tree as if it had been permanently tethered there.

When she got out of the car at the foot of the front steps she did a quick count of the bathing suits spread out to dry on the formal swell of green lawn below the verandah. There were two women's, both bikinis: one red, one white. Two men's: one red, one grey and patterned with slim silver fishes. Nine children's: three for boys, six for girls. But she was already late. She quickly walked up the steps, preparing her face to meet Declan or one of the wives, rang the bell.

But there was no sound and no one came.

She tried the bell again.

Another wait.

She decided to knock.

Then to knock more loudly.

Once more, with feeling.

But when still no one came she let herself in, stepping cautiously into a hallway that smelled like the vestry of a very old church. To her right there was a large room with a low sofa and chairs and there were also several tall old oak doors (all closed) leading off to the other rooms. She wondered which door led to Declan's office. She closed the outside door firmly behind herself, then stood, expecting a receptionist or Declan to come out. But there was only a deep spring-morning quiet. Barefoot, her sandals swinging from one hand, she walked carefully into the big room and sat down on the sofa. The coffee table was a square of glass resting on a bed of chrome tubing. There were stacks of magazines on it, but she was much more curious about the books, in a tall built-in bookcase behind leaded glass panels.

After a moment's hesitation, she got up and went over to it and soundlessly opened one of its doors. She cocked her head to read the titles: *The Function of the Orgasm, The Boat Who Wouldn't Float, Sunshine Sketches of a Little Town.* There was also a green and black paperback titled *Sexuality, Self and Survival,* a slim little book whose title was set against a background of outsized neon-green blades of grass and a black post-nuclear sky. She carried it back to the sofa with her, then leafed quickly through it, promising herself she would ask Declan if she could borrow it, but not till some future time when she wasn't feeling so anxious.

But where *was* he? And was this even the right house? The right town? Only one thing was certain, the books were the right books. But now a new fear presented itself: he would open one of these doors to discover her with this particular book in her hands. A mad worry, but apparently a real one, to judge from the way she'd gone so shaky and damp. She slipped back to the bookcase, not making a sound, and fitted the green and black book into its slot. She was also aware of the fact that she was by now very much more anxious than curious; she had, after all, made the trip out here with a certain elation and hope, and to find no one here was not only weird, it was a bizarre disappointment. And so she stood, wondering for a moment which door to try, then went over to the nearest door and knocked, and when there was no response, pulled it open.

A long table suitable for one of the grand halls of Versailles was crammed into a small sunlit box of a room with a bay window, and the chairs were tall-backed and ornately carved from a dark foreign wood. So much pomp, and way out here in the country. But it was a cheerful pomp, the only dark note in the room a floor-to-ceiling wall rug, its red eye glowing out of a field of black yarn. She edged past it warily, its primeval eye watching her to see what she planned to do next.

What she did next was open the door to what she guessed must be the kitchen. And *it* turned out to be more spacious, human-looking. A woman's puckered navy-blue bathing suit was hanging over the back of a chair, and in the tall windows, spring-like sprays of ferns were hanging in hazy fountains of green. There was also the damp ginger fragrance of cakes stored in tins, the sensible smell of banana loaf. A cuckoo clock, carved to look rickety, ticked its folksy and woody tick. She opened a door to the left of the stove and found a sun porch with nothing at all in it except a billiard table. It was a room that made her want to hurry back to the room with the books again. To the sofa, to dig around in her bag for her appointment card.

She ran barefoot back to the library. But when she pulled her appointment card out of her shoulder bag she saw that she hadn't made a mistake about the date. And so she decided to slip outside to take another look around. But as she was hurrying toward the front door it was pulled open from the other side and there stood Declan. "I've been waiting for you down in the basement. That's where I see my clients."

He spun around, and so she was left to kick her feet into her sandals and humbly clatter after him down the broad steps from the verandah.

As she followed him down the little path that ran along the front of the house she saw an arrow-sign saying OFFICE IN BASE-MENT. It made her feel foolish. She had been too busy check-ing out the number and gender of bathing suits to spot it.

Declan quickly rounded the corner and when she caught up with him he was opening a tall door in a brown-shingled porch that could have doubled as a guardhouse. More steps followed, old stone ones, and she was momentarily gripped by a far-fetched childish terror – into the dungeon, into the dungeon – but the room they came down into was reassuring: a whitewashed grotto converted into a doctor's office with a corkboard and a mammoth oak desk and behind the desk a large gloomy-skied old oil paint-ing of a tree with most of its pale yellow leaves blown down to the ground. But how predictable, she thought with anxious con-tempt, for he was still making her feel terribly uneasy.

He looked down at his watch. "We don't have much time. My next client will be here at eleven-thirty." And he led her into a room that had only one very small and very high window. "Did you bring any clothes to work in?"

She said no, she didn't know she was supposed to. "Should I have brought a bathing suit?"

"Working in your underclothes is okay. If they're com-fortable enough."

But then the phone rang and while he was talking in the other room she made use of his absence by unbuttoning her blouse and stepping out of her skirt. She also quickly took stock of the room. One brown canvas director's chair and one unpainted kitchen chair, and down on the grey carpet two bleached cotton mats that looked like Japanese meditation or prayer mats. This will be like being at a gym, she thought, but at the same time like being at church and at the doctor's.

As Declan came back into the room he was already sizing her up in his clinical way and so the moment wasn't really all that awkward after all. Whatever awkwardness there was as she was standing before him in her white cotton camisole and her sensible white cotton underpants came from the fact that even only partial disrobing always made her so unhappily aware of the intensity of the feelings she had for her body: pure love and pure hate. She hated her legs most — in black nylons and high heels they were more or less passable, but exposed and naked they looked like little girl legs, too thin below the knees and too plump-thighed above them, as if her body, once it had gotten down to her knees, had forgotten how to be a woman.

But he was already pacing around her. He looked into her eyes. "Your pupils are fairly dilated."

"They're always dilated. It's because I'm nearsighted."

"You see nearsightedness as a cause. I see it as an effect."

"What is the cause, then?"

"When you were a little girl, something made you open your eyes much too wide. You tried to see everything all at once and you ended up seeing not very much. My guess is that you let people push you around."

He paced around her some more, speculating and frowning. She felt like a horse or a slave on the block, his gaze was so shrewd and total.

"You would believe almost anything anyone told you," he told her.

She wanted to say to him "As a matter of fact I have very fierce opinions," but instead she decided to smile at him to say, "I'll believe anything. I even believe *you* as you're telling me this."

He didn't smile back. "Also, you keep your knees locked."

"Oh, do I? Why do I do that?"

"Fear," he answered, in a light voice.

"Of what?"

"Somebody was always at you when you were small, wouldn't let you be." And he knelt to her knees to unlock them. Then he looked up at her: "That's right. Cry."

She tried to wipe her eyes with the backs of her hands.

"But do you cry right? Do you cry with your body? Or are you just crying up in your head?"

"I cry as quietly as I can, usually."

"Well yes," he said in a professionally serious and gratified voice. "That's what I see when I look at your body. A tremendous stillness. You've stilled your body so much. It's as if your body is saying, 'I'll be quiet, I'll be good, I won't have temper tantrums, I'll work hard, I'll study hard and I'll think, think, think.' You must get very, very tired of being so good all the time."

Whereupon she was overwhelmed by such an ashamed pity for her falsely good self that it was a moment before she was able to answer him. But when she could she said, "I do."

When Claire came down into the room with the great tree on the wall the following Thursday afternoon, Declan was waiting for her. He even allowed her to babble on for a bit, but he didn't really want her to talk, he wanted her to breathe, and to breathe properly. That was her job here.

A tedious session of grounding and breathing exercises followed, then there was the work of breaking up the tension in her lower back and legs.

But the next appointment, for acupuncture, was in town, at the Institute. In one of the rooms at the back of the clinic she studied a bruise on her left thigh as she waited for Declan. She had always bruised easily, but before leaving home she'd circled the bruise's mauve thumbprint with a ballpoint pen and drawn a furious little face inside it, and above the face a cartoon balloon containing the words THIS BRUTALITY MUST CEASE IMMEDIATELY!

But he wasn't alone. Another voice was coming down the hall along with his voice, and the owner of this other voice turned out to be a short bearded man in a lab coat. Hearing their voices and then seeing them come in together, she felt ashamed. With this other doctor to witness it, her little joke would seem flirty and tacky. She kept the words on her thigh covered with the pressure of her left hand as Declan introduced the younger doctor to her. "Claire, this is Gus Gustavsen. I was just wondering if it would be okay with you if Gus had a little look at your eczema."

She looked up at the younger doctor. He had kind eyes, the eyes of a respectful medical sightseer. But she wanted him to go. She wanted them both to go. She decided to try for bravado. "I am not a leopard," she said to Declan. "And so I don't show off my spots. And I am not a leper either." The younger doctor looked startled, but Declan only said, "That's okay, Claire," then told her that he'd be back with her in a minute or two. At this, the two men stepped out of the room to talk together in low voices out in the hallway.

She couldn't stop thinking what it would be like when he came back in to see her again. She was afraid he would dislike her for putting him on the spot about her spots, she was afraid he would dislike her for being so childish and rude to him in front of the visitor doctor. But the eyes of the younger doctor had been so expressive that she'd had a disloyal moment of wondering what it would be like if *he* were her doctor. She might prefer him, with his compassionate eyes. He might be more the sort of person she could talk to. He also might not be so heavily into the calisthenics of therapy, which were so boring, really, at least to her; with him it might be more a matter of talking about dreams and having useful conversations about what was going on in her life. That is what I would really prefer, she thought, to discuss the particulars of my life. But at the same time she couldn't help but be convinced that the body therapists

were really spookily right in some ways — one of the tellers at
her bank on Sparks Street had been beaten as a child, she was
sure of it, she could tell by watching her walk over to the filing
cabinets at the back of the bank — she had such a drifting, tail-
between-her-legs dog's walk that it gave her a whipped look —
and it was true about anger being stored high up in shoulders
too, there were angry shoulders everywhere, at least in Ottawa,
you could see anger in shoulders at least as often as you could
see it in eyes, and yet this kind of therapy still seemed too
simple, too much beside the point of whatever was wrong with
her, and if she really and truly felt that what she was doing
with him wasn't going to work shouldn't she just get out of it
now, before it was too late, and also, if this was really the case,
wouldn't it make sense to tell him today, wouldn't today be the
right time and place? Out in the country he was too solitary to
allow her to leave him. He was too alone and lonely out in the
country, he was a sad host trapped among all the Ottersee trees
and flowers, the scent of new-mown hay carried on the warm
wind from the meadows that circled the town.

But when the door opened again, he came over and sat down
beside her and began to rub her shoulders through the flowered
back of her blouse while he told her about a recent weekend
he'd spent on an island on Georgian Bay where for three days he
had lived on nothing but roots and berries. His thumb kept
hypnotically rubbing her back as he talked while she kept feeling
that he was leading up to something, something he'd be wanting
her to do, some ritual or boring exercise in grounding or breathing. But no: he went on to speak about white-water rafting,
which he said was one of his great passions. They did not speak
of the spots of eczema beneath the flowers of her blouse, or

of her refusal to let Gus Gustavsen see them. He made a half-handcuff with his thumb and fingers and moved it up and down her right arm as he talked to her, an absent-minded caress that made her feel like a horse who'd just run a good race and so had earned a reward from her trainer. And because of all the little consolations of being touched by him, she had a moment of doubt before beginning to say what she'd planned to say. But then she made herself say it: "I appreciate all you've done for me so far, but I don't know if I'm really a good candidate for this kind of therapy." And then, like a vendor in a street market displaying her wares, she laid her objections out, one by one, before him. "Things aren't all that clear-cut, I don't think. Out in the world. In a way what we've been doing — the exercises, I mean — seems like a lie we might tell ourselves for our own comfort, a pleasant little story about how much we've changed, but it just seems too —" and here she was wanting to say "simple-minded," but didn't quite dare to, and so she only said "athletic." Then she said what she'd been building up to: "I think I'm more the sort of person who needs to just sit and talk to someone . . ."

"But that could be exactly your problem. You intellectualize too much." This statement made them both sit quietly for a moment and gaze down in unison, as if his words were the embers of a sensible fire. "Do you know what would really do you good?" he asked her — he had gone back to rubbing her back again — "It would really do you good to live in absolute silence for three days. And not talk to anyone. And don't read anything either. Not even the newspaper. Don't concern yourself with what's going on in the world at all for three days. Just go for long walks and be alone with your thoughts."

Even though his prescription had a certain appeal — it sounded Buddhist, it had that heartless and cagey Eastern purity — she still felt it was a prescription much better suited to people whose lives were utterly different from her own. Civil servants who partied too hard and vacationed in Vegas or raced around in their sports cars with their car stereos turned up. Or military men who were loud but morose alcoholics. But she was a person who already spent all of her free time alone with her thoughts. She was a person who spent her whole *life* going for walks. But now he was running his hands down both of her arms in tandem, a gesture with which a parent might send a child bravely out into the world. "I want you to give yourself over to the process more."

He went out of the room to get his tray of needles then, and when he came back again she was still sitting up to frame the bruise and its cartoon balloon with the sideways cup of her hand so he could read it.

He smiled down at it, then said something about women bruising more easily than men, something about women and collagen.

She stretched out on her belly to wait for the needles, then lay listening to the music and waiting for them to do what they must do. And after he'd removed them, they talked for a few minutes. She buttoned up her shirt as she stood listening, and as she was drawing the strap of her Moroccan bag up on a shoulder she said, "I'll try to try harder." But his tenderness puzzled her, and when it was time for her to go he puzzled her even more by saying "Goodbye, love."

A week later it turned hot, but there was still a leftover damp ache in the air from the morning's earlier rain as Claire sat with her friend Libi in Libi's kitchen. Libi yawned a fierce little yawn with a fist held tight up beside each breast, then went over to the sink to fill up a kettle. The backs of her legs were pink with a sick flush of sunburn, and she was wearing one of her bright Mexican cotton skirts, this one a harsh red. It gave off the raw stinging new-crayon smell of cheap cotton. "I fell asleep out on one of the lawn chairs after I came back from the dentist's, that's why I'm burnt to this incredible crisp." She must have rubbed baby oil into her legs too, Claire could smell the sweet babyish seep of it, coming from the thick white-banded grey woollen socks she was wearing with her heavy sandals.

Libi poured tea into a flowered cup for Claire and coffee into a brown coffee mug for herself, but her eyes became baleful as she studied her friend. "And you're quite sure that this Farrell person isn't a quack . . ."

Claire was sure he was not. "He's really an incredibly dedicated person, Lib."

Libi was getting the cheese from the refrigerator when Claire asked her if men ever said things to her.

"Things?"

"Yes," said Claire, feeling doomed, the way she'd felt at twelve when she was unwisely asking her mother questions about sex. "Do they say things to you when you're out on the street?"

"No, they don't. Do they say things to *you*?"

"Sometimes they do."

Libi was by now gazing at her with the doubtful, measuring look that a woman will give to another woman when she suspects her of having delusions of grandeur about her looks. "Be explicit. Flattering things? Unflattering things?"

"It all depends on your point of view," said Claire. She sliced herself a thin slice of the pale cheese that Libi had set out on a pink china plate. "These things are either all insults or all praise," she said, trying to sound dispassionate. The words that Libi might say to her (no, she would never say them, but she would think them) flew at her, smacked her in the heart. *Tart, slut.* She wished that she could attach Libi's puzzled expression to Libi, to Libi's history, instead of to some moral or esthetic deficiency in herself. "'Hello, Fat Tits,' is one thing," she said. "'Oh, baby' is another." On two different occasions recently, men had also made flatteringly quick little sexual grunts as if they were lifting heavy objects just as they were passing close by her, but she wasn't able to tell Libi this, Libi would be too revolted. "'Hubba, hubba,' and 'Oh, baby, let's fuck' are two others." She had to stop, or Libi would decide she was totally vulgar. Shy and vulgar and stubborn and really pathetically naïve to be impressed by this kind of male attention. To defend herself, or at least to pretend to put it all into perspective, she said, "It's all pretty predictable."

Libi was looking either sad or disapproving. "I don't look at men," she said. "And men don't look at me."

"But you're the beautiful one."

She didn't dispute this, she only said, "But I don't look open."

"And you think that I do?"

Libi studied her for a long moment. "Yes, you do," she decided. "But you also stare at people too much. This is why men say things to you on the street: you give them the eye."

~~~~~
~~~~~

On the following Thursday afternoon, Declan told Claire that he wanted her to bite down hard on a plastic shampoo bottle.

She stared down at the bottle, a flask with a dull gold label on it. "No," she said. "I don't want to do that."

The moody glance he gave her surprised her, it was so virulent with impatience. "We can't do *anything* with you, can we," he moaned (or almost moaned) and then he alarmed her even more by picking up the shampoo flask and pelting it against the basement's far wall. But it was only a flexible clear plastic flask, after all, and when it bounced back and landed with comic precision at the toes of Declan's sandals, Claire – caught in the grip of a fearful nervousness – laughed, then stood and continued to laugh silently and desperately into her cupped hands, trying to stifle herself.

Her laughter enraged him. He said that of all the people he saw she was the one who was most difficult to work with. He said that she challenged him on every little thing. He said he was getting sick and tired of having his time wasted by someone who wasn't willing to do the work required.

She seized his wrists: "Now you listen to *me*, I have something to say to you."

He surprised her by becoming immediately calm. "Say it, then."

"You can't just order me to do things that are totally bizarre without giving me any good reason why I should do them."

"If I explain, you'll have time to prepare. An explanation won't ever give you what I'm willing to give you . . ."

"And what would that be?"

"The chance to think on your feet."

But the next time she drove down to Ottersee to see him – after a week of brooding – she was ready to do battle. She ran down the steps to the dungeon, then sat down on one of the exercise mats in her black jersey and a wraparound skirt – bamboo shoots against a background of black-eyed mauve ovals – her hair tightly tied back with a hazy blue scarf.

When he came into the room – but she was by now beginning to think of it as the Room – he looked surprised to see that she hadn't changed into her shorts for the session.

"I have some things I want to say to you," she told him, and she warningly stood.

"Go right ahead." He met her gaze evenly, directly, but he stayed standing too.

"I'm not convinced we can work together any more."

"Why is that?"

"I don't think you even want to work with me."

He looked shocked at this, but she was certain it was only a bogus shock. He's like an actor, she thought, and not even a very good actor. And then he was asking her (still in the false voice) when he had ever said such a thing.

"The last time I drove down here."

He raised his eyebrows at her.

"You implied it."

He hitched himself up on the treatment table and gazed at her mockingly. Like a triumphant husband. A triumphant and amused and husbandly look. And, like a husband, he made a conductor's gesture that was a kind of perversion of encouragement. "*How* did I imply it? Go ahead — enlighten me."

"You said of all the people you work with I'm the most difficult. You said, 'We can't do anything with you, can we?' You threw the shampoo bottle at the wall."

"I don't own that."

"What do you mean?"

"I don't own saying it."

"Do you mean you didn't say it?"

"I don't own it, no."

"You mean you didn't say it."

"I don't own it."

It was like a dialogue from some insane version of the Theatre of the Absurd. She could imagine two clownish vaudeville actors having just such a mad repetitive conversation. She could imagine one of them turning out the ludicrous boats of his shoes and strumming his trouser braces with his thumbs. She could hear his cracked voice nasally croaking, "Well, if ya won't *own* it, will ya *rent* it?" She said, "Do you know what I think?"

No answer.

"I think you're ashamed that you said what you said. I think you're trying to browbeat —"

He held up a hand. "*Browbeat* you?" He looked diverted. "With *what*? My *silence*?"

"Yes, exactly," she said. "With your silence. I think you're perfectly willing to encourage me to have doubts about my own perception of reality if that's what's required to save your own skin." She folded her arms tightly up under her breasts and regarded him coldly, then looked away. She wished she had a decent window to gaze out of while she stood with her back turned toward him. As it was, she had to make do with the too-high and too-small panel of dirt-freckled glass that only showed, like an illustration in a science text, a rim of green grass above a taller cross-section of damp silt and gravel. What a sad and self-conscious joke this whole mad little world was, in any case. The little dramas and melodramas. And these self-righteous words she was using. And yet to *not* use them — to give up, to give *in* — did seem to her to be an act of the purest cowardice. But at the same time the part of her that could (however briefly) see things clearly, was thinking, Yes he's an enchanter, he's the real thing in his way, and also (like any bully) he has no use for the past. And so I can never, ever know where I stand with him. But she was already deciding that the time had at last come for her to put a stop to all that. "I don't believe I can work with a liar," she said.

He said nothing.

Things had gone much farther than she had imagined he would permit them to go.

"And so I'm leaving." Her voice broke, mid-sentence, like an adolescent boy's. Again her words sounded theatrical, unreal.

"So leave then."

She gathered up her shoulder bag, her sunglasses, her shaggy Guatemalan poncho. But at the door she hesitated. "I just wish I didn't think you were glad to see me go."

And when he replied in a drained but surprised voice, "I'm not glad to see you go," she knew she hadn't been entirely honest with herself and again she felt swamped by a sense of herself as melodramatic, unreal. But she only said in a sad voice, "Goodbye then."

He didn't answer.

She closed the door carefully behind herself, then walked up the steps and out into the cold sunlight. She walked through the back garden. The biologist's children were helping the Farrell children make a tent out of rag rugs and old blankets, and at the far end of the pool the two oiled wives were sitting smoking in their tiny kerchief bikinis. One was a tense little blonde, the other had brown hair cut in a perfect and shining Cleopatra cut. Were they her age? She thought so. Late thirties, early forties. The fair one was scratching at something on her ankle, and even glancing at them from a distance she got the feeling that the conversation between them was stilted and polite, too polite for them to join forces against a third woman and scoff.

She threw her poncho into the car, crawled in after it. The seat burned her hands and the world tilted. It occurred to her that she might be too dizzy to drive. She sat quietly for a moment while the delicately hesitant, changed-my-mind little drops of perspiration explored different parts of her body. When she felt steadier, she turned on the ignition, then made her way bumpily down the laneway to the highway.

She drove through the ugly pink and green outskirts of Ottersee and then on through the shaded and more beautiful heart of the old part of town. Then briefly into sun again, the town hall square, a park, the Ottersee Library. He's ordinary, she decided, ordinary and afraid his ordinary little secret will get out, that's why he acts so temperamental and loony, I'm well rid of him, I should have figured all this out weeks ago, saved myself all the money I've squandered, and on the car rental too, but at the same time the thought of hurrying back to Ottawa when she could be sitting out here in the sun in the clear country air struck her as a really uninspired thing to do, she had hired the car for the day after all, and so she parked on a shaded side street and then walked into the library park, breathing in the cool morning air and carrying her shaggy poncho under her arm for company.

Last night's violent rain had so battered the park's orange and red tulips that at first sight she mistook them for poppies. But she must be mad, they *were* poppies, the tulip season had long since been and gone, it was already July, where had she been, by now all the earlier flowers were even drying out and there was a hot wind jogging the rose bushes that guarded the hooded front entrance to the library and the flower beds flanking the rose bushes were filled with hydrangeas, a name that had always made her think of an illness. Everything was smelling so sad and sweet drying out, everything except for the library's diamond-paned windows whose frames were painted a

new and oily dark green that smelled poisonous and sticky.
They gave the building the foreboding prettiness of a witch's
cottage and, realizing this, she all at once could not bear the
place, and before she'd even so much as sat down on one of the
green benches, she was off again, back to the car. And then
found herself driving in the wrong direction. But it must be
what I want, she thought. At least till the end of the hour. Get
my money's worth.

The two oiled wives were sitting exactly as they had been
when last seen, down in the bright well of light in the little
hollow to the west of the house and the pool. Out of the wind.
One of them (the fair one) was even still massaging the front
of her left ankle.

Claire ran down through the churchy cool of the stone
stairwell to Declan's office. There was no sign of him, but the
door to the Room was still closed. She knocked on it lightly,
then called to him to tell him that she would like to stay till the
end of the hour.

"Come in, then."

He was sitting exactly as he had been sitting when she'd left
him, looking straight ahead, into his own thoughts.

She sat down beside him. His eyes looked as if he had been
crying. How could that be? She covered his hand with her hand
when he asked her what she was feeling.

She said, "I don't want to leave you."

Far below them down in the orchestra pit the insect musicians were tuning up: cricket chirps and the attenuated little tropical-bird cries of the violins that seemed so to cry out the news of life's small excitements and sorrows. Their seats were high up in the balcony and so they had to climb up and up – vertigo country, and how like a precipice a theatre balcony was (don't wear high heels, don't lose your balance) – then the lights went completely down and they had to slink their way to their seats through a deeper darkness, squeezing past five or six pairs of irritated knees to the sexy lunge of the legendary nasal and achy music, a hidden voice already harshly crooning, "Oh the shark has pretty teeth dear . . ."

During the intermission – their first chance to elbow their way out of their coats – Libi told Claire about the production of *The Seagull* she'd seen on her recent trip to New York. She'd also gone to the Botanical Gardens, where she was treated to a buffet in the Insectarium. She was reciting the menu – meal-worm cake, Mexican locusts, ants in sugar, silkworm pupae in

pasta shells – when a small crowd of Elmwood girls in their
green school tunics started to excuse their way past them, on
their way out to the lobby for smokes.

Smokes and mirrors.

When the play was over they let the girls squeeze past them
again, then made their way down to the pictures of playwrights:
Shaw looking Shavian, Brecht looking like a brat and not very
bright – but how could that be? – and once they were out in
the night air they walked in a cool wind along Sussex until they
found the café that always made Claire think of a café in Prague
or in London. Its newspapers were even hanging sideways from
grooved sticks, the way they did at the library.

Claire stirred her tea, set the tiny spoon in her saucer: "My
mother called. Last night after supper. And when I told her I'd
been taking driving lessons and could now actually drive a car,
she laughed."

"I'll bet you didn't tell her why you wanted to learn how to
drive though, my friend –"

"No I didn't. For the simple reason that I never tell her
anything."

"You're not going to fall in love with him, are you?"

"Of course not. Why should you think that?"

"Your voice always sounds so hushed and unreal whenever
you talk about him."

"If only you could see how earnest and serious he is, you
wouldn't even ask."

But Libi said that patients were forever falling in love with
their therapists and that it was really just so boring and banal
and in bad taste and predictable.

Claire stirred her tea again and said nothing. She wondered if Libi and Rolf were happy together. They are either utterly happy or utterly unhappy, she thought, but why is it always so impossible to tell which? "He's humourless, Lib. It's not easy to fall in love with a person who has no sense of humour."

"You fell in love with Steff," Libi said.

〰〰〰

Claire went into the little washroom whose toilet always made her think of a hissing toilet on a boat, then changed into her shorts and a T-shirt before crossing the hallway to the Room for her session.

A few minutes later she could hear Declan coming down the back stairs.

But instead of their beginning with the usual breathing exercises, he surprised her by sitting down next to her on one of the mats and asking about her week, about her work, about her not sleeping and was it beginning to get better, and only then did he tell her to stand up. But when she stood he began to step-dance around her, taunting her. "You like this, don't you?" Taking quick little licks with his hand at her shoulder, one breast, her face. "Sure you do. Why shouldn't you like it? I'm just being *friendly*. Come on, Clairsie, Clairsie, push me away if you don't like it. Come on, push me away, little Clairsie." And at this he began to lightly, maddeningly slap at her. "You can't, can you?"

She seized his wrists, swung his hands out of the range of her face. But in two seconds he was right back pawing at her again, hardly shackled at all by her hands, now locked like oar-locks around his two wrists. She then turned herself into a swimmer in a swimming hole, hanging her whole weight on two limbs of a tree, trying to drag his arms down. A swimmer who breathlessly warned him, "I'm going to do it to you, then you'll see how awful it is," but when she let go of his wrists, he at once dropped his arms to his sides.

"Okay, do it."

But almost right away she cheated, touched his face much more slowly than he had touched hers, was much more tender, exploratory.

He closed his eyes. "It's not awful," he said. "I like it."

~~~~

A Sikh family sat waiting to see Dr. Tenniswood, the husband in a brown suit and brown turban, his wife in balloony white trousers, her long tunic patterned with gold coins cast onto a miniature gold plaid woven into gold silk. Their little boy (who was four, Claire thought, three or four) played near them with exquisite tact, whispering to himself, carefully busy. A grave and beautiful old man who had a disfiguring skin condition that bubbled like black asphalt from his left ear to the left side of his neck sat watching him. But the patient who'd arrived before all the others was an irritable woman whose right arm and right foot were both in plaster casts so heavily autographed they were hazy with names and friendly insults and exclamation points. She warned her two children to "be good," then hobbled in to see Dr. Tenniswood on her crutches. The little girl (in a pink pinafore) hitched herself up onto one of the chairs, then sat crossing and uncrossing her ankles in white knee socks and little pink canvas shoes as she impatiently flipped the pages of *People* and *Newsweek* in a spoiled-princess sort of way while the little boy (a bit older, probably seven, six or seven) wandered around restless, at unhappy loose ends.

Claire got a pad of lined paper and a pencil out of a desk drawer and brought them over to him. He was looking trussed, in his slightly too small railway-engineer's overalls, his face flushed, although he too was by now sitting up in a chair.

"Write me a story."

He looked up at her and didn't answer, but accepted the pad and pencil, then squirmed a little in his chair, trying to get settled.

As she made phone calls from her desk, Claire occasionally glanced over to see him looking out the window, but at last she saw him begin, with childish deliberation, to write.

She had just finished trying to pacify Mr. Singh (irritable from the long wait) when the little boy came around the doorway of her cubicle to show her his story.

"Ah-*hah*. And so is this for me?"

He nodded, speechless with excitement.

"Well this is very kind of you."

He was waiting to show it to her.

"And so what's it called then?"

"War and Peace."

"What a wonderful title. Did you think of it yourself?"

But he was already beginning to read in a high little voice: "Write, write. Erase, erase. War is starting. Pencils are attacking erasers. When war is finished, peace starts. The pencil sargent and the eraser sargent meet. They make a team. The pencils write and the erasers erase the mistakes."

"This is a really terrific story."

He stayed standing beside her with his head bowed. But he was really quite pleased, she thought.

"And so could I take this home with me then?"

"Yes."

"Write your name on it for me," she told him while she was picturing herself saying to someone, "Today, at the doctor's office where I work, I met the author of *War and Peace*. A really great guy, although extremely short."

He printed DAFYDD in the lower right corner.

He must be Welsh. Unless he was so young that he just automatically spelled his name with too many consonants. Although a little boy who could almost spell "sergeant" couldn't possibly have any trouble spelling his own name.

But at this point she glanced up to see that little Miss Pinafore was gazing over at her with a resentful, bleak look. A look that said, We are both women of course, but I am infinitely the superior woman, more sophisticated, more charming . . . Claire got a pencil and another pad of paper out of the paper drawer and brought them over to her, but when she asked her if she would like to write a story too, the child shook her head vehemently, then squeaked her skinny thighs over to one side of her chair and slid sideways off it to take her scowl and her perfect posture over to the window.

"We're going to break up some of the energy blocks on your upper body," Declan told Claire the following Thursday morning, tapping her left arm just below its short sleeve while she stepped out of sandals gone damp from the walk across the wet lawn to his house. "And so it would be best if you could just pull this off."

Pulling her T-shirt over her head, she felt like a child being watched by a parent while awkwardly getting herself ready for bed. But at the same time she was feeling (in spite of her sexless navy-blue gym shorts) delicately sexual, offered.

Declan went over to the window. He folded his arms across his chest and watched her from there. "You're locking your knees again, Claire. Try to let them relax. Then if you get broadsided unexpectedly you won't topple over."

She tried to unclench her muscles, to let her feet make true contact with the cold floor.

He came back to her then and placed his hands on her hips. "Also, there's a lot of holding and blocking in here," he told her, but his voice was sounding a little strained and formal in the cold Room.

They then did their usual tedious breathing and grounding exercises until Claire, at the end of the hour, asked him, "How do you see your own body then? Do you see yourself as having rewritten your own history, muscularly speaking?"

"Not yet." And he began to walk around the Room for her, shyly instructive. In the dull rainy light his white T-shirt gleamed. A smell of damp garden blew in through the window. "You see how high I'm carrying my shoulders? All the anger I carry in them?"

But all the time he was moving around her in a circle and all the time his voice was pointing out blocks and flaws, it seemed to her that his body was beaming an entirely different message to her, a message completely at odds with his words, and in this message his body was crying, *Look at me, look at me, love me, love me*, at least until he came to a stop and the message became formal again. "But I'm afraid we'll have to stop here for today." And he went out to the reception room to get his appointment book.

She reached her cardigan down off the chair and stayed sitting on the mat while she pulled it on, then got up and went over to the full-length mirror to brush back her hair.

When he came back into the Room he stood watching her dart her shirt into her shorts. Then he sat down in his chair and flung a leg over one of the armrests while he held the open book in his lap. He looked into her eyes as if announcing to himself that he felt nothing at all for her, but then he surprised her by saying, "You look so lovely right now. So beautiful, really."

She turned to the mirror to see. And then she could see it too, an alluring brief glimmer. "I hope it's not just a fluke."

And in an impatient voice he answered, "Of course not. It's your real self. It's the way you really *are*."

As she was backing out of the Farrell driveway, she caught sight of a child sitting alone up on the front steps of the verandah, eating an apple. It was the first time she had seen one of the children of the ménage doing anything by herself. Declan's brood and the biologist's even bigger brood seemed always to be part of one of the grand military manoeuvres of childhood. They were the Charge of the Light Brigade, Ottersee Division, or they were the Babylonian hordes swarming back and forth over the Ottersee lawns in a flapping, conspiring pack. Now that she was at last seeing one of them alone, solitary – and there was no doubt in her mind that this particular child was Declan's child – she felt a desire to see her more closely, to really look into her eyes, but she could think of no pretext for getting out of the car and walking up the lawn to talk to her. She was also afraid she might startle her, and to give herself time to think, she stopped the car and then began to comb her hair in the rear-view mirror. It occurred to her that she might ask her the directions to somewhere. New Dublin or Newbliss. Children loved, above all things, to be asked for directions. You could make a child's day by asking the child to give you directions. And so she rolled down the window and called up to her, "Can you tell me how long it would take me to drive from here to Newbliss?"

The child set down her book and her apple and came walking down over the mound of dry grass to the car. She was nine or ten, a grave little girl in cut-off jeans and a faded yellow T-shirt. She also had extraordinarily quiet and thoughtful grey eyes. Declan's eyes in the face of a child. "When you go on the bus it takes half an hour."

Claire, who had never before looked so deeply into the face of a child, had to remind herself to look as if this news was of interest to her. Her gaze felt so fixed she was afraid the child would become frightened. She could smell her apple breath as the little girl told her she would have to turn left at the end of the lane, and as she listened she could barely hold back the desire to say to her: I love your father and I believe I could love you too. And still looking into her eyes — for she could hardly bear to withdraw her own eyes from the child's eyes — she thanked her. Then she rolled up the window and drove off.

At the bottom of the driveway she turned left toward Newbliss (as if her lying request for instructions must be turned, with all possible speed, into the truth), then after five minutes turned left again, this time onto a side road flanked by green meadows and deep ditches, their weedy grasses still fogged by mist. She drove past a long field with a dark grove of trees at its crown, then decided to back up and park on the cow path that ran up the hill.

She got out of the car and walked up through the buzz of a field in full bloom, clumsily climbing through fireweed and Queen Anne's lace and goldenrod, feeling the hazy moisture seep into her skirt. Blurred islands of mauve and yellow flowers (asters and daisies) stretched out to the west as she climbed, along with the more scattered pink and white islands of clover. Caraway flowers were bumping and nudging at the dampening hem of her skirt too, as she was wading upward, and it struck her as strange that in all the times she'd sprinkled caraway seeds into the red cabbage dish she liked to make on foggy or snowy winter nights, she'd never once thought of caraway seeds as coming from these yarrowy cottage-cheese flowers.

But the dark grove of evergreens and poplars turned out to be a disappointment, it was so itchy and resinous and sad, its granite-grey flanks of stone spotted with a mildew of scratchy blue rock-moss. She sat down on one of the damp but still moss-bristly slopes of stone, then opened her string bag with its block of hard cheese and a banana. But the cheese had a sweet sickish flavour of barnyard and grass: it was rich, but at the same time so dry she found it almost impossible to swallow. She quickly peeled the banana – by now so ripe it had been almost liquefied by the heat – and pushed it into her mouth with the cheese to discover that the mix was startlingly delicious, a bizarre delicacy that if mixed with brandy and cloves, say, might very well make – in a small way – a famous dessert. She kept the taste in her mouth, like a marvellous mouthful of wine, then after a few minutes gathered herself together and waded down through the fireweed toward the car until she found an almost dry patch where she could lie down in her spongy field of flowers.

She stretched out on the grass and thought of Declan. She wanted to hold a hand to his forehead. Almost clamped there. A firm pressure; diagnostic. Testing for fever. But a pressure that could somehow still him. Still him or help him. She wanted to cover that part of the forehead where the forehead met hair. And then stroke it back with a firm pressure, as if stroking back the fur on a dog's halted forehead. She also wanted to take deep breaths of the clean country air, breathe in the largeness of the world, the sweep of this fragrant field while so many other lives were being lived in the city or in other countries, and she thought of a story she'd read in the morning paper about a French aristocrat who, after he'd been shackled to the guillotine, looked up at his executioner to ask "Are you sure this thing is safe?" God, the bravery of it, to joke about death at the moment before death, and she thought of love, too, different kinds of love, she thought of how certain members of the animal kingdom (the lovebird, the rat, and the dolphin, what a trio) fell in love in exactly the same way people fell in love. Unlike the chimp, who thought only of sex. Which made her recall a book she'd looked through once when she was over at Libi's house, a book that was a compendium of responses to a sex questionnaire, and the woman who'd written about the moment of penetration and of how it always led to "a great and large feeling." She wondered if she was also the one who'd ended her questionnaire with the words that when sex was over she always cried and felt a fierce tenderness.

But she had to go, she had to get up and pull the back of her skirt away from the backs of her thighs. She was feeling weakened by it all, the fields of buzzing beauty, and drugged by the flower smells. But she was also itchy from where great convoys of ants had passed over her thighs, on their way to somewhere else, an itch that made her gather herself together to lunge through the daisies and fireweed on her way downhill to the car.

Damp was still blooming like dark grasses up the sides of the barns as she was driving back to the city. Landscape after rain, the far hills a mild blue. The ramps leading up to the barns were drawbridges over moats of wet grasses and the ravines all had new little fjords in them too, from the rain. Not a breath of wind anywhere, the water reflective, European, historical, still.

Urgently whimpering to herself, Claire plundered pants pockets, jacket pockets, then plunged down the stairs to the kitchen — she was by this time already ten minutes late — fiercely swinging her shoulder bag, then unzipping it to violently shake and rattle its contents out onto the tiles. As she was squatting to sort through all the plastic cards and receipts, breathing hard, enraged with herself, the phone rang, and when she picked it up to hear Steff sing into the receiver "Hullo, hullo!" she said, "Oh." And not in a kind voice. "Listen, Steff, I need to use the phone right this moment," she told him, "to call for a taxi —"

"A taxi!" said Steff, in a voice that sounded astounded and social, as if a taxi were not a taxi at all, but some marvellously exotic and extinct creature. A prehistoric bird, perhaps, with a stone beak and stone wings.

"Yes!" cried Claire, doing a desperate little jig while whimpering again to get him to say goodbye. "And so could you call me back? But not now! Later! This evening!"

And then on the way out into the country in the cab she decided that the real test of character would be whether or not she would tell Declan the story of the taxi. The grown-up thing, she decided, would be not to tell. She looked out at the green fields in the rain and thought of all Steff's efforts to be charming and of the way they seemed always to somehow sadly misfire. Even the affair he'd had when they were still married had been short-lived, banal.

The one thing she missed about him was ironing his shirts. Pressing the fine cotton of his shirts – poplin, batiste – had filled her with joy. It was the rhythmic nosing of the iron into armpits and up to collars, the peppery smell of the hot cotton as she stood ironing in the hot summer sun. And in the winter too, breathing in the smell of poplin and perspiration rising up in the steam while watching the snow densely falling in its stately evening way beyond the tall windows, "Sisters of Mercy" playing on the tape recorder and the little surge she would feel in her heart whenever she heard it, the little surge she would feel as she stood shoving the iron back and forth and then neatly back again, soothingly but firmly pressing the hot cotton as if the act of ironing could earn her her escape and perhaps even happiness.

But when she got to Ottersee, she did give in and tell Declan about the taxi. And when she did, he didn't ask, as Dr. Gleidman would (Freudianly) have felt obliged to ask, "But *why* do you think you lost your driver's licence?" He instead looked at first startled, and then (on reflection) really quite touched and pleased.

There was a busy signal each time she tried calling Lakeside Taxi after her session, and so she had to remain perched on the edge of the chair behind Declan's desk to keep on trying. Which was how she came to hear the descent of the next client. Someone on steel crutches: the staggered, war-veteran sound of a careful series of aimed-for spaces being metallically captured. A claim being staked out again and again, the ring of steel on stone.

To her surprise the invalid turned out to be not an old man or a veteran of foreign wars, but a girl of fifteen or sixteen, a lolling spastic girl who was being helped by a remarkably glamorous fair-haired girl who was a year or two older. But who had done this terrible thing to this spastic girl? Who'd had the spite to hire for her the world's (or at least this town's) prettiest possible caretaker? Unless the blonde — with fate's physiological sadism — was actually and cruelly her sister.

But now Declan, who'd gone up to the kitchen to fetch one of his notebooks, was coming down the stairs to see the handicapped girl while Claire, still sitting behind his desk, was calling the cab company again.

The fair girl, whose plump breasts were supported by the slings of her blue and white gingham halter and whose fat little hips had a smug look, brimmed up at him flirtily, and it seemed to Claire that in a more dignified way Declan was flirting right back at her, the air between them was so charged and amused, the formal questions being asked allowing both asker and answerer to ask and answer quite different questions with their eyes.

And so this handicapped girl was their helpless witness, then. Their perfect excuse to meet and flirt. But now someone at Lakeside Taxi had picked up the phone and, after giving him the address, Claire was told someone would be there right away, and so she had to pull on her jacket and escape up the stone stairs into the surprisingly calm and grey afternoon.

By the time she got home the day was sunny again and was throwing windy rectangles of light to tremble on the far wall of the kitchen: a blurred blowing pattern of new little leaves — minnowy shadows that in the late-afternoon light seemed to speak of the afterlife. Unpacking the groceries, she thought of Steff again. She pictured a scene in which she stepped into the kitchen to answer the phone and discovered one whole wall was on fire, heard herself crying "Steff! We have an emergency here! It's a fire! And so could you get off the phone right away please? So I can call the fire department?" Then his madly chatty reply: "A fire! Is it a big one? It must really be rather pretty . . ." He must be lonely, she thought as she was on her way up the stairs to the top of the house.

In her room, she had a fear of too easily finding her driver's licence. She lifted up magazines, books, then went to her closet and felt inside at least twelve pairs of pockets. She knelt on one side of her bed and peeked under it, then stood up next to her bedside table and picked up a teacup. Then the saucer. And there it was, lying in wait to reproach her for her criminal extravagance, her only consolation being that nobody else would ever need to know this, it could be yet one more secret shame.

The following Thursday Declan told her to make a face. She felt wary, she was so convinced that a trick must lurk in this particular assignment, but then she thought, Oh why be vain? After all, he's only trying to teach me to be less so, and she screwed up her face so tightly that he laughed.

After today, she thought, I won't bother to come back.

As for *his* face, it had gone pale, unhappy. He made her think of a boy who was so bitterly bored that he wanted to hurt something. He said, "How old are you anyway? Fifty?"

She stared at him, astounded. The one thing about her looks that she was sure of was that she looked young for her age. Perhaps even too young. "I'm thirty-seven."

He came over to her and placed his hands on her hips to guide her through a series of steps, showing her how to put her full weight (and trust) into one foot, the other foot, then he asked her to hang her hands on his shoulders as he steered her around the room. It was almost like dancing, it was so formally warm and measured, it was like dancing in a room filled with sunshine in a Russian novel set out in the country. She wanted not to be hurt, or at the very least to pretend not to be hurt. And, besides, wasn't it to his credit that he seemed always to know when he had gone just a little too far? Or was it yet another black mark against him? Surprising herself, although not all that much, really, and in a way that depressed her, she spoke in the social voice of a woman politely dancing with a man she's just met: "I like your amulet, where did you get it?"

"My wife gave it to me." The way he said "wife," it didn't rhyme with "knife," he drew it out much too adoringly, tenderly; it had too much of a voluptuous rise and fall in it.

"I thought it might be from Arizona, it looks so Navajo."

"You're right. It *is* from Arizona. But it's not Navajo, it's Hopi." And then (dance over) he went out into the next room to get his appointment book.

Left behind to draw on her corduroy trousers and pull an elastic band around the frizzed plume of her hair, Claire wondered what was wrong with her. And why were her feelings always taking leaps to land in opposite corners? Because what she now felt for Declan was tenderness, she even felt that in saying the word "wife" so caressingly he was trying to make her jealous and that his wanting to make her jealous must mean that he cared for her, so that when he came back into the Room it seemed it was the most natural thing in the world for her to smile at him with her most radiant smile.

He looked surprised. "You look so lovely right now. So feminine, really."

That night in bed she picked up a book and read from where it fell open: "God has his merciful, if daft, devices." But when she slept she dreamed that she was in Dr. Tenniswood's drug pantry, pouring pills into medicine glasses no bigger than liqueur glasses, their measurement levels marked in glass braille. She'd made a terrible mistake, but was hoping that if she could be very quiet and quick, no one would notice. Declan was in the dream too, hurrying by, while Dr. Tenniswood's hallway was flooded with panic and too bright a light.

～～～
～～～

On the following Thursday (a blue car this time) she drove out to Ottersee with a bottle of cranberry juice rolling around on the car seat beside her. She hadn't had cystitis for months and wondered what had brought it on this time. Not sex anyway, unless it was sex with herself. Her thighs felt fat and sticky in the hot car as she reached out to steady the bottle, then lifted her hand to her forehead. It felt unhealthily warm. She pulled the car over onto the side of the highway and climbed out, then after a quick walk up a path's speckled shade had to fight her way into a thicket of fir trees to painfully relieve herself. She squatted down beside some leaves that looked like poison ivy, they were so shiny and three-leafed, like leaves in a fable, while her hot and sick-smelling urine made the pee-beaded leaves bob wildly. What did women in the Middle Ages do when they had cystitis? They went to see herbalists. Or they went to see homeopathic doctors. But no, homeopaths didn't come along until the eighteenth century. Or was it the nineteenth? So they went to consult alchemists then. Magicians who could turn fever into dew and dew into gold. After she'd crept back into the car she leaned back against the seat with her eyes closed for a few minutes, collecting herself, then sat up to drink down what was left in the bottle.

On the stoop of an old schoolhouse attached to the gas station she pulled in beside half an hour later, two men were playing a game of cards in the mild country sunshine. As she got out of the car, the more handsome one glanced over at her with an unimpressed weariness, but the other one – a small man who'd tucked his sun-faded purple shirt into his jeans – had the sort of observant, shy presence a woman could fall for. He was also the one who got up to fetch the key to the washroom, and when he handed it to her he looked into her eyes with such a watchful sexual seriousness that she felt, at least for a moment, utterly in love with him.

But she could feel the two of them watching her from behind as she was crossing the tarmac to the whitewashed station, and their inspection gave her that awful watched-woman sensation, a rumpled, skirt-crinkled-up-in-the-back, jiggly-buttocked feeling, paired with the localized splinter of stinging discomfort in her urethra. The wind was hot. Wind for a fever. At the side of the building, she pushed open the paint-stuck door to the Rest Room and saw that one of the toilets had flooded. Someone had dropped paper towels all over the floor to soak up the wet, then thrown wet armloads of them into a wastebasket that looked like a lacquered pink basketball net. Chills overtook her as she was washing her hands. Was it an insane thing, driving so far out into the country when she was feeling so shaky? Maybe it was insane, maybe it was even illegal. There were moments when she felt almost delirious and odd thoughts came to her. Maybe it was the fever, but while she was combing her hair she felt frightened.

~~~~~
~~~~~

Declan was wearing a grey T-shirt with his jeans, along with a new amulet, this one tied with a tight leather thong around his throat. They stood talking for a moment while Claire unbuttoned her jacket, slid her feet out of her sandals. She didn't know too many men who wore amulets; the world had been taken over by boys who wore little Thai hoops in one ear. This amulet looked like quartz and there was a vein of rust in its white part and a cloudy bloom of rust in its clear glassy tip. It matched the small stain of rust in the iris of one of his grey eyes.

He told her he wanted her to yell as loud as she could.

She tried — a self-conscious shriek, almost comic — but neither of them laughed. But then she stopped. "I find it hard to yell when I need to go to the washroom."

"So go then."

She went into the little cubbyhole toilet. Her urine came weakly out of her, hot as hot tea, and while she was tucking her T-shirt into her shorts she started to feel chilled again. It was the little pulse of natural daylight, high up on the wall. Along with the sound of the flush, it was giving her the shivers.

After she'd crossed the hallway to Declan again, she told him she had cystitis. "I have a fever." She lifted his hand and held it flat to her forehead. "I'm burning."

He let his hand rest there a moment, neutrally. "You'll live." But he was already looking watchfully into her eyes, hatching plans for her. Then he said that he wanted her to do some pushing exercises. "Push at me," he told her, and he danced a little dance in front of her in his holistic sandals, in some kind of therapist's imitation of a taunt.

But she stayed self-conscious. She halfheartedly pushed at him while she could hear his children happily ordering each other about, up in the windy green garden.

"Come on now, you can do better than that."

She did get better at it but it still felt artificial to her, seemed to grow out of the wish to be good, not assertive.

He told her to yell at the top of her lungs.

"I don't know if I can do that."

He wanted to know why not.

Because there was a danger she would only be doing it to be compliant. "What good can it possibly do me if I just stand here and acquiescently holler?"

He said that an uninhibited person would just seize on the act as a way of finding out what happens next. "And might discover that a good deal of tension and anger comes out."

"An uninhibited person might really enjoy it."

"He might. She might. Right."

She opened her mouth and gave a thin yell.

He looked judgementally amused. "Is that your best offer?"

She tried again. Another self-conscious but higher-decibel bleat.

There was an answering yell high up in the garden. But it was a yell in context.

"Lie down," he told her then, his voice a little kinder, and he hunkered down beside her and began to give her a lecture on bioenergetic theory, spoke of the localization within the self of a living universe, spoke of a charged field within the body; squatting like a farmer at the edge of his crops, spoke — gazing out over *his* newly planted field, and beyond it, perhaps, to the memory of other fields, other bodies — of the body's light, the body's fire. He said that "streaming" was the fundamental function of protoplasm and that protoplasm under a microscope streamed and pulsated. He said they would be working toward tissue-states that were pulsing and rhythmic within her body, and that the more these feelings deepened, the more in contact she would be with herself and the world.

She felt moved by his words, even though she sensed that he was mainly quoting from some treatise on the body. She supposed this would have pleased him if he had known. Possibly he even did know. So far he had been able to pick up even very slight tremblings deep in her body, had seemed to psychically sense them. No, it was more than that. Even if she felt a trembling or excitement was very hidden, very inner, it was as if he could actually see it moving over her skin, a light wind over water.

But the theory and practice that were involved in curing the heart via the body did not enthrall her. Sometimes she was even convinced that the only explanation for her having grown fond of Declan came from her need for a diversion. And so did he bore her then? Up to a point he did. Or at least his beliefs did.

At the first intersection coming back into town, a big man waiting for the light to change made her think of Steff. But something was wrong: a riding crop was held at ease in one black-gloved hand, but his other hand was holding a pistol on the top of his riding cap. It gave her a jolt, but then she saw that the gun wasn't a gun after all, it was only his other black-gloved hand, its thumb stuck up. He looked flushed and fussy. And he wasn't really all that much like Steff, after all – Steff was leaner and more handsome, and yet Steff did also have some of this man's sour and imposing mid-life grandeur, and she remembered all the times they'd gone out for drives, but then detoured down bumpy roads to visit building sites. Some of their worst fights had followed visits to building sites: Steff driving home in a wounded snit and once they got there extending his rage by accusing and cursing in Russian and banging about.

And she would always agree to go, that was the terrible thing, although she hated (and had always hated) touring building sites: all the climbing around among concrete blocks and scaffolding while breathing it all in: concrete dust, the creamy but chemical odour of new paint, the sacks of powdered cement slumping against walls like sacks of grey flour, all the possibilities for injury if one wasn't vigilant. Then the tour. From one grey room to another. Future classrooms smelling of construction dust, but soon to smell of chalk dust, and with the lecturer (the chief engineer) already in them. She could still hear Steff's voice, a soothing drone, describing the problems, the challenges, what he'd had to do to meet them, while she (like a good little dog) was following behind him and warning herself to pay close attention. *Don't let your mind wander!* And yet there had even been the odd pleasure here or there – or at least that mix of pain and pleasure that could make her remember entire afternoons – because she could also so clearly recall looking through a wall that was all window (recently unpacked and dusty new glass) toward a melancholy but oddly comforting vista: a field of vivid green grass, the hills in the distance dead with the bushy greys and browns of an earlier spring.

Rain blew against her window as she sat up in bed that night, reading *A Writer's Diary*, the part where Virginia Woolf had an idea, while dressing, about how to make her war book, she could pretend it was articles editors had asked her to write ("Should women smoke; Short skirts; War etc . . ."), then there was a bit about windy rain battering, dogs barking, dark out, English night, while over here in windy and somehow too modern Canada it was a wild night too, the rain coming down even harder after she'd snapped out her light.

It didn't stop until late the next afternoon, leaving behind it a mist she walked through while asking herself, Why can't I be happier? What is the impediment? Apart from myself? Apart from all the mistakes that I've made? She walked past wrecked gardens that were petal-littered, everything rained down onto gravel, walked home down Sunnyside past children who were playing in cold little groups at the fronts of verandahs, passed by four little guys of nine or ten as she was walking along deep in thought on the subject of her life and what would she do with it ("What'll it be then, madam?" "One rye and lithium." "Right you are, madam, one rye and lithium coming right up . . .") when one of the little boys experimentally sang out to her, "Hello, *bitch!*"

Although she knew that these words were no more un-friendly than the barks of an overexcited and even friendly little dog, she was too preoccupied to think of a clever reply and so she only hurried on by, speaking almost in a mutter to say, "Hello, bitch bitch . . ."

But even this small acknowledgement seemed to excite her tiny tormentor, she could hear him cry out to the others in a squeaky and thrilled voice, "Did you hear *that*? Did you hear what that lady said? I said hello bitch and *she* said hello bitch bitch, did you *hear* her?"

She turned on them to speak to the boy who'd called out to her. "Honey, why don't you just try to grow up?"

After a moment of stunned silence, they all followed behind her, dancing and chanting on their cold little stick legs: We don't *want* to grow up! We don't *want* to grow up! We don't *want* to grow up!

She supposed she could tell them it was a universal lament.

"Suck on the heel of my hand," Declan said to Claire, and after a moment of fastidious resistance she did. It turned out to be a curiously clinical sensation, like sucking on a long cool breast shaped like the thigh of a chicken.

Then he wanted her to jut her chin out. "Doing this will help you to have orgasms."

She jutted her chin out. It was true, it did make her feel more sexy. But then she remembered something: "But I already do have them."

"When?"

"All the time," she said.

When he looked doubtful, she said, "With my husband." Then she added a postscript: "When we were together." But it made her feel ashamed, that he should feel the need to say such a thing to her — that he should know her so little! — and ashamed too, because of the stern way he had asked *"When?"* She wanted to say to him, You assume too much, you presume too much, you shouldn't go around acting as if everyone in the whole world (except you, of course) is, where sex is concerned, in need of instruction.

Her argument with him continued on the way home in the car. She mimicked his voice sharply asking *"When?"* But she made it sound even more aloof and moronic. *Idiot,* she harshly whispered. *Idiot, idiot, idiot.* I have them with myself too, she should have told him, and she saw herself pulling on her jacket and leaving him behind as she tossed a few leftover words over a shoulder: *"When* I feel like it."

Tiny black berries fell from the trees onto the streets, but once they'd been walked on they didn't even look like berries, they looked like squished pellets of roof tar, and now that it was twilight the leaves on the trees were black too, sharp little black leaves against a colourless sky. Claire took one of the footpaths out to the canal to find a little more light. She wanted to walk for hours, walk and think, she wanted to walk and think about Declan. Not that she was in love with him. But when was he ever not in her thoughts?

Saturday was a windy wet day, drearily dripping, and when she walked through the wet bracken close to the river she met up with six or seven sodden couples, the women grim-faced, their silk bandannas tied in tight knots at their throats, while huffing behind them came their ill-looking husbands, although some of the women were paired up with men who had observant eyes that were filled with emotion, and behind them came more couples made up of tired, decent women, their coat collars turned up, women whose men were either too sour or too grimacingly friendly. Or men who looked ruddy, merciless.

She thought: I don't want to be married again, ever. Although sometimes she dreamed of something like marriage. Like marriage but not marriage, a more emotional relationship. More intense, the two people more absolutely *for* one another.

But now, like a human embodiment of a cautionary tale, even more husbands and wives were climbing up from the river, and these final wives were wearing sectioned clear plastic rain bonnets while peering brightly out at her like inquisitive grasshoppers.

That night she dreamed that she was still married to Steff. They were living in a house whose main floor was clear glass. They could see pale schools of fish moving beneath them. Then a naked man came swimming directly in under their feet. When she turned to say to Steff, "*Look* at him. Now he'll be able to see up into our lives," Steff glanced over at her with an impatient look to say, "Well, we can put down a *rug*."

〜〜〜〜
〜〜〜〜

A handwriting analyst was being interviewed on the car radio as Claire drove down to Ottersee the following Thursday. He'd written a book – Strokes Something? she couldn't quite catch it – and was telling the host that people who made long loops on their *y*s and *g*s were highly sexed people. Claire listened with interest – her own *y*s and *g*s were long and full – and off and on all the way through the session with Declan, she found herself thinking of the words of the graphologist. They stayed in her thoughts, a taunt, so that when she peeked at her watch and saw that they had only five minutes left, she dared herself to say: "I haven't been to bed with anyone for over two years."

Having got it out at last – and it seemed, now that it was out, to have been the thing she had always wanted to tell him most – she rolled away from him and hid her eyes with her fists. But at the same time she was feeling the absolute relief of confession. She was in awe of it too, in awe of the way it still had its old power to make her wonder why she could never remember ahead of time how clear it could make her feel. It still had its old power to make her wonder why she lied to herself, and fought it, and tried to pretend that secrecy (ugly secrecy) was her friend.

Declan had in the meantime rolled in behind her, she could feel him, he'd placed his hands on her shoulders, a strong firm presence. And his hands stayed with her, bobbing with her noiseless spasms until she freed an arm, reached blindly out. "Could you hand me a Kleenex please?"

She could hear him walking fast on his knees over to the box of Kleenexes to yank out a handful of them, then she could hear the sound of his knees come shuffling back, could feel him passing the Kleenexes to her, over her shoulder. It seemed to her she could even feel admiration beaming warmly from him to her, through her back, and with this realization tears came. But at the same time she was feeling like an imposter, a fake, as if whatever she was crying about, this wasn't it, this was a performance. A phrase came to her: the awful efficiency of obsession. She was sure it must mean the awfulness of turning a person into an object that was at least as well stocked as a well-appointed desk. Awful if for no other reason than the reason that in the end – life being life – it would lead to loss. Then what you were left with? You were left with yourself, the joke being that this might have been what you'd wanted all along:

not to be bothered. But at the same time she was also thinking thoughts that were completely opposed to this, she was thinking she loved him. Just to be here with him, his whole body breathing behind her, was paradise. But now he was speaking again, speaking low — there was, after all, no need for him to raise his voice — now he was telling her that the whole culture was deprived where sex was concerned, the whole culture was deprived of true emotion, this was why there was so much emphasis on how many times and how often and how many partners and how long since you'd had it and technique. "All that bullshit," he said hoarsely, and his voice seemed to convey a kind of principled anguish, as if he, too, had not been to bed with anyone he loved for over two years.

The crying, after blocking her nose, was now also clearing her nose, and she could again smell the freshly cut lawn on the breeze blowing in through the open window. She wondered if Declan had cut it himself this morning before her arrival. Getting out of the car she had seen his children and the biologist's children running in a circle all around the garden. "Green rain!" they had shrieked. "A green rain is falling!" And they had flung handfuls of grass up into the air and then had thrown themselves down on their backs so that the grass-rain could drift down into their open mouths.

"Even the people who think they are having a full sexual life usually aren't," Declan said. "They aren't having anything like the powerful feelings they could be having if we didn't live in a performance culture." And then he said that the culture's emphasis on sex was a compensation because true sexuality was missing from the rest of life, and that if a person was living out of his true sexual feeling, then all of life was foreplay, and at this she again thought of his children, lying so blissfully flat on their backs up in the garden.

He was by this time massaging her right shoulder with one hand and she was feeling so grateful to him that she wished she could turn to the hand he was supporting himself with and dip down to it and kiss it. She didn't quite dare to do this but she did rub her cheek and hair, cat-like, against it. And when he said, "Only one percent of the population has a truly vital sex life," she didn't feel even the slightest temptation to smile at so unresearchable a statistic.

Then it was time for the session to be over. She sat up to pull on her skirt while he went into the outer room. But while she was still buttoning up her shirt he came back to say, "I want you to write me a letter."

"A letter?" She gazed up at him, puzzled. "What sort of letter?"

"Any sort of letter. It doesn't have to be long."

Driving back to the city, she remembered the morning interview with the graphologist. She imagined Declan hearing it too, a cool breeze with the smell of cut grass in it blowing in through the big Ottersee kitchen, the bitter earth smell of strong coffee.

~~~~
~~~~

She thought only of him, and missed him, and wondered what it would be like to live with him in a nearly wordless and passionate collusion. But collusion wasn't the right word. She meant bond, bond was the right word, or she meant a connection so psychic and sexually deep that words not only would not be required, they would ruin things, words would lead to attacks of integrity, words would mean there could be no future for them, ever.

After she'd had her shower she pulled on her most slippery nightgown and went down to her bookcase to find a book that was sexually dear to her because of a single phrase in it ("He was bite-kissing her"). She wanted to see the words blaze up at her, the words were an explosion and it was a relief to know that they could explode over and over again, it was even sexy to take her time going back up the stairs, to climb back up to the top of the house carrying the book. But when she saw herself in her bedroom mirror she decided she was looking too studious to make love to herself: she was, after all, still wearing her glasses, and so she took them off as she lay down on her bed and opened the book to the necessary line, felt its heat while at the same time she was longing for a man's hands to roll her over and shove down her panties. It was a longing that made her feel the need to shove a cushion up tight between her thighs, above all a cushion with a hard seam on it, although all she had the energy to do was roll over to snap out her light and reach for her pillow. But her pillow was too soft, it wasn't manly enough, she wanted a hard manly cushion. Still, the thought of turning on her light again and running down to the sofa to fetch a cushion exhausted her – it was also too exhausting to play all of the parts at once (the man, the woman, the director, the girl who had to run downstairs for the props) no matter how much she wanted the bliss of the busy final moments of arousal. And since Declan was also on her mind – he was always on her mind because she was never not thinking of him – the sexy feelings began to go, to leave her, a kind of shy respect for

him was already doing its principled dark work of censoring
the absolute thrill of sex, her feelings for him kept on keeping
him out of bounds. Her gratitude and her tender respect
for him kept on being too much at war with what was most
babyish and wild and squirmy about it, the whole greedy grab
and throb of sex.

~~~~~~

The morning she was to drive out to see him again, she sat on
her sofa in the room overlooking the muddy back garden and
wrote on a clean sheet of foolscap:

> About last week: I just want to thank you for saying
> what you said when I told you what I told you. I also
> want you to know how happy I am that I had to learn
> how to drive, and also how happy I am that I have to
> drive such a long way to see you. But I'm finding it hard
> to write to you when I see you every week. And I wonder
> why you're asking me to do this. What is it you want
> me to say? What do you want to know? What is it you
> want me to know?

She sat in the morning sunlight and read the letter aloud. It
struck her as self-centred, but self-centred in the blunt, sensible
manner of a child's letter. It was even sloppily written. She tore
a clean sheet of paper off the tablet of foolscap and wrote it
more neatly over again. As she did so, she was aware that she
was making her *y*s and *g*s very loopy.

~~~~~

Somewhere below Claire a door slammed. She quickly sat up. But it was only the children next door, in and out.

She went over to her window to watch for Libi and was surprised to see her almost directly below her, hurrying across the van der Meer lawn to the lower door, her hair braided to one side in a fat brown braid with a bow of yarn tied around it.

And then almost right away she could hear her voice, already inside her apartment and calling up her stairs, "Get a move on, Vornoff! I have to pick Rolf up at four o'clock!"

When she got downstairs, Claire drew on her jacket and hit at her pockets for keys and money. Then she followed Libi down the hall stairway and out into the weak sunshine. Walking out to Libi's car, they even bumped into each other.

"I had a nap," said Claire. "After an afternoon nap all creatures are sad."

Libi didn't respond, and so she wondered if she'd even heard her. But she must have, because once they were on their way, Libi turned to speak to her in a voice whose coolness suggested a certain angry incubation: "Do you know what *I* wish? I wish you'd get over this obsession or whatever it is, that is what *I* wish. *That* is what's sad."

Claire said that lately she'd only been seeing Declan for acupuncture treatments, now that the summer was over and he was back in the city. She kept to herself the news that she missed the car trips into the green world of the country. "In a way I suppose I don't even belong in this century," she said to Libi. "I don't even own a car. As you may have noticed."

"Actually, I think you're extremely trendy. A woman of our time."

"Thanks a lot, friend. How am I trendy?"

"All this chasing after cures."

"But you know I can't sleep. I don't need to tell you about it all the time, do I?" And at this she had to turn her face abruptly away from Libi and pretend to look out the window. My sleeplessness is like love, she thought; it's just never not on my mind. And yet she *had* slept. Had done the dangerous thing, had taken a nap, and was already trying not to dwell on the thought that because of this nap there would be no sleep tonight. She said in a low voice, "I'm also in pain, Lib."

"Give up dreaming of Herr Doktor and run three miles a day and your pain will vanish, I guarantee it."

"Do *you* run three miles a day?"

"I'm not in pain."

After they'd finished their shopping they went for tea at one of the Byward Market cafés. While they were drinking it, Libi spoke of a fight she'd had with her daughter that morning after breakfast.

"What about?"

"She took a tube of lipstick out of my purse without asking for my permission and so I slapped her across the face."

Claire stared at her in amazement, then looked down at her tea. If she had a daughter, she would be fair to her. She considered saying in a mocking voice, "And did the punishment fit the crime?" But then she decided not to, preferring the bitter safety of disapproving of her friend in silence.

Twenty minutes later, as they were driving down Elgin Street to Boushey's to buy cheeses, Claire looked to her right as they approached the Institute and saw that Declan's car was parked at the deep-shaded side of the Institute garden. Its presence seemed to turn the street into a street in a movie, it so much gave it that air of false peace. She felt that the day was now worth something, because without at all expecting to, and with thanks to a friend who did her a favour without even knowing she was doing her a favour, she had seen Declan's car.

The first snow came, and with it came a windfall: Steff sold the little house on Noel Street, then shared its profits with Claire. She decided to go to Florida for a week. She had never felt even the slightest desire to visit Florida, but Florida was the closest warm place. She planned to go the first week of the new year.

On the afternoon of Christmas Eve, she went downtown to the Byward Market. It was a mild rainy day, and the air of Christmas carnage she'd looked forward to (the fragrance of torn tree-bark, the slashed sound of bells) was partly undone by the rain and by the fleet of black panel trucks parked at the mouth of the market and stocked with poinsettias and red roses. How unreal and even ugly the poinsettias were, they made her think of flowers cut out of red fabric for a church bazaar, and why was she buying flowers in any case, she was leaving the winter behind her, but as she was standing in the Christmas rain trying to decide, she looked up to see that a woman buying flowers from the back of the neighbouring truck was watching her. This woman was wearing a glossy brown fur jacket and elegant slacks and tiny brown leather boots. But it was by her hair that Claire knew her: she was Declan's wife. They smiled small reserved smiles at each other before they both turned away, each one devoting herself to the buying of flowers.

～～～
～～～

From Florida she wrote letters home. She described the beach (how white it was) and the long ant-like line of promenaders slowly moving in nineteenth-century fashion up and down the shoreline in their overcoats. "The wind," she wrote, "blows in from the Gulf of Mexico and is bitterly cold. There are a few shell collectors, no swimmers, a few joggers wearing gloves."

The best part of her day was the night. She took a walk on the cold sand every day at sunset. She seldom met anyone, and when she did, it was almost always a solitary soul like herself. If the dark figure came toward her at a walk, her heart went on alert and her arm pressed her shoulder bag tight to her side, but if the dark figure came toward her at a run, her heart and arm didn't respond at all. All a thief would have to do, she thought, is jog. When the sky was completely dark and all the little hotels along the beach had turned on their lights, she hurried back to her room. She heated up small dinners on the hot plate in her tiny kitchen, and after she'd made herself a cup of tea she would take a long bath, then sit propped up on one of the big beds to read. She kept the door to the balcony open so she could hear the waves coming in on the beach. Her third night in Tampa it rained, and she stood out on the balcony with her winter coat tied on over her nightgown and watched the rain falling into the garbage pit and the parking lot and the ocean.

The next morning was almost warm, was almost a real Florida morning, and she decided the time had come to give up being a recluse and go down to the main floor for breakfast. She could hear the sounds of cutlery and breakfasting voices as she walked along the downstairs hallway, then entered a dining room with a long view of the cold beach. The buffet offered every kind of Florida plenitude (huge platters of sliced fruits and giant vats of eggs benedict and jugs of orange and pink juices and great basins of muffins) but the room was so crowded that she ended up having to share a table with an elderly man whose prominent eyes greeted her morosely and a young woman who must have received a similar welcome, she smiled up at her with such quick gratitude. And so there they were: three polite strangers at the same table, hyperaware of their table manners while bemoaning the erratic weather and the fact that the books in the hotel library were all old romances from fifty years ago. But as he was leaving their table, the elderly man offered to lend a few books to Claire. She said, with a kind of polite dread, "Thanks, that would be marvellous."

One of the books turned out to be a dull espionage novel, the other a book on herbs that she sat out in the sun and read for part of the afternoon. For nervousness it advised red sage and skullcap. It said that one great cause of nervousness was novel-reading. She had to smile as she looked out at the late afternoon glare of the cold Atlantic. Why did all these people who worked with the body feel such a hatred for words? Because they did. Words were their enemies, unless they were words that could be used to force people to believe what *they* believed.

A little after five a wind came up, and when she went for her nightly walk along the beach, she felt an ache in her right shoulder. She kept her left hand in her pocket to protect it from the wind because she was getting a fungal infection in one of her fingers, something she must have picked up at work before she left Canada. It didn't bother her. All she had to do was remember to keep it dry.

The next morning, down in the hotel smoke shop, she stood looking at magazines next to a young woman, then noticed that she was standing beside the girl she'd shared a table with in the dining room. They got into a conversation about magazines, about how addicting they were. At least, they agreed, they could be addicting for the first ten minutes or so. "Last year I was still reading the teen magazines," the girl told Claire, "but when I turned nineteen I made a resolution to switch over to *Cosmo*."

"A lot of advice about sex in *Cosmo*," said Claire, smiling over at her.

"I *know*," the girl responded in an eager declarative voice, flat with the vowels of the American Midwest. "In every issue a new position! I mean, I'm just not all that flexible . . ."

They shared a small laugh over that.

Later in the morning the temperature dropped again, and just after lunchtime the wind began to blow great flings of cold rain at the windows. By late afternoon the rain had stopped, but the day had turned so much colder that Claire decided to go home. But could she just do that? She thought of going home before her week was up, the shame of it. But it was what she wanted, and so she sat down on her bed to phone Air Canada's toll-free number in wherever it was — she thought it was in Miami — and to her amazement was able to get a flight out of Tampa for just before midnight. She went down to the lobby and said to one of the clerks at the front desk, "I'm checking out tonight, I can't stand the cold," and the clerk said to her, "I don't blame you." And then to her great surprise he even gave her a refund for the three days that she would no longer be a resident of the hotel. All the way back to her room she thought, That was easy, that was easy.

In the shower she shampooed her hair for the trip home, but she could only shampoo it with one hand, she had to keep her infected hand dry, and so she held her left arm raised high, a great dictator or an imposter saviour blessing the multitudes.

But after she'd packed her lightweight clothes and was leaving her room, she heard — from one of the rooms close by — the untethered cry of a woman crying out in love, a cry that was so lonely and grateful and surprised that it stilled her, made her feel that everything she'd ever done up till this moment was just nothing, compared to so ardent an aloneness.

Snowflakes bobbed in the cold air and now and then even flew crazily upwards, dead sparks from the storm. They were like the dark spots that dance in front of the eyes during a time of exhaustion. But by ten in the morning the sky outside Dr. Tenniswood's windows was so windy and white it had turned the day dim as twilight. Turned it into a lamp morning. Claire made her way through the warren of rooms on the ground floor of the clinic, clicking on lamps, then spent the morning typing letters and setting up appointments.

At noon, she went up the stairs to Dr. Tenniswood's apartment to water the plants, then wandered from room to room, looking at things. She went into the den to take a look at the zebra rug she coveted, paid a visit to the bedrooms. She examined the photographs and cosmetics on the dressers, opened a few drawers, then went on to the brighter family room where a lectern with an open atlas on it was standing over by a window, an atlas that all at once seemed to her to be a gift from the world: an open book in whose pages she could look for (or at least locate) Declan in Venezuela. She went over to it and turned its pages until she found South America. She was feeling the pleasurable humiliation of a woman who falls in love with a map because a man she adores is a tiny black dot on it. Except in this case there were two tiny black dots: man and wife. She pictured Declan walking hand in hand with his wife on the hot white sands of Venezuela. Or in ankle-deep turquoise water, veined by the underwater optical effects of tropical light.

Last stop was the little bathroom off the master bedroom. The more utilitarian furnishings – toilet, sink, lion-pawed tub – were far away at its other end, almost as distant as stage props. But they made her feel watched as she sprayed on sweet mists from five different bottles of cologne.

Night after night while Declan was away in Venezuela, she dreamed of babies. She was happy in these dreams, swimming with the babies in deep but very clear green water. But one night she dreamed she was wearing a red headscarf tied back like a gypsy scarf. She was feeling attractive in it, but when she got home from downtown (where she'd been swanning around, utterly full of herself) she felt something bulky sticking out and then shook out the scarf to discover a whole nest of sanitary napkins in it, still unused (thank God for the fastidious unconscious), but it was a strange dream for her to dream the night she'd decided to announce to Declan that she would be leaving therapy, for a while in any case, since she seemed to be making the process her life. She could also tell him (but probably wouldn't) that she couldn't even go to a movie without wondering what he would think of it, or live through a weekend without obsessively wondering how he was spending his. But she also seemed to be angry with him. The fact of the matter was, his kind of therapy was beginning to depress her: the correct way to stand, the correct way to breathe, the correct way to be like everyone else. It's really Nazi, she thought.

On Monday morning the secretary from the Institute phoned her to ask her if she would be willing to switch her next acupuncture appointment from Wednesday noon to early Friday afternoon and she agreed to the change, but when Friday dawned it was such a sleety dark morning it made her feel utterly sorry for herself for having been born a Canadian. After lunch she took a cab to the Institute through lightly falling snow, then climbed steps so slick with snow-powdered ice that she had to hold on to the railing. What bad luck to fall. And what an irony it would be too, to slip and break an arm or a leg or fall backwards and crack open her skull on the Institute doorstep on the very day she was coming to tell Declan that she'd decided to leave him. And above all to fall because the altered date of her appointment had converted itself into an unlucky number in the lottery of Canadian weather.

But sitting in one of the Institute's back rooms that had been invaded, on this particular Friday afternoon, by the dull and cold snowy light, all she could make herself say was "I'm sorry, but I'm going to have to leave." And then, quickly, to fill the silence: "I seem to be making this business of therapy my life."

Declan was over at the window, pulling down the blind, but now he looked back at her over his shoulder. She could see that her announcement was not what he'd been expecting. But then he'd invested a lot in her, in time and hectoring, and now she would be going out into the world incomplete. She sensed that it rankled. But then he seemed to rally. He even came over to sit beside her to tell her that he understood. "Life is after all also therapeutic," he told her. But it seemed to her that he said it in a dull voice, out of duty.

She was feeling dull too, having made her announcement. She had expected it to give her a great shot of euphoria and it had not. Still, it would have been completely mad for her to change her mind after having with such difficulty at last made it up. And he had passed a test, since he was so clearly (if ambivalently) willing to let her go. Dr. Gleidman hadn't been willing to let her go (even ambivalently) and so in the end she'd had to give him the slip.

"It may not be permanent," she told him, although she was absolutely certain that it would be. All she wanted was to walk out of this room and be free to live (however dully) her life.

He again told her that he understood. And then after what seemed to be a small argument with himself he said there was of course always more work to be done if and when she decided she wanted to come back and do it.

It was snowing again when she came down the steps into the afternoon, but the sky still had enough glare in it to hurt her eyes. She felt bereft, useless. The day had turned into a day with no meaning. She tried to remember the hard things, the times he had said unkind things to her, and when she remembered them she had certain regrets. She regretted that on certain occasions she hadn't had the wit or the integrity or the bravado (or whatever it was) to say to him, "You wanted to hurt me so much that you were willing to have me think less of you. And so now I do. And so who's sorry now?" But she could never bear to hurt any man (at least any man she admired) if he had tender feelings for her; to hurt a man who had tender feelings for her seemed so cold-hearted that even the idea of it made her feel physically ill and in an uneasy way even inhuman.

The next day was another sunless but glaring grey day and when Claire came down her street she saw that Lowell – the spring-water man – was parking his white truck in the van der Meer driveway. "I've bought myself a still!" he called out to her. "To make water, not whisky!" And when she got closer to him he told her that there was a distilled-water craze in this town. "I kept getting all these calls from people who wanted to know if I could deliver distilled water to them, and so I started asking, 'Why does everyone want distilled water all of a sudden?' And it turned out they'd all been to see these same two guys – two brothers, actually – who take samples of your spit and urine and then send them off to a big computer down in California and in a couple of weeks the computer people send back an equation that tells you everything about the state of your health."

Claire got out her keys to unlock the street door. The two brothers sounded so much like two crafty brothers in a fable that she wanted to laugh. "And then the two brothers put you on a regime of distilled water?"

"Yeah," Lowell said, kicking the snow off his boots on the doorstep, then following her up the stairs to her landing. "There's an ideal equation to aim for. One equation for Caucasians, one for Orientals. And then these two guys — Walter is the one I went to — detoxify your body with certain foods and minerals. They say they can even cure cancer this way." Mounting the stairs behind her, he was sounding dangerously breathless. "The thing is, you have to drink an awful lot of water. Half, in ounces, of your body weight in pounds. For a big man it could come up to three quarts."

They'd reached the landing by this time, but Lowell was still breathing heavily, holding the heavy carton of water bottles high up on a shoulder.

Claire quickly unlocked her door, then stood aside to allow him to precede her into her apartment. "I once saw a man who believed that people drink too *much* water," she told him. "He saw the kidneys as an overworked sponge."

"He must be macrobiotic. The macrobiotics could put me out of business," said Lowell. And he lined up the bottles of spring water along one wall of her kitchen.

~~~~
~~~~

The sound of barking brought Claire to her kitchen window the following evening. She drew back one of her curtains to see Dirk van der Meer down on the floodlit driveway urging his two excited dogs into the back of his car, then remembered that Judy had told her they were all going to go off to Mexico for the last two weeks of January, and so tonight must be the night of their flight, she thought, they must be boarding the dogs at a kennel. And they were sweet old dogs, really, the van der Meer dogs; sometimes at night when she could hear Judy or Lynnie calling them home she would smile, thinking of the kinds of names dog owners would give to their dogs. To own two dogs and name them after a French philosopher and an English food, say, and then to have to go to your doorway every night and call out – as her neighbours two houses up the street were obliged to call out – "Here, Voltaire! Here, Muffin!" would, she thought, be like shouting out over the neighbourhood night after night the same tired joke. The van der Meer dogs had been named after a discredited politician and an herb (Boris, Sassafras), names that seemed curiously appropriate to them once you got to know them, but she couldn't honestly say she would miss their barking, she was too much looking forward to the pleasure of having the whole house to herself.

While she was sitting at her desk the next evening, making notes for her essay on *Insight and Responsibility* for her one psychology course (and also making use of the dream about the featureless face riding by in the carriage) she heard a click like the click of giant chopsticks at the back of the house. She hurried to the back window to look out, and saw that one end of the park had been frozen into a rink that had already attracted nine or ten skaters. She was so cheered up by all this nearby life and commotion that she stayed for nearly half an hour at the cold window, mesmerized by the way the skaters' blades hissed when they braked and also by the way the ringleader skaters snaked the puck down the ice with their sticks as they were breaking away from the dreamy others, now drifting in psychic convoys behind them. There was even a father with a toddler at the far end of the rink — the father swinging in a protective half-circle around his small boy while a whole flotilla of bigger and rougher boys went gliding by.

On Tuesday night, as she was coming down her street, she could see how hugely dark the van der Meer house was looking in the winter moonlight and she let herself with more alertness than usual into the downstairs hallway in her part of the house. She felt watched, old fears from childhood. But as she was unlocking her own door she could hear the phone starting to ring and she ran to it in gratitude as if whoever was calling would have to be bringing her only good news.

It turned out to be someone from her past, although more from Steff's past than hers, a former secretary of Steff's named Elaine Chevaldayoff, and when she said "Oh hi, Elaine, how have you been?" Elaine took the question seriously, telling her that she'd had cancer and that she'd had to have six operations and chemotherapy and cobalt and how her hair had fallen out and how she had to wear a wig. At Elaine's mention of the wig, Claire was able to recall her face and along with her face her straight shiny brown hair. But now Elaine was telling her that the doctors had cut slits in the soles of her feet and shoved tubes up them and then shot dye up the tubes and finally were able to locate the cancer in some lymph nodes in the back of her stomach. She described each of her six operations, how long they took, how long she was in hospital. Claire wanted to ask her what made her suspect she had it, but Elaine was already asking her if Steff got married again.

"He's living with someone, but they're not married, at least not yet. And in fact they can't be, because we're not even divorced yet."

"I heard that he was," said Elaine.

Two nights later Claire was startled awake by a knocking on the downstairs front door. She turned on her light and picked up her watch to see that it was nearly three, then pulled on her robe and hurried downstairs to turn on the overhead light in her kitchen. She let herself out of her apartment then, looking anxiously to both left and right on the landing, then proceeded much more slowly down the dark second stairway, step by peering step, until she could see that the man who was standing motionless on the other side of the window glass was a stranger; a bare-headed man in a raincoat standing in a way that looked formally humble (a professional man, then: detective, cop). Her heart thumping killingly as she squinted down at him, one hand shading her eyes, the other clutching together the tops of her lapels, she at last reached the street floor. But although her visitor couldn't possibly have seen her, he must somehow have sensed that he was being watched because he was already hurrying to stand under the nearest tree. And so what now? But she already knew what now: she should flush him off the property with light, but as she was feeling her way with her free hand for the panel of lights she saw him unzip his pants and then urinate against the trunk of the tree in the cold night – he's only a drunk then, she thought, and she felt so weak with relief that she wanted to both laugh and cry at the craziness of it all – but then she heard a noise like a firecracker going off at

the back of the house. No, the sound was coming down from
upstairs. The man under the tree was a decoy then, a distraction while the real work — robbery; robbery or worse — was
going on at the back of the house. But, no, it was definitely
coming down from above. She ran back up the two flights of
stairs to her bedroom, looked through her window to see two
men in black caps and black windbreakers skating at high speed
while taking renegade slapshots at the slats walling the rink.
Gracefully fierce and black against the pale ice, they were skating
with their black dogs — the skaters fleeing the dogs, the dogs
racing the skaters: it was a scene that seemed spookily medieval,
sinister, the scene and the late hour — but at the same time the
skaters were making her feel protected (they were dog owners,
after all) and so they made her feel she could call out to them
if the man under the tree (or his accomplice) — if he now was
even anyone to worry about any more, being drunk — tried to
break into the house, but when she ran down the stairs to check
on him again, it was to discover that he'd gone. Besides, the men
down on the rink were hardly to be trusted, making so much
noise while in the houses all around them people were doing
their best to stay asleep.

Once she was back in her bedroom again she went to her
window, then stood looking down at the skaters with a kind of
puzzled fury until twenty to four, when they at last skated off
the rink and out over the bumpy ice that led to their car, the
biggest black dog nosing the backs of their skate blades. But
the smaller dog was wanting to linger behind to sniff out the
message trail left by other dogs, and so didn't leave until he was
hailed by a sharp whistle, then he too ran off the white ice, the
shadow of his own little legs running neatly beneath him.

At first the little blue pills were magic pills, bringing a deep perfect sleep without dreams, but on the fifth morning Claire woke to a merry-go-round of obsessive dark thoughts, the world turned fated. She had to keep watch over it. On the sixth morning she came to a shaky decision: she must give her tiny blue saviours up. She was afraid to throw them out in the garbage, she was already too addicted to the deep sleep they could give her and she could all too easily picture herself — already tonight at two in the morning — going down the icy back stairs in her nightgown and snowboots to root around among slickly freezing orange peels and deeply cold coffee grounds in her search for the vial, and so she flushed the little pills down the toilet, she was that afraid (and that certain) they would drive her mad. But the moment she saw them whirling away was a desperate moment, whirling with it a wobbling question: What if I can never fall asleep again?

That following night was the stormy night of St. Valentine's Day, and the Tenniswoods were throwing a party.

And although she knew she should stay home to work on an essay for her psychology class, linking Gurdjieff's enneagrams with *I Ching* hexagrams and the kabbalistic Tree of Life, how could she not go? She even wanted to, to escape from her essay. The guests were all to wear something red. But she had only one red dress and although she wished it could be more shiny and alluring (exposing, at her back, a nearly heart-shaped V of white skin) it was only a stiff brocade, a demurely ugly dress that she craned around to zip up as she was squeezing her feet into the pinch of her tall leather boots. She also slid on a ring – bought for her by Steff on the Ponte Vecchio – a ring with a dull red stone set in an oval of silver bubbles.

The downstairs rooms of the clinic were crowded with cold coats and laughter, but the food and most of the guests were upstairs in the main part of the house. She excused her way past the talk and guilty smiles of the smokers to go into one of the clinic's examining rooms to tighten her bra straps and put on her (red) lipstick. She was tempted to pull her shawl off and stuff it into her shoulder bag, but she needed to somehow warm her cold arms. She dreaded having to go upstairs to meet people. She spoke to herself in the clinic mirror. Pull yourself together, for heaven's sake.

But when she came up into the living room, she was immediately taken under the wing of Dr. Tenniswood, who wanted to introduce her to an architect whose name was Mitchell Kinkaid. "This is the genius who's building us our new house."

Claire had seen this man before, but she wasn't able to quite recall where. He stood leaning against one of the tall bookcases and they talked for over an hour while she held, in one chilled hand, a glass of tonic water with a slice of lime in it. He was wearing a wool scarf tucked into a V-necked sweater and now and then he gazed at her with a briefly surprised look, then turned sharply away from her to sneeze into his cupped hands. His wife (or the woman Claire took to be his wife) decided to leave the party early. Were they estranged? This woman said "Bye-bye, baby," in a coldly wifely way, holding up her right hand and wiggling her fingers at him, but as she was walking past Claire she smiled a smile so sweetly eerie it was unearthly. This was the way an angel might smile. Or a psychotic person.

After she'd gone, Mitchell told Claire he could see that she was a really open person.

She was pleased, although she knew that it was not wise to be, because in her experience the people who told you you were open invariably ended up telling you you were hard. "I don't think I'm so very open," she said.

"What I mean is, I can see that you're not a hard person."

"I can be a tough person," she said, trying to hide the fact that she felt vaguely offended.

"We've met before, I think."

"I've been trying to remember where too. And now I do: it was at the Health Alternatives Bazaar. Last spring, out at Earlton."

"Right. We sat on the grass listening to one of our local charlatans giving us instructions on how to breathe."

"You thought he was a charlatan?"

"God, yes. The man was dog*matic*, and besides, all that breathing stuff is *ancient* news, it's yoga stuff, even *I* know all that stuff, it's incredibly old hat. The yoga way is the better way, believe me . . ."

Shouldn't she somehow at least try to defend Declan

Farrell? Say: Look, I happen to know this person, and he's really just not like that at *all*. But she was silent.

~~~~

From her window that night she could see a lone speed skater doing his side-stepping laps all around the perimeter of the rink. She pulled a ski sweater on over her nightgown and stood watching him while she brushed her hair, nearly hypnotized by the way his elegant speed skater's stance — part sports fiend, part scholar — still left him free to skate with such grace. A mystery man striking off for far away even within the small confined space of the rink.

That night she slept only a few hours and when Mitchell phoned her at work on Thursday morning to ask her if he could come over to her place to give her a yoga lesson she said, That would be great, terrific. Because she was thinking: Yoga could be good, it might help me sleep.

"Could I come tonight after supper?"

But it couldn't be tonight, tonight was the night for Dr. Tenniswood's diabetes clinic.

And so they settled on Tuesday night. "But my wife knows much more about yoga than I do. And so maybe she should be the one to teach you, maybe I should bring her with me."

"If you like."

It snowed on Tuesday evening, a snow that by seven seemed on the point of turning into rain, and when Claire looked out of one of her front windows to see if she could see Mitchell come walking (with or without wife) down her street — he was by now half an hour late — she saw a man in a black parka who was standing down on the white lawn bring a tube of lipstick up to his lips. She saw him apply it with two bold male strokes, and it was only then that she understood that it wasn't lipstick, it was Chapstick. Was this Mitchell? But it would have to be Mitchell; the man in the parka was now turning to squint up at her windows, causing her to quickly step back. A little ashamed to have been seen (but did he really see her?) she went to check her face in the mirror.

When he got to her door, she told him to bring his boots into her apartment so they could get dry.

"We'll also be needing a blanket."

She told him she had an old camping blanket somewhere upstairs. But as she was walking along the upstairs hallway, she could hear him walking along the downstairs hallway to her kitchen. She could hear where his feet stopped. Coming down with the blanket, she met him on his way back into the living room.

"This is very rude of me," he told her, "but I've been reading your appointment calendar." Looking hugely pleased with himself. Looking for other men's names, she supposed.

"And what did you find on it?"

"That you go belly-dancing."

"Oh, that was a terrible experience. I was so uncoordinated. I only went to one class."

"Who was the teacher?"

"I forget her name, this was over a year ago. Some glamorous blonde shrew, very impatient."

But he didn't seem to be listening. He was crouching to spread the blanket out on the floor. "And who is Declan?"

Would he remember that this was the name of the man he'd called a charlatan? She didn't think so, and so she felt it would be safe to say "A friend."

"I want you to lie down on your back."

She stepped out of her shoes and onto the blanket. She hadn't changed her clothes when she got home and was afraid she might be smelling a little too sour and female. Or at the very least of a medical scent from the disinfectant at work. "You don't want to have a beer or something?" she asked him. "Before we get started?"

"Let's just do the exercises first. And then after we're finished you can make us a pot of tea."

When he had her placed on the blanket he began pacing around her. "Relax. Let your legs go limp. Close your eyes." He paced some more. "This is called the corpse position and it's very relaxing."

She smiled up at him, but kept her eyes open. On the sofa she spotted what looked like a peddler's bundle. "What's that?" she asked him.

He opened it. It was his yoga pants, tied up in a T-shirt.

She asked him if he wanted to change. "The bathroom's at the top of the stairs."

He sprinted up the stairs, but he didn't go into the bathroom. She could hear his feet running instead into her bedroom. She thought of the shirts and unwashed panties she'd thrown onto her bed, and the bed not made either, and then she did close her eyes.

When he came down again she could feel him easing himself onto the blanket beside her, could feel him place a hand on her belly. Then she could hear him whisper, "Now I'm going to teach you how to breathe."

After the yoga lesson, they sat across from one another at the kitchen table to drink their tea. Snow fell beyond the windows as Mitchell talked with the speed and desperation of a man who feared he might be thrown out at any minute. But whenever Claire had something to say he responded vivaciously. An odd word for a man, she thought, but the right one. In fact there was an over-vivacity in him that suggested some fundamental lack of attention. Finally she said, "Mitchell, listen, I'm going to have to ask you to go. I'm dead, and I'm going to have to get up early tomorrow morning."

At the door, his kiss grazed her cheek and she didn't offer more of her face to him than that. He ran from her then, down into the mild wet night.

Three days later she called him. When she said her name she had to say it two times before he would even acknowledge that he knew her. And yet when she invited him to lunch the next afternoon he accepted quickly enough. She told him that she could get an hour off from work and he said he could do the same. Then she told him that she'd been thinking about the other night and that she was probably too elusive. But then she found him too intrusive, she said, so it wasn't a simple thing.

"Too *what?*"

"Too intrusive."

"And you were too *what?*"

"Too elusive."

"Oh," he said. "Well." He yawned. "You know how it is." He yawned again. "C'est la vie," he said.

After she had put down the phone she felt her face go hot, and wished she hadn't called him.

Walking down the steps to the fish store she could see the fishmonger in the cold hallway leading to the back of the shop, unpacking his crates of fish and crushed ice. Maybe she should buy something a little exotic, she thought, like shark steaks. But was shark truly a delicacy? She tried to recall what she knew about the dietary habits of the shark. Wasn't the whole point that they didn't have any? Didn't they eat anything unlucky enough to go floating by? Men, mercurochrome, rubber boots, tubes of toothpaste? She decided to play it safe and buy smoked trout or smoked salmon.

A man's voice called out to her from behind a glass tank of mottled brown lobsters: "You should be happy today!"

She tried to see him, whoever he was. "Why should I be happy?"

"You wanted a lobster, right? Well, today I got you a whole tankful of lobsters!"

"I think you must be confusing me with someone else," she told him, still trying to see where he was. She was also trying to look pensively pleased. But she was secretly feeling the dying fall she always felt whenever she reminded anyone of someone else.

The owner of the voice now appeared behind the main counter, and he was just a boy, really, a part-timer. He weighed the smoked trout for her, wrapped it up in butcher-shop paper.

As she was on her way out of the store she glanced down at the glass display case to see a black plastic platter. Not quite an oval, it was a platter with shoulders. A platter on whose mirrory black surface an octopus had been laid out. Slippery and feminine and faceless and grey, its armless and slippery grey body came to an end in a nightclubby swishy skirt of pearl-buttoned tentacles. How alien and un-dead (although deflated) it looked, a flapper in a shimmery grey flapper dress, a flapper with her inks among all the glum fishes.

〰〰〰

At lunch Mitchell presented her with a bottle of wine before pulling off his coat. It was a cheap one, she noticed – during the winter with Al, the only man she'd gone out with since it was all over with Steff, she'd become an expert on wines – and after they'd finished eating their cold salmon and avocado salad (the sun was by this time shining down on the backyard's small hill of snow while she was running hot water on their flowery plates) Mitchell told her that the last woman he was involved with turned out to be a very hard woman.

This news made Claire decide then and there that the woman must be a decent woman; anyone other people called hard was in all likelihood someone decent.

"I was first attracted to *you*," said Mitchell, "because of your eyes. Your pupils are so dilated. And there's a lot of new evidence out now that people with dilated pupils are incredibly open people."

"My pupils are always dilated. It's because I'm nearsighted."

"No more nearsighted than I am. And look at mine."

She peered at them. They were skeptical pinpoints. She lifted off his glasses, tried them on. They were incredibly strong: his face swam before her, amoebic, pale. Only his hair was the same, a bushy gold sphinx shape. She whispered, "You look sort of distorted."

"I *am* distorted," he assured her, speaking low. He was standing close to her and they were both smiling. She didn't want him to kiss her. All she could do was massage his arms as he stood with his hands on her hips. And say, "I like you, Mitchell." It sounded tepid, even to her, but it was the best she could do.

He said, "I'll drive you back to work," and they pulled on their coats, then went down the stairs and out into the glare.

He had a great raft of a car, battered, heirloom of an earlier decade. The door on his side didn't work, and so he had to go in on her side and hitch himself over to the steering wheel. They drove in silence through the winter stillness of the southern part of the city. As they were passing the icy streets that ran down to the lake, Mitchell reached over to take her hand. But when they got into heavier traffic she withdrew it, then was afraid she'd hurt his feelings and so made a big show of pulling on her mittens.

At the next intersection he started to talk about his wife (Liz) and about Liz's sister who he said was a bitch. In what way, she wanted to know, and he told her some of the things this sister had done to Liz. What about some of the things *you've* done to Liz, she was tempted to ask him, but then considered that this would seem — under the circumstances — to be a curious question. Instead she asked him, "Do you think *I'm* a bitch?"

He was cleverly, judiciously slow to answer. Yes, all in all, he did rather think she had the potential to be a very difficult and demanding woman.

They drove on in silence after this, until they reached the clinic. But as she was getting out of his car he turned to smile at her. "Listen, Signora Vornova, I'll call you . . ."

She touched his hand, an appeaser again, but then she said, "No, Mitchell. Thanks. But please don't call me."

As she was running up the steps to the clinic she could hear the careening sprint and whine of his tires on the bare parts of the cold street.

She felt quelled, at least a little bit quelled, and when Dr. Tenniswood came into the examining room, where she was taking the blood pressure of an anorexic aerobics instructor, and asked her if she had any plans for the evening she said no, thinking he might have a pair of free theatre tickets to give away. But what he was wanting to know was if she could she stay after work to type up the notes for a speech he had to deliver at a medical conference in Cleveland at the beginning of March.

Once she was alone – the patients gone, no noise coming down from upstairs – she sat and typed at her desk under the illumination of only one lamp. The warren of dim rooms behind her, with their smell of sterilized towels and denatured alcohol, made her type furiously, she was so hungry for fresh air. And Dr. Tenniswood's handwriting was ill-looking too, its clots and reckless clumps of letters unravelling downhill on page after page. But although he was a Luddite (and proud of it, not being the one who had to type up the monthly bills), he had made one very small concession to the new wired world: he'd bought a second-hand typewriter that had a line of memory behind a clear bar of plastic. Still, in her hurry, she kept jamming the keys and after she'd been whimpering and cursing to herself for almost an hour, she heard a noise somewhere upstairs (but weren't the Tenniswoods all out for dinner somewhere?) then decided it was only the joists of the house contracting in the falling temperature, but then – perhaps because she was working under a single light and this lonely light was turning the office into a stage-set – she began to picture scenes of terrifying drama: Mitchell Kinkaid throwing open the door and striding into the clinic to tell her he'd been sitting parked in his car the whole afternoon watching everyone leave Dr. Tenniswood's office – "Everyone but *you*, Claire . . .," or a gunman kicking in the door and yelling that he'd shoot the place up if she wouldn't give him drugs, and it was at this moment that one of her fingers hit a wrong key and the typewriter began to type by itself. She stared at it in stunned wonder as it typed onto the page: WHAT IS YOUR NAME? *Oh*, she felt like wailing, *What will happen now?* When she obeyed, typing CLAIRE VORNOFF, the machine galloped off on its own once again, this time to type WELL, CLAIRE VORNOFF, LET ME SHOW YOU . . . And this time, although still alarmed, she thought, What? *What* are you going to show me? She was even sitting with her raised hands backed up in spooked reverence, like a poor girl in a fairy tale, as if she expected a prince to rise up, then neatly climb right up out of the machine. Or he could turn out to be no bigger than a caterpillar, a reclining miniature prince leaning back against the steel stems holding up their fan of inked letters that were like intricate numerical flowers. But what the typewriter was now typing, after

its LET ME SHOW YOU, were the words A FEW OF MY SPECIAL
FEATURES, and as it began to type a long list of the office chores
it had been programmed to do, Claire sat alone in the dim
office, feeling as if she'd had an amazing future predicted for
her by a ouija board. Or as if she'd been given the perfect solution to a problem after throwing down the sticks for the *I Ching*.
She was still feeling chosen as she ran through the smoky cool
of early evening on her race to reach Habib's store before seven.

When the lights came up again, the two actors, by now wearing bathing trunks, were gazing out over a beach that was apparently to be played by the audience. They were talking about women, the pale actor pointing at the spot in the dark that was Claire to say *"There."* And as Claire tightly crossed one plump thigh over the other, the taller actor turned to say in an awe-struck voice, *"Oh,* yeah." To which the first actor wistfully said, "My sweet goodness." A ripple of laughter moved across the audience then as the taller actor said, "Uh-huh," and then the first actor said, "What a sensitive young lady," and the laughter surged down the rows of chairs in the mercifully small auditorium.

By the time they were moving on to admire other spots in the dark, Claire could feel that the nearly bald man who was sitting next to her was shifting his position in what appeared to be wary sympathy for her. He seemed young to be nearly bald, and as they were pulling on their coats at the end of the play he asked her how it had felt, to be singled out like that.

For a moment all she could think of as a response was "Seduced and abandoned," which also happened to be the title of the movie she'd seen at her local repertory house two weeks ago. "Praised and accused," she said, doing up the buttons on her long winter coat. "Adored and offended."

"No one wants to be called sensitive any more."

"And no one," said Claire, "wants to be called a lady." Then she said that at first she'd been afraid they were ad libbing. "And that they'd picked me out earlier in the evening and decided I was the one it might be fun to humiliate —"

He squinted down at her. "But it was definitely scripted. You could see the way they had practised choreographing it. First spot in the dark: lower left. Second spot in the dark: upper left. Third spot in the dark: upper right —"

They were by this time walking past backdrops for other plays: parks and farmyard panoramas painted with the cartoon innocence and spectacular clouds of a children's book, the whole place smelling so strongly of paint and dust that it was an extreme relief to step out into the cold evening air. It was even a relief to hear the crunch of snow underfoot.

~~~~

The following Friday evening, her head aching, Claire stood at her kitchen sink, hulling strawberries. She hulled them until her fingers turned red, then she waggled them under the faucet. I'm Lady Macbeth, she said. But these particular berries were too hard, white-knuckled at their tips. She poked them in a circle around the cake's white field of whipped cream. She wished she had something more inventive to add. Mint leaves.

Or tiny blue basil flowers. But the anemic berries would have to do. Besides, she was going to be late, she would have to run.

In the foggily mild evening she walked up the dark steps of the verandah of her hosts — both architects and old friends of Steff's — and, once inside, made her way through all the shouting and laughter toward the kitchen. In the long dining room, illuminated mauve glass mushrooms were hanging low over long rows of salads, hot deep trays of lasagna, black bowls of wild rice. It was scarily crowded, she couldn't see anyone she knew, and the noise level was making her feel solitary, ill-equipped for the evening. She set her cake on a counter next to a surgically gleaming sink in the vacant and glamorously utilitarian kitchen, then went up the stairs to take off her coat.

In the bedroom, what looked like a hundred women's coats were heaped on the low bed; she could smell the expensive and sweetly peppery aroma of perfumed fur, perfumed fake fur.

She was on her way over to the mirror when she heard someone else come in. It even turned out to be someone she slightly knew, Maggie someone, who'd worked with Steff when he was still at the National Capital Commission. She was dressed in a long brown skirt and a slouchy brown jacket, expensive, mannishly elegant, and after she'd inspected herself in the mirror, testing the bounce in her hair, she turned at the door to look back over her shoulder and narrow her eyes at Claire: "You really *do* know how to do the best for yourself, don't you?"

Then she was gone.

Claire wanted to run down the stairs after her to say: "Just tell me this, Maggie: why is it that you . . . are the way that you are?" But as retribution this did seem to be just a bit on the lacklustre side. As she was walking down the stairs herself, though, she remembered that Steff had once said in a scornful voice, "Oh well, you know Maggie, she's not exactly one of our brighter lights," and this was a comfort to her.

While she was taking her time serving herself at the long table under the glass mushrooms – to extend a moment in which she actually had something to do, and while she was also looking for her cake (was it too pathetic? it hadn't been set out yet) – a voice just behind her said, "My sweet goodness," and she turned to see the man who'd sat next to her the night she'd gone to see *Sexual Perversity in Chicago*. "If it isn't the sensitive young lady," he said, and they laughed.

"Try this," she said, pointing with her spoon at the bowl of wild rice, and he did, and after they'd both helped themselves to a little of everything they made their way toward the fire. Walking down the shallow steps to the living room they sank through waves of jokes, waves of laughter, women glancing coolly back at them over a shoulder, over backless dresses, while a barefoot man in jeans who was wearing a black T-shirt under his tuxedo jacket was mimicking a politician he'd heard being interviewed on a talk show, a Montrealer who'd wanted to assure the interviewer that he wasn't Satan but who'd kept pronouncing Satan as Satin as he'd shouted into the microphone, "I am not Satin! I am not Satin!" At that same moment, a woman who was at the centre of a group of women over by the back windows was (as if in explication) moaning in a laughing, protesting voice, "No, no, he's an absolute monster!"

When they got to the fireplace there was talk about someone who'd married a woman some of the people there seemed to know, and a man sitting on the sofa was saying, "Don Greenlee was her first husband —"

Which led a woman who was sitting lower down on a hassock to cry up at him, "Which makes you wonder about *his* judgement . . ."

"Yes. But he did try to drown her . . ."

"Then all is forgiven."

Claire's companion made space for her on the opposite sofa. "I'm Tony O'Bois, by the way." And he picked up the nearest bottle of wine so that she could see the label, raised his eyebrows at her.

"Thanks, Tonio, yes."

"Actually it's Tony. The o doesn't go at the back end of the Tony, it goes at the front end of the Bois. Half-Irish, half-French." But he was, he told her, actually British. "An army brat who grew up north of Birmingham. I was actually born in London, though, at the London Fever Hospital . . ."

"But wouldn't a hospital that called itself the London Fever Hospital be only for infectious diseases?"

"I think my mother was admitted with a fever and then while she was there she just happened to give birth to me." He was by this time giving off a jaunty sexual glint — making him seem much less of an uncle than he'd seemed to be the night of the play — and after he'd loosened his tie, he told her he was teaching history out at Carleton.

She was out at Carleton too. "But just in the evenings. Taking English courses. So I can teach." Although what she'd really like to be, she told him, was a bibliotherapist. "Isn't that what they're called? Therapists who treat their clients by suggesting that they read certain chosen novels or stories or poems?" Walking along a street past a glisten of ice caught in morning sunlight – but this was years ago – she'd glimpsed a copy of Sylvia Plath's *Ariel,* its cover the deep blue of a place-mat, lying on the back seat of a car with a child's rattle placed next to it like a bulbously humanoid pink plastic spoon. "What I really want is to force my opinions on people. You could take a poem by Wordsworth – 'Strange Fits of Passion Have I Known,' say – and you could tell your patient to take two doses of it at bedtime."

"And call me in the morning . . ." said Tony O'Bois. "Anyway, when you do get to be a teacher you'll be able to force people to read things. At least in theory. You'll be able to say 'Before your exam take three doses of this sonnet: "Steamboats, Viaducts, and Railways."' Which, by the way, is the only sonnet I can remember from high-school English."

She asked him who had written it.

"Wordsworth," he said.

This made them laugh, although Tony swore it was true.

Sometimes, Claire told him, she got almost frantic, trying to match the person to the book when she was riding the bus on her way to work, and she described the absolute silly anguish of sitting next to a stranger who was holding a book so that she couldn't quite see its title. And then there was the way all this seemed somehow to be connected to her compulsion to give the right person the right book.

"Or connected to feeling left out of the sexual secrets that might have been in the books your parents were reading when you were a child," said Tony O'Bois. "Wouldn't Freud have said that?"

"Yes," she said. "I'm sure he would." She was ashamed that she hadn't thought of this herself. But his referring to sexual secrets then led to their talking about sex and love scenes in books and movies, about how they were either too romantically hazy or too clinically precise. "When the only thing we really need to know," she said, "is how people get into bed with one another in the first place. The unexpected ways it can happen."

He was watching her, over his drink. There was a moment of quiet, then a familiar voice made her turn to see Janine Mills, who four or five years ago had been one of her closest friends, and who was now listening, in her stoop-shouldered, disapproving way, to a woman in a dress patterned with weedy blue flowers. Why had they decided to stop being friends? But she already knew why: Janine was a person who could not tolerate listening to other people's complaints. Claire recalled a farewell note she had once planned to write to her: "You gave me so much advice! But you mustn't reproach yourself. (And I know you won't) . . ." She also remembered complaining to her because Dr. Tenniswood had, over a question about a lab report, treated her unfairly. She remembered the impatient way Janine had listened, then the way she had rushed to defend Dr. Tenniswood — a man she had never met! — even going so far as to tell her that Dr. Tenniswood was a terribly busy man and that she (Claire!) should make at least some effort to get over being so thin-skinned and always imagining things. And wasn't the first requirement in a friend that she have the tact to scoff at your enemies?

But now she could see that she too had been spotted, and so she stood, feeling false and doomed, to excuse herself to Tony O'Bois and walk over to say hello to Janine. The two women talked until Janine's husband at last came to the rescue, and after they'd gone off, Claire looked for Tony, but he was by this time sitting next to the fireplace and talking to Maggie.

She detoured into the kitchen to check on the whereabouts of her cake and saw that a few kind souls had helped themselves to three or four slices of it. Her poor fallen little cake. Just for tonight it was her humiliated child. But she should be getting home, she had a fever.

On her way back upstairs again she felt dizzy, and up in the bedroom she quickly pulled on her coat. And then as she was coming down the stairs she could see Tony O'Bois talking to a bearded man and a tensely skinny woman in a black dress who'd hung their arms around each other's waists like schoolgirls. She didn't think he was looking her way as she was saying goodbye to their hosts, and so she stood pretending to read the titles of the books on the top shelf of a bookcase just off to his left. She held onto a nearby chair to steady herself. She didn't want to walk alone out to the bus, particularly not along so many dimly illuminated and slushy streets. But at last he appeared to have noticed her, she heard him excuse himself to the lovers, then he came over to stand beside her. "Listen, I'm about to leave too, let me give you a lift home."

But on their way down the steps to his car he asked her if she would care to go out for a drink.

She was still feeling shaky, but she didn't want the evening to be over yet either. "Or could we go for a walk? It's so mild."

"Sure. How about a walk on the beach?"

"Isn't it still winter?"

"It feels like spring."

As they swung past the university on their way out to the beach at Mooney's Bay, he told her about all the in-fighting in the history department and about all the trials of applying for tenure-track, but his words — although alarming — were, after all, only the familiar words of everyday speech: back-biting, nefarious, nepotism, incestuous, internecine, cloak and dagger. Then he began to sing, "We were sailing along, on Mooney's Bay, we could hear the something singing . . ."

"Mermaids singing . . ." sang Claire.

"We could hear the members of the tenure-track committee singing . . ." sang Tony, and then together they shouted, ". . . they seemed to *say!* 'You have stolen our hearts! On Mooney's Bay!'"

But at Mooney's Bay they were quiet again and sat looking out over the cold river. There was still snow on the beach. And there weren't any joggers running their dogs along the wet sand close to the water. No joggers, no dogs, no gulls, no moon. But there was a nearly warm wind. Claire rolled down her window to breathe more of it in, but after a few minutes the breeze made the air inside the car get too cold and so they got out to walk through the warmer outside air down to the river.

When Tony spoke of his wife, a lecturer in the history department at the University of Victoria, Claire was surprised. She had thought of him as a balding young bachelor. "Twice a year I fly out to Victoria to see her, and twice a year she flies back here to see me . . ." They began to walk along the tideline, kicking at little stones as they talked, and after they'd walked to the far end of the beach and then back almost as far as the other end to get to Tony's car, he looked at his watch, holding his wrist up close to his eyes in the dim river light. "We still *could* go out somewhere for a drink, we could go to a little bistro I know that's close to the National Gallery . . ."

But the bistro, when they got to it, was closed up for the night. There were people huddled inside it though, eating and drinking under the low reddish lights. It was like peering into a stage version of an extremely cosy hell. "The owner's family," said Tony. "And the cooks." The owner's family and the cooks shrugged apologetically as they waved from the darkly glowing interior, then Tony invited Claire to come back to his place to help him finish off a bottle of Algerian wine.

The wine might be helpful, it might even kill the infection, and so she said yes.

On their way across town it started to rain. Claire looked out at the little houses with their single dark evergreen trees standing on little hills of dry grass in a sinking sea of old snow. It was windy and wet by the time they pulled in beside a tall house, its bricks already darkened by what was becoming a dense rain. In the wallpapered warm hallway, she unzipped her boots, then carried them in one hand as she followed Tony up a carpeted staircase.

While he was out in the kitchen she arranged herself sideways on his leather sofa with her stockinged feet tucked neatly beneath her. On the wall across from her were rubbings from tombstones, Inuit prints. The hardwood floors shone. She thought, He's a better housekeeper than I am. She helped herself to an apple from a hill of apples that had been tumbled into a grooved pewter bowl, then ate it in experimental bits, her stomach was still feeling so rocky.

When he came back into the living room they spoke of

landlords, insomnia, music, and his psychiatrist, a Freudian from Glasgow.

She then told him that she had just recently stopped seeing someone who worked with the body. "Psychodrama," she said. "Breath work. Primal scream. A spooky gym class for only one student."

He sat down beside her.

"But my feelings for the therapist were very conflicted."

"In what way?"

She drew up her knees to clasp them, even though this made her skirt slide back to the tops of her thighs. She felt like a girl at summer camp, her pale hefty legs hugged to her while she sang the praises of a boy she adored. But a rising wave of nausea forced her to slowly let her feet down to rest flat on the floor. Her arms felt damp in their crevices, her head ached. She tried to breathe slowly, evenly. "He was so moody, but at the same time he was just so incredibly helpful and decent. He was also enigmatic and magnetic and sporadically vile . . ."

Tony's eyes were looking amused, observant. He took another small sip of his wine, then gave her a swift look. "So. Were you in love with this guy?"

Her eyes started to fill, she had to turn her face quickly away from him.

"Hey," he said kindly, stroking back her damp hair. He poured her a second glass of wine. He rested a hand on her shoulder while he was pouring it and she could smell the wine in his skin.

"Nothing bad happened," she said. "Nothing unethical. I was just getting more and more attached to him and so I made myself leave him. There was quite a lot of touching, though, but then that's the kind of therapy it *was*. A lot of pushing and shoving and embracing and howling . . ."

He smiled, but he was also looking a bit puzzled.

And so she said that she supposed Freud was right, really: the therapist shouldn't touch the patient, ever. "Not even to shake hands. Because it muddies everything . . ."

"I suppose it would."

Her face was feeling flushed. "And so I left him," she said. "He also gave me acupuncture treatments," she told him, thinking how inconsequential it must sound to be adding this.

"A more delicate form of torture," he said. "Unless it was *less* delicate."

At the beginning of the last acupuncture treatment Declan had given her, he'd poked the skin of her back with the tiny needles that so seldom caused pain, then he'd thrown something ticklish over her back that had felt as light as gossamer or a spider's web. But before leaving her he'd turned the knob of a dial somewhere off to her right and the spider's web had electrically metamorphosed into a giant hairnet of tiny dancing shocks. Still, the effect had been more pleasant than not.

When they'd finished the wine they went out to Tony's kitchen, passing by a master bedroom whose wide bed was under a grey bedspread patterned with black triangles, and got themselves cold drinks of water, and again Claire felt almost faint, but when they came back to the sofa again and Tony stretched his arm along its rim she felt she would be able to quell her uneasy stomach, if only out of a social terror of throwing up. But then

Tony was saying that they needed food and music, and he got up to go over to his tape deck and put on a tape that he'd made of songs he'd liked on other tapes. "Everything from Bach fugues and Schoenberg to country and jazz," he told her as he was on his way back to the kitchen.

Over the music Claire could hear dishes being washed, taps being turned on and off, the opening and closing of cupboard doors, and she again felt queasy, but she also thought if she ate a salted cracker it might help to settle her stomach.

As Tony was coming back to the coffee table carrying a tray of crackers and cheeses she smiled up at him to tell him that almost every song she'd ever loved seemed, by some miracle, to be on his tape. But by this time the room was turning surreal and it even seemed to spin just a little as he was sitting down beside her again.

"But which one was your *most* favourite?"

"Most favourite, most favourite . . ." she said, trying to make her voice sound musing, smiling. "But I have too many favourites, especially some of the really old ones. 'Mack the Knife,' 'Suspicious Minds,' 'Bye Bye Blackbird' . . ." When I die, she thought — well, *before* I die, actually — I must arrange to have "Bye Bye Blackbird" played at my funeral.

"How about 'Come to Me, My Melancholy Baby'?"

When she smiled, he hitched himself over to her and more than ever smelling of being married (of perspiration and laundered denim and of the wine again), he began to rhythmically rub a thumb behind one of her ears. I must tell him, she thought — but what must she tell him? — she was feeling the urgent need to communicate some vital information to him, but the room — why was it so bright? — was making her feel an

even more urgent need to clap a hand to her mouth, which she
then had to do as she jumped up to run in the direction of what
she prayed was the washroom and as she was running she could
hear him running swiftly on sock feet behind her, could feel
how he'd turned into a basketball player shadowing another
player who was guarding the ball (her nausea), keeping it
hunched up close to her, and when she dropped to her knees
in front of the toilet bowl, then supported her arms on its cold
rim, she could feel him ponytailing her hair back for her, then
he was kneeling to one side of her to smooth the sweat back
up into her hairline so he could support her forehead for her
while she was, in between bouts of throwing up, weeping-
laughing to cry "Sorry, sorry, sorry, it's not *you*, it's the *flu* . . ."

"I know, I know," he sang down to her as he walked her,
hugged sideways to him, over to the sink where she bowed over
a smaller and pinker porcelain bowl to rub toothpaste on her
teeth with her fingers and rinse her mouth over and over, then
he walked her on down the hallway to a shining spare room
where she let herself be helped to lie back on a narrow bed
covered with an itchy blanket that was patterned with grey and
blue stripes and smelled slightly of mould. He pulled a white
waffle-weave blanket up over her, then sat down on the floor next
to the bed, his head tilted back to rest against the prop of her
nearest thigh. "The corner store doesn't close until midnight,
so maybe I should just nip down there and get you a bottle of
ginger ale or something. Isn't that supposed to be good?"

"Tonic water would be even better, if you can get some."

Tonic water he already had in his fridge, and when he
brought her a cold glass of it, she raised herself up on an elbow
to drink it down in small sips. After she'd handed him the

empty glass she could hear him set it down on the floor somewhere off to his left, then he sat down with his back to the bed
again. She reached out to smooth back his thinning hair, which
he seemed to like, but at some point he caught her hand and
pulled it down in front of his face to nose level, then held it
steady by holding its two outermost fingers milked down to a
stop. Then he blew air at the middle of it. "Did you know that
the Emperor Haile Selassie, instead of calling Mussolini 'Il
Duce,' called him 'My enema, the Douche?'"

She laughed weakly into her pillow. She felt like a child
being entertained with bedtime jokes by her father.

"I just thought this might be an appropriate story to tell
you under the circumstances . . ."

She smiled, feeling quite certain that even with his back to
her he could tell she was smiling.

"Tell me about your husband," he said.

"He really wasn't so terrible. But at the same time he *was*.
It's hard to explain."

"Just another guy who was sporadically vile?"

When she made a noise that was more like a reverse sniff
of amusement than a laugh, he planted a small kiss in the
middle of her palm. Then he said, "Are you divorced yet?"

"Not yet, but I hope to be quite soon."

"And so now why don't you tell me all about this psychodrama person."

She was quiet for a moment, thinking, then said, "The thing
was, he reminded me of a boy I knew the summer I was eight.
I was eight and he was eight. His mother had an old dog who
needed some kind of surgical attention, and the day of her
appointment with my father, who was a vet, this boy (Ralphie)

stayed and played with me the whole afternoon. We played Monopoly and charades and tag and baseball and croquet and whenever I'd sit down to rest for a minute he'd start shrieking 'Play! Play! We may never see each other again!' Just like the sorcerer in *The Sorcerer's Apprentice* screaming 'Dance! Dance!'"

"It sounds pretty intense."

"It was the most exhausting afternoon of my childhood."

He stood up to stretch and turn off the light, then sat down on the side of the bed, next to her hip. "So what are the fashionistas in the department of English teaching their students these days?"

"Identity is a bourgeois illusion, a construct created by material objects and ideology."

He laughed, then said he thought he might lie down for just a little bit too. "Keep you company for a while."

She shifted herself over to make room for him, and once they were lying tightly side by side, one of his arms awkwardly supporting her head, he began to stroke her behind one of her ears, then moved down to her mouth with little beckoning sideways caresses of his index finger, little caresses that felt both repetitive and tender — but then repetition *is* tenderness, she thought — which was when he turned to give her a quick kiss on the forehead. "To make you get better," he whispered.

"Thank you," she whispered back in a flirty little squeak, lulled by the furtive convenience of it all.

He stroked back her hair. "You have such beautiful hair, my darling Claire, how did it get to be so goddamn fair?"

It was from her fair German father. And her fair Danish mother. "Although my fair Danish mother is not at *all* fair emotionally. In fact, emotionally, she's a Danish Hitler . . ."

"A Danish Hitler . . ." he said, and she could feel him smiling in the dark. "So which parent do *you* take after then?"

She swiftly turned to him, dragging the blanket with her, to bite his nearest earlobe, but he was too quick for her, hitching himself up over her to kiss her much more seriously on the mouth, and she felt a kind of triumph then, as she began to kiss him deeply back, she was all at once feeling so creamy and convalescent, willing, weak as a baby, although she did also feel that when she came up for air she should ask him if he wasn't afraid of catching it from her. "Whatever it is?"

But he said no, he never got sick, and right after this they began to undo each other's clothes while making drunken little whimpering noises of practical gratitude. But the whole time this was happening they both seemed to be feeling the need to console one another because they were both thinking of others, then she was afraid that her dampness wasn't only from being aroused but also because she might have wet herself just a bit while she was throwing up. But now he was pushing down her underpants with his thumbs and she was raising her hips to help him and this was like being a baby too, like being a baby getting her rubber pants pulled off her. But her breath. It must smell, at least slightly, of vomit. But he didn't seem to mind.

Rain on the windshield at 2:20 A.M., the windshield wipers tock-tocking while she was gathering herself together to make the lunge across the wet lawn to her door.

"Except when I was throwing up," she told him, "I had a marvellous evening," and she gave him a quick kiss that collided with the corner of his mouth, a kiss meant to convey that she was a grown-up after all and so wasn't going to create difficulties by expecting to see him again. "And the walk on the beach too," she said. "It was amazing."

He pulled her against one of his shoulders to speak into her hair. "Hey, it was just sexual perversity at Mooney's Bay." Then he ducked a little, to squint up, turned up her coat collar for her, gave her a kiss above an ear. "Which floor do you live on?"

"The upper. Well actually, it's the two uppers, there's a bit of space up under the gable, with just enough room enough up there for a bathroom and a bed . . ."

As she was climbing the stairs to her apartment she reproached herself because practically the last word she'd said to him was "bed." What if he thought she was hinting that she was hoping to see him again? She went up the stairs to look at herself in the mirror over her bathroom sink. She slipped out of her coat and let it droop over the rim of the bathtub. She wanted to see if her low-cut taffeta suit still looked devastating but beguiling. Especially with no blouse underneath its fitted jacket. But first she had to bare her teeth at her reflection to see if there were any little bits of food stuck between them. There weren't, but it seemed to her that her face was looking too stiff, as if she hadn't smiled enough. But it was also partly the flu. She thought of Tony's hairiness and his kindness and their little island of fever and wine, but she was also feeling like a betrayer, as if she'd been unfaithful to Declan, this was perhaps why her face wasn't looking as flushed or happy as she'd expected it to look, and to make herself feel better she recalled a photo that Judy had shown her, of a woman who'd been a patient of her brother, a psychiatrist in Kapuskasing, until the brother had ended her therapy so he could marry her. The photo was of a dignified woman in a mustard cotton shift, a skinny black braid hanging down over one skinny breast, a perfect silver necklet encircling her tall sunburned throat. There was something stern and even biblical about her as she stood holding something odd in one hand, what looked like a scroll or a diploma carved out of wood. But it was her face Claire had most studiously scrutinized, searching it for signs of a pathological vulnerability or madness. No such signs were apparent, and yet something about the photograph had made her feel sad, as if the woman, in marrying her therapist, had annexed herself to a wealthy landowner instead of cantering off to freedom on a pale horse, leaving behind her a great cloud of pale golden dust.

Memories of Tony O'Bois made Claire want to smooth sheets and the blue Swedish tablecloth out to the edge of the bed, the table. She also wanted to get her ears pierced, and so on a mild Saturday afternoon in late March she did, sitting perched up on a dunce's stool at Dash of Sass while a cosmetician in a lab coat used an implement that looked like a staple gun to make holes in her earlobes, then screwed stainless-steel studs into them. And very soon after this she became the owner of a pair of elaborate Mexican silver earrings that she dropped into one of her raincoat pockets every morning as she was leaving for work. She hooked them into her ears as she was walking along Wilbrod Street, this small morning ritual making her feel like a femme fatale. As good in its way as smoking a fierce cigarette on a fast morning walk out into the day.

The following week a blue-skied postcard arrived from Saskatoon: Helmut was flying to Ottawa in two weeks to oversee a horse sale out in Manotick. He would stay, he wrote, at the

Château Laurier. News that filled Claire with extreme relief, she so hated having people stay overnight. Above all her family.

~~~~~

Torrents of red poppies were rushing down a dark hillside on the end wall of the gallery, and Claire — peering at them while feeling fat-breasted and pregnant (but could she be? all she knew for certain that she was two weeks overdue) — had to remind herself to smile and mingle. To her left, fields of orange poppies filled the top half of a green canvas called *Poppy River*. And red poppies blowing under a black sky had been painted on a small black rectangle of shellacked wood. There were also studies of bluets and cowslips, and fields of fireweed, and on one of the really huge canvases a scratchy mauve haze of thistles was swinging in the wake of a tractor toddling over a far hill.

The painter, Dorothea Hickey, was still surrounded by fans at the east end of the gallery. Claire had known her since childhood. But she must be in her early seventies by now. Not that she looked it, being impish and ageless in her black heels and black nylons and a slim Black Watch plaid suit with a beret. She had come to her own exhibition in the company of her newly married (and younger) sister, a stately cadaver in glimmering shantung who looked much more ravaged by age than Dorothea did and who was also filled with a trembling pride in her doddering bridegroom. How much more I would prefer, thought Claire, to grow old as Dorothea has grown old, and it was at this appropriate moment that she looked up to see Steff.

He was walking across the gallery toward her, smiling one of his uncertain small smiles. When he got closer he bowed to

her, kissed her hand. Impersonating a German diplomat, perhaps.
Or an icy Swede. He even clicked his heels together. "Madame
Vornova." Then he stood holding her hand, making her feel the
physiological oddness of standing with her hand in his while
she was possibly carrying another man's child. It was almost as
if he had been turned into the baby's father (if there actually
was a baby) by the rights awarded him by proximity and history.
She was even lulled by his holding her hand until it occurred
to her that holding hands with him was the very last thing in
the world she wanted to do, and so she wormed her hand out
of his to ask, "And so how are *you*?" But he had already turned
away from her to say hello to Dorothea, who had rushed over
to tilt her face up at him like a child.

After she got off the bus, Claire walked deep into Rockcliffe
Village, past every kind of architectural jewel and aberration,
not quite sure of the way. She passed stone urns with pink gera-
niums in them, women in tennis dresses coming out of grand
houses, the green of their lawns turned to sparkle by sprinklers.
But the house, when she got to it, didn't look like a house
designed by an architect, having been built in the style of a tra-
ditional hacienda – poor Mitchell, he would have wanted to do
something less folkloric, then it occurred to her that he would
probably be here, in fact he most certainly *would* be, he would
have to be, and she wondered what she could possibly say about
it when she was speaking to him. She tried to spot him beyond
the trees walling the side garden off to the west of the house,
but all she could see, through a screen of new leaves, were ten or
fifteen people who had the casual look of neighbours, including

a number of women and small children – all of them sunburned and in bird-of-paradise colours. As she turned in at the gate, Zuzi – baby-blue jeans, shiny tropical midriff blouse (yellow grasses against a black sheen) – came out through the front door looking amused, as if surprised to find herself living in Rockcliffe, of all places, then she was saying in her bored voice, "Oh hi, Claire, have you come to check out our new abode?" and Claire was following her out to the kitchen to get herself a drink of water.

Trays of pink punch in champagne glasses were waiting on a large tiled counter in the vast Spanish kitchen. Zuzi said, "I better get this stuff passed around," then she was gone, carrying one of the trays down the back steps in her platform sandals, leaving Claire to sip her drink and plot ways to steer clear of Mitchell.

But coming down the steps of the back verandah she caught a glimpse of him (in a formal dark suit and silver tie) standing out on the lawn talking to Kit Tenniswood, and so she changed direction and made her way up two sets of stairs to make a tour of the bedrooms. She visited a small upstairs den, then turned to enter a bedroom that looked out over the back garden, a sunken and peaceful room, its walls a handsome matte red. As she went down its three shallow steps she was met by the most gigantic bed she had ever seen, but it was really two queen-sized beds shoved together and covered with three or four stitched-together antique white cotton bedspreads with a phantom pattern of white wreaths woven into them. And on the wall above the bed, a painting of a village common dominated by a very large leafy tree. The sky was the kind of sky that almost always appeared in paintings of this primitive sort, an inversion of skies out in the world: where it was cloudless, it was not blue, but white, and high up where it was curdled and cloudy, it was not white, but blue.

But it was so strange to think of any sex happening in here. It was like being a child again and trying to imagine sex between her parents. She tried to picture herself sharing a room like this room with a husband. Breathing the same air. She was not at all convinced she would like it. Living alone had become an addiction. Imagine being permanently tied to someone. Someone like Jack. Imagine him getting sick, or even only being Dr. Tenniswoodishly boring, it would be a kind of endless genteel hell. But how did people manage to live their lives in this way? Without leaving a mark?

She went over to the windows and looked down on the guests, all the while thinking that when it came right down to it what she really wanted was to live in peace, to not have to bother with love, to be left alone. And yet when she tried to imagine a future in which she hardly thought of love at all any more it appeared to stretch out before her, endless and dumbstruck, a future afflicted by the sunny and melancholy taint of the eternal.

When she came back down into the garden, she wondered if she would have to sit at the same table as Mitchell, but she ended up seated with strangers who all the way through the cucumber soup talked about city politics.

A grey-haired woman in a grey velvet suit with a touch of white blouse at her throat then began to talk in a guttural voice about robbery. Which was when it turned out that the people at the table all had something in common (all except Claire): all of their houses had been broken into during the last year.

"In safe little Ottawa." This from an amused woman with sad but bright eyes.

The man sitting next to her said that Ottawa had really been a safe city for him. "Everyone on our street's been robbed at least once since last summer, but we've got off scot-free every time —" and at this, his tall, eager wife aimed her toothy smile democratically all around the table: "We have a system. And it's just two little doorbells mounted beside our front door. The bottom one has our own names printed under it. But the name that's printed under the top bell is Corporal L.C. McWilliam, RCMP."

"So is the cop your landlord?" The guttural woman asked her. "Or are you the cop's?"

"The corporal doesn't actually exist," the wife told her. "But we've been thinking of giving him a promotion."

"For his many long years of faithful service," said the husband. "Make him a staff sergeant."

And then while people were still standing out on the cold lawn drinking their coffee, Claire had to squeeze past a laughing crowd of men grouped at the bottom of the stairs. She tried to make herself inconspicuous, just one of a phalanx of women in pale dresses, some of them with coats and men's jackets caped over their chilled shoulders, but Mitchell's glance passed over her, looking rehearsed, even though his eyes were so brimming with laughter at something one of the other men had just said that it was impossible to tell if there was resentment in them. Then, and this too seemed rehearsed, he looked quickly away.

On Monday morning, it was warmer again, and the wind smelled of wood-rot. Claire ran down the stairs to pick up the morning paper. Her worry that she might be pregnant was making her feel so queasy that she decided to drop off a bottle of her urine at the pharmacy down by the Byward Market on her way to work. The one thing she did not want to do was take it to her neighbourhood pharmacy. She knew the pharmacist there and so had no wish to have him know any of the misleading details of her essentially innocent life.

When everything was turned down to simmer, Claire went up to her room to change into a clean shirt, but before she'd even finished buttoning her buttons, the doorbell buzzed down below. Helmut then, already here, and on her way down to the lower level she detoured into her kitchen to feel for her feather earrings in a teacup on the shelf next to the stove. She hooked them into her ears as she was running down to the street door to let him in. Once they'd climbed the stairs to her apartment, Helmut dug a bottle of red wine out of his briefcase, along with a bag of red grapes, then sat at the kitchen table in his grey raincoat, eating the grapes and talking to her as she diced green peppers and long-tailed green onions. Dapper but breathless, he kept watching her stir the soup as he was spitting seeds into the cup of his right hand. He said he liked her earrings. "You really go in for those dangling claws and feathers, don't you, kid?"

Yes she did, but how could he know this? But as the herby green soup was swelling up, she remembered a pair of feathery clip-ons she'd owned when she was in high school.

Helmut pulled off his raincoat, but then he sneezed. "I think I must have picked up some kind of bug on the flight east."

Claire went up to her room to fetch him a sweater.

A muffled voice addressed her from the cave of grey wool: "You pour yourself some of that wine now." And once Helmut's flushed face had emerged and he was sitting at the table spooning up his soup he talked about illness and money. The bad news was that five people from his graduation class were already dead. "Three from cancer, two from bad hearts. And remember Floyd McArdle? Donald McArdle's father?"

Claire brought a basket of bread over to the table. "What happened to him?"

"He's been through hell is what's happened to him. I could give you all the gory details – and I *do* mean gory – but first I need to know: are you squeamish?"

"I work for Dr. Tenniswood, remember? I'm utterly heartless."

"So here we go then, here's the story of poor Floyd: Floyd had to go into hospital for routine surgery. Rotorblading or rottweilling or whatever it is they do to old guys when they have trouble with their prostates, but his own doctor was called out of town, and so another doc had to come in to take the case history. And this new doc took one look at our Floyd, then told him he had macro-something, can't remember what exactly, just that it's caused by a tumour on the pituitary gland, and the reason he knew this was that Floyd's head was like a monster man's head, his bones were so overgrown. Jaw bone, nose bone, forehead bone, everything. Even his shoulders and hands had grown so much that they were like a giant's shoulders, a giant's hands . . ."

"But wasn't that painful?"

"Floyd is a farmer, he's accustomed to pain."

"But didn't anyone notice the way his looks were changing?"

"It happened so gradually. And he never travelled. Day in and day out he saw the same people, the same people saw him . . ."

"And so then what?"

"And so then he had to be operated on by a neurosurgeon, no time to waste. The tumour was behind one of his eyes – his left eye, I seem to remember, and so they had to take the eye out and put it in salt water or something, whatever they do with eyes when they take them out, then they had to scoop out the tumour and spray in the disinfectant or whatever they spray in behind an eye and then stuff the damn thing back in again."

Claire was silent, he had her attention.

"But here's where it starts to get even weirder. After only three days they send him home – you must know how they are, they need the bed – and then on Monday or Tuesday of the following week Donnie drops by to see how the old guy is doing . . ."

And Claire could so easily see it: Donnie McArdle coming into the dim house, that decent sweet guy.

". . . and finds him out cold on the kitchen floor. So then it's back to neurosurgery again, back to taking out the god-forsaken eye again, because this time there's a massive infection in behind it, and this time they can't put it back in again, not right away, the area's too inflamed, and so they stuff some kind of plastic sheeting into his eye socket until the damn thing heals up . . ."

It was as if one of the great city-stomping monster men of their childhood comic books had come to terrible life. It seemed almost in bad taste, after this, to talk about anything normal. But they did. And after they'd finished their soup Claire served Helmut buttered baby spears of asparagus and fried sausages and new little Prince Edward Island potatoes browned in the sausage fat. She hadn't had time to make anything special, there was only the dash on her way home to pick up the kind of food she knew he would like, and in fact he did seem to like it, having eaten up his sausages as if they were marvellous, she in the meantime getting up from the table to go and get more things to bring back to him: a dill and cucumber salad, pickle relish, a bowl of black olives, a pot of black tea. Between mouthfuls of everything he talked to her about his problems with back pain, asked her if she could tell him how to treat it.

She gave him her brutal prescription: no tomatoes, no potatoes, no eggplant, no red peppers. "All members of the nightshade family," she told him. "Also no salt, no fat, no milk, no cream, no sugar. Now that I know you've got back pain, I know I shouldn't have fed you what I just fed you."

But he wouldn't allow her to take the dessert back to the kitchen. "I'll reform my diet tomorrow." And after they'd spooned up the last of their strawberries and cream (Claire too had decided to give in to temptation and spoon up in the strawberry-flavoured slope of sugar gone sweetly grey from the cream) she turned to him. "Want to go out for a quick spin before you have to go?"

And so they went down the main stairs to the car. Cool spring evening, smoky and breezy. "Let me drive!"

He tossed the keys over to her. "So when did you learn how to drive?"

She slid in behind the wheel. "Not that long ago. And then whenever I needed a car I'd just rent one. I used to rent one sometimes to drive out to see someone in Ottersee, a little town about an hour from here."

And as she was driving at hearse speed along Grove Avenue, she told him, "And I can't even begin to tell you what a high it was, driving down that highway . . ." she could feel him studying her as she was speeding up, ". . . to see this person," she said.

And when he said, "And so do you still see . . . this person?" she thought how kind he was, engaging her as he was in a sweet bit of brotherly teasing. Of course if she were to say "This person was my therapist," he would in all likelihood stop his teasing at once and even be a little offended that she'd led him on. She would be like a child boasting to her parents about a make-believe friend who lived at the bottom of their garden. She said, "No, I don't." And then: "I think I'll just drive you up to Brown's Inlet, it's so lovely up there."

"You didn't find it hellishly expensive? Renting a car?"

"No!" she cried out in a wrenched voice. "It's much *much* cheaper than *owning* a car, believe me." But then she spoke more quietly, lethally. "Do you know who's always most concerned about my extravagance? People with not just one car, but two cars! People with three cars! It just makes me wild —"

"Okay, okay, *okay*," said Helmut. "Calm *down*, for Christ's sake, I'm sorry I asked." He looked out his window to speak in a lower voice to the night. "*Damn* sorry," he said.

But this was the way it always was between her and Helmut. They began well enough, but they could not keep up their good behaviour for long. And yet Helmut was the brother who'd saved her life the time they were caught in a blizzard and she'd

fallen down so often that she'd finally just decided to sleep in
the storm for five minutes or so, her other brothers (even Max)
having long since disappeared in the squalls of snow. Helmut
was the one who'd trudged back for her, pulled her up, shouted
at her to keep her awake, then bullied her all the long way back
home. But she had saved his life once too (or tried to) when
she was six years old and therefore young enough to be deluded
into believing she was a hero. An older boy named Buddy had
started teasing Helmut at school, calling him names: Hellie and
Hell-Cat and Hell-Nut and Nazi, and she, a whirling mittened
little fatty in a red snowsuit, had flung herself at him, her fists
pounding again and again into his soft bully's belly, and when
he'd fallen down on his back on the frozen field next to the
school she'd straddled him and then continued to flail and hit
at him while all the other students from his grade-eight class
had stood in a laughing circle around them. All through the
early years of her childhood the memory of this episode had
filled her with great pride in her own power and bravery; it
wasn't until she was thirteen or fourteen that it finally dawned
on her that she'd been crazed enough for everyone (even bullies)
to come to the conclusion that she was hilarious.

But now they were driving around perfect little Brown's Inlet,
and Helmut was asking her to park at the end of it because it
was so pretty. "That's the thing about the East," he told her.
"You've got scenery down here." And so they sat and looked out
over the water while Helmut inhaled the view and Claire thought
about Floyd McArdle. But how lucky they'd been, the people in
her family, considering the things that happened to some people.
Awful things. Select visitations by Grimm's fairy tales made to
certain chosen unfortunates in the modern world.

Then it was time for her to drive back to her place so that Helmut could go off to the horse farm in Manotick.

"By the way," she asked him as she was getting out of the car, "how's Mother these days?"

"Mother is Mother," Helmut darkly said.

And then just before he drove off, he got out as well, to give her a loose hug goodbye, then he pushed her glasses back up to the bridge of her nose. "Just because you're a college girl now you don't have to go around looking like an absent-minded professor . . ."

She batted his hand away. "What are you trying to *do?* Don't *do* that . . ."

But he must have been wanting to make amends, because just before he took off he reached out and touched one of her feathery green earrings. "Christ, that's pretty." Then he was off, sweeping up the hill in his rented car, turning at the corner, gone. She walked up back up the stairs to her apartment to get herself a glass of cranberry juice. Her refrigerator, so old that it sometimes mewed like a kitten, this time decided to creak like a saddle.

There was also Helmut's news of the boys of St. Walburg to mull over, all those farm boys who'd done so well once they'd stepped out into the wide world of Saskatoon and the cities. They'd become plumbers, real-estate agents, fast-food entrepreneurs. And where was *she?* She was nowhere. She, who used to be a star among dunces. But Donnie McArdle was never a dunce, he was observant and belonged to that small clan of boys she'd considered passionately decent. One afternoon the spring she was twelve, she'd gone for a walk in the woods with Donnie and Helmut. They'd packed grape jelly sandwiches in wax paper

and had sat down to eat them in a clearing a mile west of the
McArdle farm. She could remember what clothes she was
wearing, even — her slick and sour mauve nylon parka and her
short dark tartan skirt, closed with a kilt pin stuck into a ver-
tical fringe that looked like a fringe of dull green and black
hair. And everywhere the smell of pine needles still damp from
the rain. She had a memory of being paralysingly shy (this was
her chief memory of herself in those days, the fierceness of her
shyness) but half the time she was also in a secret fury because
people acted as if they really believed that she was as she presented herself: a girl who was dull and desperately prim. But
she didn't think Donnie McArdle saw her that way, she was sure
he saw through her as he saw through everyone, she was sure he
understood that she was pretending to be less than she was in
order not to be hated. But then Helmut had made some joke
about her, she could no longer remember it, she could only
remember pulling her tartan skirt tight over her knees and
saying, "Don't do that," while Donnie McArdle had sat on the
slippy floor of pine needles looking as if he would die for her,
he had so much seemed to want to be her true friend. Of course
both of these memories — and this must be the explanation for
why she'd remembered them — were utterly self-serving, pre-
senting her younger self to her as (1) a hero, and (2) adored.

She was finding it hard to concentrate, but at last, after half an hour of doodling, she finally wrote:

> In this metaphysical whodunit — did God do it? did the devil do it? — the crime to be solved being the anguished sojourn of the soul, in human form, on this man-maimed ruined planet — many clues, false leads and riddles are provided for characters and readers. The book is a thriller both as a genre and in its verbal pyrotechnics. Metaphysical jokes abound and rebound —

She was writing ". . . graceful and enigmatic; disdaining speech rather than speechless, he is a figure of eerie glamour and power . . ." when the phone rang.

She picked it up to hear a professionally mournful voice ask, "Ms. Vornoff?"

"Yes," she said, her own voice almost dead with distrustful caution.

"Your urine sample tested positive, Ms. Vornoff."

She wanted to cry out that this could not be so. She wanted to say that Tony O'Bois had taken precautions. But had he? She was amazed that she was able to make her voice sound so calm. Normal, even. "But there still could be an element of doubt, couldn't there?"

"If it had tested negative, that would be very possible," the pharmacist told her. "False negatives are relatively common. False positives, on the other hand, are extremely rare."

An India ink drawing of bodies blissfully falling upside-down from a fort's ramparts was tacked to the wall above the table. Happy bodies with arrows stuck into their hearts. Would she get an abortion then? She would have to. She would hate to, but she would have to. She who more than once had been afraid that she would give in to an urge to just grab a baby out of its carriage and spirit it home, hide it under a leaf. But was she one of those women who could raise a baby without a father? She didn't think so, the thought of being raised without her own father was too terrible to her. Still, the temptation to keep it would be very great, and a baby that looked like Tony could be sweet — a little bald baby like tall, almost bald Tony — but now the pharmacist was speaking again and she disliked his voice, an irritating, self-satisfied falsetto. He was saying — unpleasantly, she felt — "Of course, you might take a sample of your urine to a *lab*. You might get an answer more to your liking from a *lab*."

What would really save her time would be to set her little jar in with the test tubes and bottles to be picked up by the lab boy who came late every afternoon for the urine and blood samples in Dr. Tenniswood's wire basket. But what she should really do was go back to see Declan again. She had, after all, a dilemma to bring to him. A dilemma that was both medical and moral.

But on Monday morning when she got to work and called the Institute to make an appointment with Declan, the receptionist told her that he'd already moved out to the country. "A bit earlier than usual this year." And so she couldn't give her an appointment until Thursday afternoon, out in Ottersee.

Footsteps were coming down the back stairs, and now here was Declan, looking pale in a pair of black chinos and a black shirt with green stripes. But his eyes were warm with a smile that he seemed to have carried down the stairs with him. Claire was feeling nervous and wanted to tell him why she'd come back to see him again. But he was hiding something behind his back and after giving her a brief glance of assessment he tossed it.

It flew at her – a flowered cushion – and when she caught it he said, "Be your mother."

But wasn't the whole point to *not* be her mother? "Do you mean be my mother as *I* see her? Or as she sees herself?"

"Just *be* her."

"You want me to make her sanctimoniousness heartfelt –"

"Right," he said. "After all, what's more heartfelt than sanctimony?" And he dropped another cushion onto the floor across from her and sat down on it himself. "And I'll be *you* –"

But this was all really just such a silly waste of time — all this play-acting — what was the use of it? She also had a longing to say to him, "I think you are a real amateur at being *me* . . ."

Still she would have to try, and so (being her mother) she said, "All I want is to love people. To love people and be loved."

"But I don't *feel* loved by you, why is that?"

Very good, she thought, this answer (if I dared to give it) *would* be the answer I'd give to my mother. "You are so selfish, little Claire," she said, squeezing her eyes into a squint of disapproval. "You are a selfish, selfish person."

"All I want is to love people. To love people and be loved."

"So what *is* this? Is it just some kind of game?"

"What do *you* think?"

I think I might be pregnant, she almost said, but instead she said, "I think I want to go back to being my mother." Although really she didn't.

"So do it, then."

"Can I help it if I have a generous nature?" she cried. "*Can* I? I just can't seem to be selfish no matter how hard I try. I've just been afflicted by too kind a heart, so be it."

"But you don't *act* generous, do you?"

"Who are you now?" she asked him. "Are you you? Or are you me?"

But by now he seemed to have tired of the game too, because he stood up, held down a hand to her. "Stand up," he told her, "and we'll do some breathing exercises."

On the way home a violent slam of leftover winter hit her windshield — a wind-driven spring snowstorm that periodically snowed out the world and made her eyes and the bones in her wrists ache. In the end she'd completely forgotten to tell him that she might be pregnant, which astounded her, since the news of her possible pregnancy had been her reason for going back to see him in the first place.

The sun came through now and then and shone on the damp highway, and driving with the windows down, she could smell the wet trees everywhere. Wet weeping willows and wet poplars, a whole grove of wet maple trees with their new little leaves, beautiful turncoat trees standing in formal green groves down here in the green and civilized heart of formal Ontario.

But the chilled row of pink tulips running the length of Declan's verandah seemed to be warning her: We have our own lives. We have nothing to do with either you or the town.

She didn't hear his footsteps come down the back stairs until she was already in the Room. And even then he didn't come right in to see her. She could hear that he had a cold. She could hear him blow his nose with a short-tempered honk, then cough, then speak briefly, in too low a voice, to someone on the phone. A woman, she was sure of it. It was a conviction that made her feel depressed and crabby but at the same time too shy to be crabby.

The moment he came into the Room she stood, feeling white-faced, to tell him about Tony O'Bois and the pregnancy test.

He had wound a black scarf around his pale throat and pulled a hairy brown sweater on over his T-shirt, and everything about him suggested sick itch and fever. He said in a croaky, raw voice, "Get undressed. I can probably tell by examining your breasts."

She unbuttoned her blouse and unwrapped her skirt, then stood in the cold May morning in nothing but her pink underpants while he felt her left breast. But then he had to stop to go into the open-mouthed cringe that comes just before sneezing. And when he did sneeze he blew his nose violently, then rammed his Kleenex into the back pocket of his jeans. He hoarsely said that he couldn't tell for certain if she was pregnant. He cupped her right breast to thoughtfully weigh it, but while he was holding it his eyes were looking so sick and the cup of his hand felt so warm that she lightly touched his wrist with the tips of her fingers. "You don't think you should be in bed?" and then frightened herself by pretending she'd said, "You don't think *we* should be in bed?"

"I'm fine, don't worry about *me*, okay?" But then he asked her if she would mind if he gave her a vaginal examination.

She was surprised, but she only said, "No, I'd be grateful."

"I'll just go upstairs then, to get a surgical glove."

She waited until she could hear his footsteps reach the top of the back stairs, then she quickly walked over to the mirror and tensely massaged her hair to give it more body, sniffed her armpits. And once she'd heard the creak of his footsteps on the ceiling above her fade away to creak their way up an even more distant stairway she quickly peeled off her underpants, neatly stepping from foot to foot, but then was afraid to do anything more for herself because he'd be coming back down any minute and she was feeling too shaky to allow him to see that she'd been making preparations. He'd never done anything medical at all for her, not before today, not even the time she drove down to see him with a strep throat and a fever of nearly a hundred and two. No, it wasn't *that* high, but it *was* over a hundred. And not the time she had cystitis either. He had turned totally against ortho-dox medicine and no longer practised it. He even despised it. And again she thought of how sick his eyes had looked, almost tearful with fever. She folded her underpants into a pink square and darted them in between her folded-up black blouse and pale cotton skirt, then eased herself down on one of the therapy mats and told herself to get calm. She wished that she'd rubbed apricot lotion into the insides of her thighs after taking her shower. But she did know one thing: in a more relaxed situation a person would have to smile – the scene was such a far cry from a scene in one of Dr. Tenniswood's examining rooms: the jacked-up cold steel stirrups and the snapping of a sheet like a disinfected tablecloth out over the patient – but now the creaks were start-ing up in the ceiling again and footsteps were beginning to make their descent down the back stairway. For a panicked moment she considered grabbing something to cover herself with, but there was nothing, not unless she wanted to hug her own blouse and skirt to her.

When Declan came back into the room and closed the door behind him she could see how pale he still was. It was a pale-ness that seemed to her to be a nervy paleness and also seemed to be connected in some way to quick-wittedness. But now he was dropping to his knees and starting to untie the ties of a beige linen napkin-like packet. He has a cold, she told herself, that's why he seems a bit shaky. But she also wondered if she wasn't telling herself this in order not to risk thinking things she was too nervous to think in his presence. She imagined driving home and thinking them then. She imagined telling herself, This is normal, normal, normal. She would tell herself it was normal so she could tell herself it wasn't. It wasn't normal and so it must mean he loved her.

But now he was only telling her to take a deep breath. "And don't hitch your hips back — that's what most women do when they're being examined vaginally. Move them toward me instead . . ."

She shimmied down the mat and as she opened her legs she felt shy, as if her shyness might save her from everything. She could hear the adjusting snap of the latex glove on his wrist, then felt she could dovetail the snap to the way his voice seemed to be losing its way. The way it is when you are being entered in love, she thought. But then she became afraid that he would know she was thinking this, as if his hand coming inside her body would allow him to know her thoughts. She could also see that his eyes had a listening look, the look of a man trying to diagnose what his fingers were feeling. She felt no pain, she only felt as if (in her body) she could hold her breath forever. Wanting to somehow console him, she allowed one of her hands to rest close to his free hand, a small curve of fingers whose fingertips just barely touched him between his first finger and thumb. She thought: He has broken every rule to help me. Out of gratitude to him she even found herself feeling the need to relieve them a little of their joined shyness and so she spoke to him in a small formal voice: "I think my uterus might be prolapsed just a bit?"

"No, no," he reassured her. "Everything's fine." He sat back on his heels. "You're not pregnant." And as he pulled off the glove it seemed to her that his eyes were filled with feeling for her.

At the end of the session (after they had finished their breathing exercises for the day) they sat side by side, just as they always did, panting in unison like two winded athletes. This morning they were even in their usual spot, their backs supported by the panelled wall that faced the room's one tiny high window. "About that person I went to bed with," she then managed to say to him, "he was fine, really, he was really a good person, but I just didn't have any sexual feeling at all for him." But was this really true? She was rubbing a thumb up and down the leather T-strap of one of her sandals. "Do you know what I was thinking, the whole time I was with him?"

After a nearly alarmed look at her he asked her what.

"All I could think of was coming back to you and saying, 'Okay, so I did it, so I went to bed with someone, and all I ever learned from it is that you are the one.'" Now that she'd at last come out with it, her heart began to beat like something that had lived its whole life in terror and she understood that what she was feeling most was a fear that he would feel the need to subject her to some kind of ethical humiliation, that he would feel it was his duty to make a fatherly little speech to her about how her feelings were understandable "under the circumstances," the implication being that it was exactly this flaw in them that must always prevent his taking them seriously.

But instead there was a moment of almost unendurable quiet. And when he at last spoke he said that feelings like this didn't exist in a vacuum. "If one person is feeling them, you can be sure the other person is feeling them too."

She looked down at her hands. She was overwhelmed by a longing to say to him, thanks for treating me like a human being, thanks for not being a coward, but she couldn't speak.

On the way home she was in torment. Because she already knew: any personal relationship between a patient and a therapist was doomed beyond doomed, everyone knew that. If only they could meet again, for the first time, in some other place. But they couldn't. Not in this life. They already *had* met for the first time, there couldn't be a *second* first time. But then two minutes later she was telling herself that people were more important than the theories that people had invented about people. And that love was love. At the same time she was sure there were those who would think (and say!) "*So?* He's a doctor! He examined you because you were afraid you might be pregnant! It meant *nothing!*" But she wasn't one of those people who could be convinced that something was nothing, she wasn't even one of those people who could be convinced that nothing was nothing, she would always think there was something, and so by the time she was coming into the city again she knew she would have to leave him, and for real this time, knowing she wouldn't ever go back. And she would have to leave now, while there was still time for her to make an escape. She also knew that she couldn't bear to, and so it was to appease the part of herself that saw danger ahead that she made a vow to herself: if her period started before midnight tonight she would take it as a sign and give all idea of him up. But even as she was making this promise to herself she knew it was a ruse — a ruse, a false vow — it had to be, because she was already so certain that her body would see to it that she wouldn't have to honour it.

She was thinking of Declan's smile: of the way it carried within it an even more amused smile than the smile he was smiling (or his eyes were smiling). By now her undressing for him seemed to have acquired a more sensual depth as well, as if she really hadn't been all that awkward after all, as if she'd even been almost statuesque and warm-breasted, more like an artist's model than a patient, but at this point she was startled out of her reverie by Judy's voice calling up from downstairs to ask her if she wanted to go for a swim. And she called back down to her, "Sure, great!"

But then she wasn't able to find her swimsuit in its usual drawer, among her silk scarves and sun-halters, although when she ran down to tell Judy she wouldn't be able to go after all, Judy told her that her daughter had just got back from the pool at her school and that since Claire had a similar build, Lynnie's suit might just fit her.

"But won't she mind?" (And won't *I* mind?)

"She won't mind."

And so Claire carried the borrowed swimsuit, still damp from the younger woman's body, wound tightly up in the twist of her towel. But walking to the pool house in the cold spring night she was already regretting that she'd agreed to the swim. If she couldn't be with Declan, then the next best thing was to be by herself and thinking of him. Other people were only an impediment to thinking.

Swimming pools made her feel anxious at the best of times. For some mad reason they always made her fear an injury. Something to do with the winter. All those loud fifteen-year-old boys emboldened by the sound of their own yelling, all of them bouncing their powerful feet up and down on the ends of the diving boards and making them thrum. They always made her fear she would be hit by something. Some winter thing. A hockey puck or a too-hard snowball. She would always feel braced to duck something.

In the pool house's locker room she considered waiting until Judy had safely closed herself away in one of the stalls, her plan being to rinse the crotch of Lynnie's bathing suit under hot water while she was pretending to wash her hands, but she instead decided to keep her panties on underneath it. She walked down to the most distant stall and pulled on the damp borrowed suit: quick cold nudge of a dog's nose hauled up between her legs, her lace panties a warm barrier against the cold shock of where it would shock her most, then there was only the hitched-up bite of each damp flowered strap.

Judy led the way down the corridor to two giant chrome doors and as the two women pushed their way in, coming shy and white into the splashy bedlam of the pool area, the steam-bath warmth of the chlorinated air moving toward them, across the sloshed tiles, in that great booming hall of hygiene. The place was an aquatic madhouse: yells and shrieks and gasps and splashes and small children swimming and cough-ing – their foreshortened splashes like coughs, their coughs throttled short splashes.

Judy's back was freckled, powerful. She looked like a crack swimmer in her channel swimmer's black suit. She dropped her towel and took off for the pool, aimed cleanly in.

Claire crept down the ladder to make the water's acquaintance much more slowly, then let herself sink backwards into the chair of the water — the chair that was never quite there — then swam in scooping and awkward lunges on her back, up to the pool's deep end.

Judy popped up beside her, disappeared, popped up again on the pool's far side, then yelled over to her about the marvellous water.

"Yeah, it's great!" Claire called back to her, and the phrase "great with child" came to her. Oh, she thought, I should smile at myself, that here I am, feeling pregnant at last, and on the night of the day I've been medically assured that I'm not, and what do I feel pregnant *from?* From the look on Declan's face. From Declan's finger. Wouldn't anyone who could read her thoughts decide that she'd have to be either deluded or crazy or pathetic? But she didn't feel she was any of these things; these were only states of mind her conscious mind was trying to bully her into feeling. As she grasped the railings of the swimming-pool ladder and came breathlessly up out of the water she felt far from such states of mind, she felt loved, she felt cherished. Then she walked out to the end of the lowest diving board and with a deep bow fell into the pool and forgot everything, she was only aware of a heavenly extra fullness in her breasts and hips as she sank, then swam, then sank into the lower layers of floodlit chemical water.

Back in the locker room again, pulling off the wet swimsuit and the lace skin of her wet panties and feeling hormonal and happily pudgy and above all marvellously free with nothing on under her skirt, she recalled a woman she'd briefly known years ago, a woman who'd had an affair with her psychiatrist, a woman who'd seemed, of all the women she had known in her life, the most sunken-eyed and lost. She recalled this woman sitting on the beach at Mooney's Bay on a dull September Sunday, obsessively smoking while talking ad nauseam of her psychiatrist lover. A dull-eyed woman in a white-flecked grey sweatshirt and white-flecked grey slacks and wine-coloured socks and heavy Birkenstock sandals. But why think of her? Why not think of the photo of the woman who had fallen in love with Judy's psychiatrist brother? The afternoon Judy had shown her this photo, her eyes had been lit by disapproval as she'd said she considered her brother somewhat unethical, stooping to fall for a patient. "Selfish, basically," was Judy's diagnosis, made while pouring Claire a fresh cup of coffee.

"But is it really?" Claire had cried up at her. "I mean, isn't that what passion *is*? Having the generosity to be selfish?"

Judy had raised an eyebrow at her through the steam. "We'll just have to pretend we didn't hear that," she had said.

It wasn't until she was lying back in her bath and thinking of *Anna Karenina* (above all thinking of Kitty looking at Levin with her frightened caressing eyes) that she swished the washcloth between her thighs and saw a cloud of red rising like red dust up through the clear water.

~~~~

But she couldn't stop seeing Declan, it would be unkind (and perhaps even immoral) to stop seeing him just because she now

had physiological proof that she wasn't pregnant, she must see
him at least three or four more times, as a patient she owed him
that, *then* she would leave him. And in fact when he came into
the Room the next time she drove down to Ottersee it seemed
to her that they were even a little more stern with each other than
usual, that they were both primed to cry out "Nothing happened!" They seemed to be tired too, or they were using what
they were pretending was exhaustion as an excuse to touch each
other more often. Certain things could go on, but they must not
be acknowledged. A careful but secretly tender formality seemed
to be what they were in need of, and it was in order to counter-
act it a little that Claire, toward the end of the session – they
were lying on the exercise mats by this time, breathing in unison
– smiled at him disbelievingly when he told her that he could
read any number of childhood events in her body.

"But it's true, you *can* read certain very specific historical
events in a person's body," he insisted, and he hitched himself
up on his side and cupped a hand around the calf of her nearest
bent leg and then allowed his hand to travel slowly down to her
heel. "Words are so ambiguous," he said, and she had the
impression that his voice was coming out much more emotionally than he had intended it to.

She ran a hand up the back of his bare arm to his elbow,
then beyond his elbow, up under the sleeve of his shirt. She felt
gifted in touching him. And for a minute or two, with her hand
resting on his bare shoulder, high up under his shirt, they were
quiet together, listening to the footsteps of his wife creaking
back and forth in the kitchen over their heads.

But after a few more moments had passed, he sat up. "I can
hear that my wife is making the tea, and so I'm afraid we'll have

to stop here for today." And it seemed to Claire that although
he was struggling to keep his voice neutral, he wasn't able to
purge it of real regret.

All the way back to the city, she drove the car with the
bizarre automatic precision of a woman in a dream, not at all
knowing when she passed other drivers or when she was passed
by them. She was in a state of grace, if love was grace. She felt
tender toward all lovers and was convinced that lovers all over
the world must recognize one another on sight, across the
boundaries of language and race and gender and caste and class.
She recalled herself at twenty-four, twenty-five, and remembered how she would sometimes be judgemental about certain
love affairs, love affairs between people who were sleeping with
people they weren't married to, or sleeping with people who
were of the same sex, or sleeping with people who were much
older or much younger than the people they were with, but now
none of that mattered to her, now all she could think was how
beside the point the marital status of the lovers was, or the
gender, all she could think was that there was some boundary
of risk or tenderness you crossed if you were a lover and once
you had crossed it there was nothing else in the world that could
possibly matter.

The weeks were now measured only from Thursday to Thursday, and this particular Thursday was windy, a little cooler, a heady taint of leaf decay in the air. Claire drove through a wide valley and the leaves of the world seemed to fly toward her windshield from every corner of it, the car a magnet, the day playful. She thought about nothing or she thought about Declan. She thought about how they had been these last weeks, how high-minded and touchy. Extremely pleasurable in its way, to act like that, but only if it didn't go on for too long. There was a point when you couldn't do it any more, the game would be up. Up or over.

Being in love herself, she had begun to notice illicit love all around her. Even at her local library, where one of the youngest of the librarians, a sad-eyed but definitely glamorous blonde in her early twenties, was too casual by half when she briefly rested a very large ringed hand — why did pretty young women so often have such very large hands? — on the back of the most fatherly of the middle-aged librarians as he bent to a cupboard to look for a book. And then the fatherly one, although he was careful to keep his expression neutral, really did look — at least in his body — too sweetly eased by her touch. And Claire could see it too, why the younger woman found him so attractive. He wore rimless glasses and he had dull hair, a dry moustache, but his arms looked strong, and below his warm eyes his smile was responsive.

She parked the car under the usual tree and ran down the stone steps to discover that the door to the Room was standing open and there was nobody around, but then sometimes on Thursdays she was the first person Declan saw. She ducked into the low-ceilinged little bathroom and splashed her eyes with cold water.

When she came back out into the room with the desk she was struck by the fact that everything looked exactly as it had always looked. This was a puzzle when she herself felt so altered. But the potted plants were still hanging in their macrame slings and the pale-yellow leaves of the painting's great tree still littered the ground. They made her think of someone saying that someone had thrown all of his cards on the table. They made her heart feel out of control in the deep country quiet.

She went over to the desk to look down at Declan's appointment book. A spy's trip she had made several times on earlier visits, and one that made her feel more like a child than anything else she could do when she was alone in this room. She read the names: Carol Schmidt, Terry Glass, Claire (a little hop of the heart here), Barbara, Sheila Leblanc, Gerry Meek, Alison Stackhouse, Elspeth Frewin, Brian Duchemin, Barbara Seidman. Which meant what? That the first Barbara was a Barbara he was closer to than he was close to Barbara Seidman? The suspicion that he was closer to some of these people than he was to others made her feel more uncertain of her own hopes and boldness. Also, he was late. She was already ten minutes into her hour and there was no sound from upstairs.

She went back to the sofa and picked up a magazine from the low table and tried to leaf through it, but her heart was only waiting for the sound of his step. The whole place seemed deserted, except for the cries of the children. She could hear their happy shrieks as they raced around the garden, and occasionally there was a glimpse of them too, or parts of them — their legs, their running feet, a half-view of a bridal party, the bride's train a beach towel dragging by on the grass above the high window until she dropped her bouquet of daisies into the window well and one of the smaller boys hopped down in a squat to retrieve it.

She flipped through the magazine again and when she came to an ad for a holiday in the Bahamas it made her remember the first summer she was married to Steff and a drive they'd taken to an isolated lake. They'd had to drive toward the water on a grassy track, tree needles brushing the car roof until Steff parked under a giant rowan tree, then make their way through the small forest single-file. When they'd come out on the other side of the woods there was the shock of a vast sky and a wide sweep of water blown into bands of grey and brown near the far shore and a convoy of great white flat-bottomed clouds passing slowly in the almost colourless but bright air above it. A long row of birch trees stood on the lake's other shore, their leaves precise in the late-afternoon light.

No one else here, was her first thought, thank God was her second thought, and so she foresaw a heavenly afternoon of reading her book while Steff took one of his heroic swims far out in the lake. It wasn't until she'd started to smooth suntan lotion on her pale legs that she'd noticed a woman in a lime-green bikini asleep on the soft green hair of the rich grass that grew in the shade of the dock farther down the beach. The sun-bather had shoved down her bikini bottoms and untied her top so that, folded over, it lay across her nipples like a rising and falling green ribbon, her appearance on the shore of the lake leading Claire to conclude that on every beach there was a sun-bather waiting for Steff to find her, like a penny in every slice of a child's birthday cake. At that same moment it had become clear that Steff had noticed her too and had consequently decided to also read for a while. And so the game had begun: his pretending not to look toward the dock followed by her pre-tending not to see him looking, then his finally going for a walk and on his way back pretending to stumble as he dropped his towel on the sleeping woman's feet. Which had led the startled woman to jump up, then bend forward to pour her breasts into the top of her green bikini. But as she'd straightened up again she'd revealed that she had a bearing that was somehow too solid, unanimated. She was doing biochemistry at McGill, she told them when she came over to join them for a glass of lemon-ade. But the whole time she was talking she hadn't been able to stop shoving the heel of her right hand up her forehead, as if trying to push the pain of a headache back up into her hair.

Fifteen minutes had by now ticked by. Then another ten. And so where *was* he? The suspicion that he might have forgotten her appointment was eating away at her, and today of all days, when she had planned to come with so much of her feeling for him showing in her face. But then wasn't this so often the way it was in life? At the very moment you decided to give in and be open, fate rapped you smartly over the knuckles for your hopes, and the next thing you knew you were ashamed of even having them and then you didn't have them, they were gone, and then you almost hated the person you loved for not arriving, and then you did hate him, and then you felt a kind of double hatred because now you even hated him for making you hate him when all you ever really wanted to do was to love him.

But at long last, when there were only twenty minutes left before her hour was up, she heard a tentative creak on the floor just above her, and then, quickly following this, the more orderly progression of creaks that would mean someone was walking down the back stairs. The door opened, and there stood Declan supporting himself against the door frame and looking puffy around the eyes, as if he'd been crying. "Claire, look, I'm sorry, I'm not feeling too good." As he said this, she had the odd feeling that he wanted to welcome her into his sorrow. But he only stepped down the last step, then said in a shaken voice, "Come on in."

She followed him watchfully into the Room, her shoulder bag hugged close to her side. He hadn't forgotten her then. But what had happened? She felt afraid, almost, to hear. She dropped her bag onto the nearest chair, stepped out of her sandals. But as she was starting to unbutton her shirt he held up his hand. "No!" And then, more quietly: "No. Don't take anything off. We'll just do a few breathing exercises." He sat down then, like someone who no longer trusts his legs to hold him up, and Claire, to keep him company, sat down as well. But as she sat, she understood something: he was leaving his wife and so would very soon be free. She felt a careful tenderness curiously mixed with dread.

There was a moment of profound quiet. Then he said that he'd just been through a crisis of some kind, something he didn't even begin to understand. "I was supposed to come down and see you and then I couldn't. I started to cry and then I couldn't stop."

She lifted her hair over the back of her collar, held her damp hands pressed to the sides of her knees. There was another long silence. But they were accustomed to silences. It must have been because he had spoken about his own life that this particular silence began to seem as unbearable as a social silence that two people might be made anxious by, out in the world. And then at last, as if he had expected some response from her but had now been forced to conclude that none was forthcoming, he told her that his wife had been wonderful to him. "I was lying on the living room rug and crying, and then my wife lay down on the rug with me and held me."

All of her shy apprehension was draining away from her, she felt physically ill with jealousy. She had seen his wife getting out of their car late one Thursday afternoon two or three weeks ago, dressed in sandals and red satin jogging shorts, the kind with the upside-down tulip cleft at the sides. The recollection made her feel inadequate and unsure of herself, a too-easy blusher. A face, she thought (trying to cheer herself up with a bad joke) that too much wears its heart on its sleeve. She also understood that he was only looking at her as he had planned to look at her before coming down from upstairs and so wasn't really seeing her. As for the breathing exercises he was now standing up to recommend for her, she couldn't at all attend to them, and when he told her he'd made arrangements to go away for two weeks to China, where he'd be visiting acupuncturists in Shanghai and Beijing, "and also for a bit of a holiday," she thought yes, I was expecting this, I just didn't know it was coming so soon.

She climbed the stone steps up into the day, dead-hearted, and was surprised to see a new visitor waiting in an old Volkswagen beetle parked under the elms. A gypsyish young madonna in a bright yellow skirt, she was sitting smoking in the open doorway of her beetle, watching the world go by from it, barefoot and pleased with herself in the hot sunlight.

Claire's car was parked out in the open sun, a little way off from the rectory. She said hi to the madonna, and the madonna, her eyes cool with a younger woman's appraisal, answered in a deep voice, almost a man's voice, "Hi there."

In the furtive second glance Claire stole at the girl under cover of picking a leaf off the windshield of her car she saw that she had a disfiguring birthmark. At first glance she had taken it to be elm-shadow; this time she saw that it had a mulberry stain to it. But it was huge, it ran down the right side of her face and down her neck to bloom at her throat. Too big to be a birthmark, it must have been caused by a burn. Unless it was the symptom of some awful medical condition. The young woman did not seem to be cowed by it though.

Claire drove bumpily down the lane to the highway, and on the road again she thought about Declan's wife, her perfection. But wasn't there always something surprisingly unsurprising about such perfect women? Less perfect women had their good days and bad days, their faces flew open or brimmed with feeling, they could look hurt, they could look euphoric, they could look a thousand ways, they were flawed and variable, there was even a proverb that saw right through the kind of perfect beauty Declan's wife possessed, an Italian proverb (Italian or Spanish): A woman who is always beautiful is never beautiful. But she found herself wanting to believe it more than she really *did* believe it, because driving back to the city she wasn't able to think of Declan's wife with anything but envy. She also thought of Declan's power to make a woman inventive. Because this was where his power did come from, with women, at last she could see it, he would come into a room, and a woman would think, This man is going to force me out of myself in some way, he's going to force me into invention, I must love him. Even a woman as physically unimpeachable as his wife was in all likelihood capable of being frightened by him into invention. And she pictured the legions of other women who were probably in love with him too, and it seemed to her that if she ever could have an affair with him it would be a relationship made truly romantic by its prohibitions, a relationship that would blaze out of a century in which all the barriers but one had been trampled, it would be the modern version of the love of the woodcutter's son for the king's daughter.

But meditations on her jealousy and the other women he saw got her somewhere she hadn't expected to get. It was as if the thought of jealousy and other women ("other women" by now including his wife) had a life of its own and had hopped and skipped its way to its own conclusions, and one of the conclusions it had hopped to was that there had been something fishy about his story of lying on the rug and crying in the arms of his wife. Not that she didn't believe it had happened. She believed it had happened, but now she saw the reason. And the reason had to do with the intensity of his emotional bond to herself. This was why he had started to cry in the first place. By crying (and crying in the arms of his wife, no less) he had absolved himself of the guilt he felt for loving one of the women who came to see him, and in the process had even managed to keep himself away from the love object or whatever it was she had become to him now. With this thought something in her heart eased, turned hopeful. It threw a whole different light on everything he had said to her, on everything he had done. Now she could re-run the whole puzzling scene over again and pick out small bits of evidence that her hurt feelings hadn't allowed her to spot earlier. Now she could even see that there had been something very watchful and even cunning about the way he had told her the story about lying in the arms of his wife. Now she could see that he had been using it to make her jealous, to use her jealousy to goad her into some action that would force them to confront each other at last, out of the true and desperate feeling of their true hearts.

She tried to imagine describing this scene, this scene and her feelings, to Libi. But she could all too easily imagine what Libi would say. "And that's supposed to prove that Farrell loves you? Oh, please."

So answer me this then: If he was as innocent as he tried to make out, then why did he bother to tell me he'd been crying in the arms of his wife?

Because he's unprofessional, that's why.

But it was none of my business!

So?

So that's the clue.

Oh, please. Or, more simply and even more woundingly, "Please." And both of these pleases translating to: Please don't torment yourself with such silly hopes.

But then that's the trouble with passionless people, she thought, thinking of Libi and just in time paying enough attention to the traffic to brake for a red light, they lack imagination so much it's pathetic. And so of course it's only natural that they live for the pleasure of being able to say to the people who have real feelings "Are you sure you aren't just imagining things?" It's because they can't bear other people's happiness, or their unhappiness either, she thought, that they disapprove so much of what they call, in their mincing, incredulous voices, "the imagination." She remembered all the times she'd wanted to grab Libi by the wrist and say to her in a hard little voice, "I know the way he looks at me. I was there and you weren't, so please don't tell me I don't even have the right to see it the way I see it." And, besides, when she looked all around her, at the lives of the married people she knew, they seemed just so dull, more filled with resentments than pleasures. It's the future I need to be saved from, she thought, and I need to be saved from it by love.

Green was the colour for this particular fall, at least in this boutique: corduroys and velvets in hunter green, forest green, Nile green and bile green. Even the sales clerk, a sour and quiet girl who was, really, much too sour for her gentle Renaissance clothes, was wearing green velvet: a quilted green velvet jacket, its pearl buttons drooping from the gold sticks of their delicate stems.

But then fall is the medieval season, thought Claire, and she couldn't help but feel the deep solemn thrill of it as she made her way past the racks of serious Shakespearean colours: blood and plum, forest green and burgundy. And claret, too, for the dresses whose sleeves were cut to show slits of peony silk. So that when Libi said, "For God's sake, Vornoff, let's go up to the next level, we're caught in a time warp down here," she felt a little regretful to be leaving a place that was so religious about the romance of dresses.

Jazz was playing up in the brighter light on the upper level, and in the first shop they came into there were carousels of lime tops and white pants for cruises, and long rows of palm-tree wrap dresses in glazed lime or indigo cotton. Libi went over to a hill of sweaters that had been tumbled onto a high table next to the windows. She picked out three and brought them to Claire, and in a voice hushed at the prospect of ownership she said, "Feel these, this oatmeal one is made out of wool from the Scottish Highlands and this one has insets of chocolate suede, isn't it terrific?"

Claire held the sweater with the suede insets to herself in front of one of the mirrors, then crossed the floor to a wide table piled high with a silky spill of spotted tops, spotted jackets. She pulled a leopard-print jacket out by its sleeve, then said in a low voice to Libi, "I'm going to try this one on, just for the hell of it."

In the change room, she slipped on the silky jacket and saw a transformation take place: the way it was cut, in panels, made her look sexy, a woman of the world. She would have to have it, never mind the price. She shoved her hair up as if she planned to step into a bath, vamped at herself in the mirror. It was on sale too, as if it had been ordained that she should find it and buy it.

When she came out of the change room, she looked for Libi, then saw her come walking quickly over to her, grim with a shopper's efficiency, a white linen skirt folded over one arm like a napkin. And when she said to her, "Lib, where can I pay for this?" Libi pointed the sales clerk out to her. "Over there. The lady in the bumblebee top." And she pulled Claire along by the cuff of her windbreaker to lead her to the island where the cashier was waiting for them up on her platform, the silk shirts Libi had chosen lying in a heap next to the cash register, then they both stood and humbly waited while the clerk, a wrecked-looking blonde in a black leather mini, her face a middle-aged cowboy's face, her body an anorexic adolescent's — it was from working with Declan that Claire now saw people's heads and bodies as improbable cartooned combinations — calculated the cost of the morning.

"Yes indeed, my dear Vornoff," said Libi as they were walking along Sussex, looking for a place where they could have a cappuccino and maybe soup or a muffin, "your little jungle jacket is very, very trash glam. You can now quite honestly call yourself a true fashionista."

In the restaurant they talked about Libi and Rolf's move to Regina while they spooned up a salty soup whose disks of fat floated among weedy black herbs and tendrils of chicken, a vile soup that tasted no better than chicken-flavoured hot greasy water. "My mother's been visiting us for the last five days," Libi said. "I forgot to tell you. To help us pack. Which she's more or less been totally useless at."

And when they got to Libi's house there Mrs. Turnbull indeed was, pitted as a stone beneath her military wedge of grey hair and sitting in a white wicker rocker up on the verandah, holding a heavy book on her lap. She called down to Libi to ask her if it was time for tea.

"Uno momento, Mother dear, I just have to try on my spectacular new togs."

Claire sat in one of the wicker chairs next to Mrs. Turnbull and looked sideways at her book (*The Great War*), then aimed her glance down at Mrs. Turnbull's orthopaedic shoes. They were tan shoes with tiny pinprick holes in them, like digestive biscuits. Then she looked down at her own feet in her tired sandals and thought, I don't want to get old! But she also thought: The other beautiful thing about the leopard jacket is that it can be worn either tucked in or left out, and when it's not tucked, it will be as elegant as a spotted short silky coat.

As soon as she decently could she excused herself to go into the house to look for Libi. The whole place smelled of cold coffee and carpets. She passed by the cats as she walked through the front room. One of them was asleep on a windowsill, but the other, sitting alertly up on the sofa, studied her for a moment, then blinked at her in a way that made her feel she'd been photographed. Something about the blink, its perfect noiseless click.

She went on down the hall to the kitchen, where she was met by a single word: Declan. Since she'd started seeing him again it was as if they were conspiring in some guilty thing that could never be mentioned. Someone had left a beret on the kitchen table, parked next to a teacup. She thought it must belong to Rolf. She went back down the hall. "Lib?"

"Upstairs!"

So then it was up the cramped stairway to find Libi in her new white skirt pulling her new shirts on and off, her eyes in her mirror the skeptically listening eyes of a person being told a story she considers somewhat outlandish but is deciding to reserve judgement on until the story is done. But then she was glancing back at Claire with a nearly imploring look: "Is this a mistake? Tell me the truth now."

Claire said no, no. She sat down on the bed. "It's terrific, you look really great in it . . ."

But the atmosphere in the room was claustrophobic and she was made even more uneasy by the flashes of what she could see of Libi's pale breasts squeezed together in the stitched rosy cones of her satin brassiere. She tried not to look while at the same time her not looking made her remember the little squirms of ignited forbiddenness she used to feel as she was watching her mother dress or undress (her mother pulling off the pale swish of her nightgown to reveal the plump and half-tanned grandeur of her breasts) or the way she, the toddler pervert, would lie odalisque-style on the end of her parents' big bed to watch her mother begin to draw on, with a nearly professional glamour, her shining nylons. All of this dressing being almost as exciting as all the *un*dressing, all the unzippings and unhookings until the final thrilling unhooking: the breasts unlocked to spill out, warm pinkish moons tipped by what looked like brown gumdrops. Which made her wonder if she would remember this day after Libi was gone, if it would take on a kind of memorial glow, Libi yanking the new shirts on and off, snap, snap, Libi taking her into the hushed little cathedral for dresses.

"I'm going to miss you so much," she said to Libi. And it was true, she would. Why then was she also so longing for her to go?

On the bus home, Claire glanced back at the other passengers and saw a boy and girl who were clearly new lovers. The girl playfully pushed at the boy, hugged him, whispered to him, ostentatiously let her head collapse against his shoulder. While the boy couldn't seem to lose his melancholy listening air as he shyly kissed her behind one of her ears, everything about his face and the way he was standing seeming to say, "I would do anything in the world for you, but please don't embarrass me in public," and then he was bashfully breathing her in as he hid his face in her hair while farther down at the back a man in a navy raincoat sat pressing his lips together as if to prevent an escape. Indigestion? But then Claire saw that his eyes were welling with tears and that he was biting his lips in order to contain spillage. She looked quickly away, humbled, having been brought up short by the discovery that it could still come as a surprise to her to see that others also suffered.

While Declan was away in China, a terrible excitement took possession of Claire, and one windy evening when she was walking in the park with Judy, she told her that she was once again unable to sleep.

"You speak as if not being able to sleep is some kind of crime."

"Isn't it a crime not to be able to admit to myself what's causing it?"

"But who can say? It could be anything."

"Or I'm a manic depressive."

"It could be an electrolyte imbalance, it could be demineralization, it could be a hundred things. You should go to see a naturopath. There are these two brothers who are simply totally amazing. Walter and Wallace. But Walter is the best. Walter is the one I went to."

"I think I've already heard of these two legendary brothers," said Claire.

The house where Mr. Spaulding was "camping out" was a white cottage with green shutters and a tiny walled garden. The garden had a gate with a latch, and there were teepees of dark wood slats already protecting the rose bushes against the future cold winds of winter.

Claire pressed the bell and the door was immediately opened by an almost bald man who led her into a narrow polished hallway. In fact, everything in it seemed to have been oiled, even Mr. Spaulding's head and the leaves of the rubber plants she could glimpse in his parlour were looking oiled, but the house was also smelling, bizarrely but pleasantly, like a field of hay.

"Come in here and find yourself a chair. I'll be with you in five minutes."

So she went into the first room to the left of the hallway and sat down in a big brown velvet chair and tried to read the titles on the spines of the books. There were also baskets everywhere. They were grouped on tables and lined up on the tops of the low bookcases. They were hung on the walls like the shields of not-very-warlike tribesmen.

When Mr. Spaulding came back to see her again, he sat on the ottoman directly across from her and intently gazed for a few moments into her face. "You have a heart murmur," he told her.

"How can you tell that?"

"From your nose. There's a cleft at the bottom of it."

"I thought you used the eyes for diagnosis."

"The eyes too. Let's have a look at them."

She took off her dark glasses and Mr. Spaulding fitted over his head what appeared to be a sort of belt with thick rectangular lenses in it. Then he held up a little wand of light and leaned forward to shine it into her left eye, then into her right eye, then he made several notes. "There's weakness in the kidneys and the liver and the heart," he finally told her. "Also, your lymph glands are backing up. In fact, you're on your way to having what is known in iridology as a lymphatic rosary."

What else could be left? "What can we do about all of that?"

"We're going to have to detoxify you." He made more little notes for her on three slips of blue paper, telling her what to eat and in what proportions, showing her which foods were yin and which foods were yang, and telling her that she would have to give up dairy products entirely.

After he'd finished looking into her eyes he told her to follow him to the parlour. Here they sat across from one another at a polished table while Mr. Spaulding kept using a pinched-together finger and thumb to precisely draw two or three strands of what remained of his hair back behind his left ear. Then he asked her a few questions and made even more notes.

Balding Spaulding, she secretly dubbed him as he was giving her a tiny paper cup to spit her saliva into, then he also handed her a bottle for her "other contribution." The washroom was upstairs, he told her, first door on her left.

When she came back down with her paper cup and her bottle, Mr. Spaulding carried them into the sunroom off the parlour, then sat with his back to her at a card table cluttered with glass jars.

But after a while she heard him go over to a sink and wash everything away. Then she heard him sit down again. One of his knees was jiggling, she could feel the vibrations, and in tandem with its jiggling she became aware of the beating of her heart.

At last he came back into the parlour again. He sat down at the gleaming table and transferred the test numbers onto a sheet of yellow paper. When he had finished his calculations he looked up at her. It was the look she'd been waiting for. The knife. "You're in rough shape, girl."

"In what way?" she asked him.

"First of all, your body salts are so high I can't measure them. Forty is the highest number for body salts and yours are higher than that. Your body is too acid. It's also throwing off one hundred times more dead cells than it should, and that, translated, means it's dying faster than it's rebuilding itself . . ."

She stared at him. But wasn't everyone's body dying faster than it was rebuilding itself? Wasn't that life, and the story of life? That the body died?

But Mr. Spaulding had more bad news to deliver and no time to waste. "The big thing to worry about is your uric acid reading. It puts you smack in the middle of the zone for a major heart attack. You could drop dead at any minute, it's that bad."

There was a silence until she said, "I hope that hearing all this isn't going to make things worse. For my heart. If it's in the shape you say it's in."

"I believe it's best to tell the truth. And, besides, there's some good news. There are no cancer cells anywhere in your body. So! Think positively!"

As she was pulling on her jacket, he told her not to be too depressed by so much bad news. "It's the times we live in," he told her. "The *times* are the pathogen." He also spoke of the many lives he had saved. People with cancer. People with neurological diseases. He had also effected more everyday cures. He had, he told her, cured a baby's colic with bottles of catnip tea. "I'm also pleased to see that you are wearing natural-fibre clothes. That's good." But as they were saying goodbye at his door he told her she had a butterfly-shaped rash on her face. "I noticed it the moment I saw you standing out there on the doorstep. The mark of the wolf," he said. "Lupus erythematosus. An often fatal disease. So you be sure to keep out of the sun now, until we can know more."

"I don't think I've ever even heard of it."

"The body turns on itself and attacks its own tissues. It can go for any organ. Even the heart."

Her poor little heart, it was beating terribly. "But what has the sun got to do with it?"

"The sun is a killer if you have lupus." But then he told her that he wouldn't know for certain if she had it until he'd sent the samples of her urine and saliva to a group of researchers who ran a big diagnostic computer in Los Angeles. "Down to my friends in California," he said.

It was a cold evening for August and the eaves of the row houses up on the hill had been hit by a low golden fall light. Steff would be shocked to see that her winter hats and mittens were still out in the hall at the end of summer. He'd always had a more housewifely sense of the seasons than she did, and when they were married he was forever after her to wash and put away the winter clothes early in March. Now that he was no longer living with her she didn't do this, and so on the shelf above the coat rack there was still a hilly wool banquet for moths, along with a small hill of mismatched suede gloves and mittens.

The following Tuesday, when she got a call from the office of her own doctor, Dr. Hardy, telling her that she was two years overdue for her general check-up, Claire made an apologetic appointment. She had lost all faith in orthodox medicine. She wasn't sure she had all that much faith in holistic medicine either. But on Thursday afternoon she did go off to see Dr. Hardy, a woman who wore her white hair in a bun and who pinned silver sprays of heather to her flowered dresses. Dr. Hardy had very high young breasts for such an old woman; she was also fond of stuffing Claire's pockets with grandmotherly little gifts: sample bottles of vitamins, tiny tubes of medicated shampoos.

Claire dreaded making the confession that would prove her lack of faith in Dr. Hardy, but by this time the computer in California had sent back its report and Mr. Spaulding had phoned her to translate it for her and she had new reason to feel fear on her own behalf: uric acid in the danger level, and she had, or was on her way to having, lupus erythematosus. But when she told Dr. Hardy about the computer in Los Angeles, Dr. Hardy said she could think of better uses for forty-five dollars than having her spit sent off to California. "We'll run a few blood tests on you, for non-nuclear antibodies, but I very much doubt we'll find anything." She also spoke about medical fashions. "Tongues used to be what they looked at, but nobody looks at tongues any more." Not that long ago, she told her, she was walking past a dress shop on Rideau Street when she happened to see an exact replica of a dress her mother made for her when she was in high school. The same voile, the same sleeves.

~~~~~~

The last weekend in September was hotter than the hottest days of midsummer, and Claire, who'd worn her new jacket out to the market, kept it on while she sat in the shade of the rowan tree in the back garden to read the Saturday papers.

But the slippery jacket was too hot, and so she pulled it off and laid it beside her, down on the dried and ill-looking lawn. Sunlight moved over its silky spots when the wind shifted in its jungly summer way through the leaves high up in the trees.

For a few moments, the light inside went too active and dark, after the brilliant sunlight. She fitted the jacket over the back of one of the kitchen chairs, then took an ice cube from the freezer, and as she was drawing it down her throat, thoughts of Declan and the warm breeze blowing in through the open window made her feel light on her feet, happy. On her way into the front room, she stopped and looked at her face in the hall mirror. There was no mark of the wolf, no mark of the butterfly. The butterfly had flown.

A spot of sunlight might have moved over the leopard spots if any sun had been able to make its way down into so deep a room. As it was, the sun only burned green in the grass up near the top of the basement window, up in the high veld of the garden.

And now that they'd finished their hard work for the day and were lying on the mats, talking, Declan, who'd been lying on one side, resting his chin in a hand, rolled over on his back and raised an arm straight up to squint at his watch.

Claire studied his raised arm. She longed to reach up and touch it, draw her hand down the length of it. It was a strong arm, but pale. He always stayed pale, even at the end of summer he was pale.

She was startled to hear him say, "We have exactly five minutes left." And then after a few moments of silence that felt oddly careful, "You have five minutes to touch me. Wherever you like. Anywhere on my body."

His voice was so expressionless that she couldn't tell if this was a therapeutic dare or something he really meant. It even seemed possible that, being intuitive, he'd picked up her longing to run a hand down his arm. But this wasn't the way he had said it, she was convinced it was something he was daring her to do, it felt like a watchful test he was putting her through, a test rigged to make her look wrong and hysterically modest.

And so a silence that felt as if it planned to turn itself into a very long silence began to take root in the Room. There were five or six seconds, an allotment, in which she might have shown amazement — in which, as a patient, she might have said "Are you out of your *mind?*" — but almost at once this allotment ran out.

They lay in silence and more silence. She most certainly should have said something at once, now it was too late to speak out in surprise. Because if you were going to speak out in surprise, dammit, you couldn't wait twenty-four seconds to do it. She laid a doubtful hand on his diaphragm, then watched, pretending to be mesmerized as it moved up and down with his breathing.

He was wearing a grey shirt and jeans and although these were the sort of clothes he always wore out in the country, they added to her feeling that he was not quite a doctor. Not a doctor in a suit who sat behind a desk. After a few more awful moments of doubt, she dared herself to move down toward his penis. Cock, she thought, although it was not a word she could say except when she was in bed. It also seemed to her that it would take more courage than she could ever possess to make her touch it. Whatever tender feelings she'd had for him were gone. She had no sexual feeling at all for him and was convinced that he had no sexual feeling for her. But it's what he thinks I don't have the courage to do, she thought. And so at last she made her hand creep down to it and shyly cap it.

Even beneath the denim she could feel how small and soft it was. It was as if they were both now incredibly young, pre-sexual, if children were ever young enough to be that. But she didn't feel like a child either, she was too tired and too afraid. More afraid than a child would feel. He's lost, she thought, and it seemed to her that she must take care not to hurt him, now that he had crawled so dangerously far out on a limb, far out into the weak little leaves at the end of a branch that dipped and sprang and then nearly swept him onto hard ground. And yet now that she had touched him down there — *down there, down there,* "down there" no longer a euphemism but turned into a drumbeat in her head — she was convinced that she could feel his excitement, could feel he was too excited to show any physical evidence of it. His whole body seemed tense to her, in a state of held-in rigid tingle while it was waiting. But he was like a little boy waiting. There was a roaring inside her head. Think! But she couldn't. Unless she was only thinking. But if she was only thinking, then thinking wasn't at all able to help her. She thought, I have failed at everything. She moved her hand back up to his diaphragm and they politely remained that way, frozen into position while they watched her hand slightly rise and fall with his breathing until the final minutes had ticked by and they could at last make their awkward little arrangements to stand up.

And when they said goodbye they also said it awkwardly, pretending not to be awkward, and she felt weak and stunned walking up the stone steps into the light, as if she had not understood his way of being close and so had given him a push that set him adrift onto a fast-moving body of water. She thought, he's a passionate person, and even if what he did felt weird and loveless there could still be a kind of watchful love in it. Still, he hadn't looked at her when he'd said what he said to her. If he had loved her, wouldn't he have looked at her?

The little gypsy madonna was sitting in the open door of her beetle again, just as before, but today she was dressed in faded and very brief frayed shorts that showed off a good tan and her thick-ankled legs. She had also cleverly knotted a flowered blouse into a midriff-blouse and was wearing a feather choker. The birthmark, mulberry-stained, was bleeding its lowest teardrops down into the flamingo-pink ruff of feathers. So openly drawn attention to in this way, the birthmark (or burn mark?) seemed more like a fashion statement than a handicap.

Claire felt humbled by the girl, by her youthful willingness to not mind having Declan see — for all this sex and exotica had to be for Declan — that she wasn't at all afraid to look as if she'd made a big effort for him, and after a moment's hesitation, she greeted the girl with the same hi as before, and the girl, just as before, man-voiced and young, answered, "Hi there."

Driving home, Claire kept trying to remember a poem about love, something about the whole process being a lie, unless, crowned by excess, it broke its way forcefully through from something (she couldn't remember what) to find something deeper — she thought the deeper thing might be a well — and then there was the part about Anthony and Cleopatra being right, something about their having shown the way, and then the lines she was sure of: "I love you or I do not live at all." He was only trying to crown it by excess, she finally but also with great and uneasy doubt decided, and although his doing it made him seem like a child, she was the one who was really a child and so wasn't willing to help him do it.

She couldn't sleep, not even after her nightly rituals: aspirins, camomile tea made with three tea bags instead of two, a hot shower. But someone else was also awake, she could see another light burning when she went to her bedroom window to look out. Someone who was perhaps studying late behind an upstairs light across the street. And so her heart felt at least a little bit eased, it was such a consolation to know that she now had a companion in sleeplessness.

Dr. Tenniswood was overbooked the next afternoon, although when Claire got a call from Mr. Wilcox, an established malingerer, she promised to fit him in as well, mainly because she was feeling too exhausted to say no. The days when she used to worry that Dr. Tenniswood's patients would abandon him seemed to be over. She used to sit at her desk early some mornings and think, what if you had a clinic and nobody came. What if, what if, what if. But now she was finding it hard to pay any attention to the patients at all. What she really wanted to do was put on her dark glasses and go out for a walk along the canal. Go out for a walk and think.

But when she drove down to Ottersee to see Declan the following Thursday he was openly cool to her, and after they had gone through their grounding and breathing exercises for the afternoon he told her he wanted her to walk in a particular way.

As he was doing a quick demonstration for her, she tried walking behind him, a dancer trying to duplicate the movements of an obsessed choreographer.

He broke from their circle, then walked backwards to watch her. "*No,*" he moaned in a low voice that seemed to carry within it a contemptuous whimper. "You haven't got it right! I'll have to show you again, so watch more closely this time." And then his voice dropped to become almost inaudible – it was like a child's voice, she thought, when a child wants to say something obscene or cruel – and in this new and young and tauntingly tiny voice he said, "You'll never get men to look at you on the street if you walk like that." She knew exactly the kind of voice it was being said in too, it was the kind of voice that said: This is supposed to sound as if you are not meant to hear it, but you really *are* meant to hear it, you are meant to hear it more than you've ever been meant to hear anything in your whole goddamn *life.*

Wounded, her first impulse was not to show it. But then she spotted a small refinement she'd missed on his first demonstration and so tried to incorporate it into the next walkaround she did for him.

With another careening whimper he cried, "No! Not like *that!* Like *this!*"

She couldn't see the difference. She tried again, feeling lost, an imbecile, she was so convinced that he'd already decided she was pathetic and droopy, too dumb to learn the tango.

"Christ," he said, and his voice was again the new and soft and terrible voice, "I can't see why you can't *get* this, it really isn't that difficult at *all*."

She kept trying and trying and still not getting it. It was like being an out-of-work dancer and working out with a deranged dance master. It was like dancing in hell.

But finally, after casting a bleak look at her, he said in a spitefully weary voice, "Oh what the hell, let's do something else," and he told her to lie face down on the mat.

Thank God, at least now she would be able to relax for a bit, and so she let her belly sink into the mat, then rested her head sideways on her peacefully folded arms. She even began to breathe almost comically, deep down in her abdomen to impress him. Herr Doktor, Herr Enemy, she thought, recalling the walk she'd taken with Libi to Strathcona Park and how they'd stretched out on the sun-warmed silk linings of their black raincoats and read aloud to each other from *Ariel*. But now Declan was straddling her, just above her hips, pinning her torso to the floor between the quick vice of his knees, and so she moaned a little, trying to shrug him off. But he seemed not to hear, or had decided to pretend not to, for he was now digging his left thumb into a painful point at the back of her neck and holding her head down while using his right hand to keep it turned sideways and clamped to the carpet. Tears came to her eyes as she tried to lift her head, but he shoved it back down again. It was like drowning or being smothered except that there was also the pain. She saw how the grey canvas

cushion was beginning to get wet with the tears that were now
running like clear sap from her eyes and nose. By this time she
could also hear herself wailing, a high keening wail, but even
as she was wailing she was aware of trying to keep her wails
within the bounds of good taste. A terrible sort of partnership
even began to be established between them — her cries weaving
in and out among his shortened breaths, which were the explo-
sive piston breaths of someone who was using all of his strength
to fiercely hold something down, and while this unbearable
pressing down was happening she began to experience curious
floating moments of feeling nothing at all, and it was at the
end of one of these floating moments — for she was now in
pain once again — that she realized that there hadn't been any
other cars parked beside the house when she'd swept up the
driveway just after three. We are all alone here, she thought,
and yet to be afraid because of this seemed foolish, dangerous
even, terror would make her even more his quarry. And so terror
made her grab for common sense: it was a test, he was testing
her to see how hard she would scream, she had only to scream
with her whole heart to get him to stop, and so she let out a
great (but still somehow tremulous) howl, and as she did so
she sucked in a sickening whiff of dust from the carpet, the Room
by now swimming all around her, swimming and whirling — her
watch-face, the cushions — the pain was making them bob, the
pain was turning the grey carpet into a river, but just at the point
when she seemed to have reached a high meadow of pure pain
and was about to black out, he rolled off her and told her she
was now free to sit up.

But she wasn't, at that moment, able to sit up.

"Are you all right?"

The Room was still a limping merry-go-round, its mats and cushions doing their slow-motion dip and spin all around her. She raised herself up on one arm and drew the back of her free hand up over her damp forehead. "I don't know."

He ran a hand down one of her arms, then said in a more strained voice than she had ever before heard him use, "You could have fought me, you could have tried to buck me off. You could have *kicked*."

She didn't answer. She was still feeling odd, a bit dizzy.

He stood, then held out both of his hands to her, pulled her up. "You're sure you're okay?"

Again she didn't answer, she had to get to her skirt, pull it up over her shorts. She held on to the back of a chair for a moment although the Room had by now come to a standstill. Really she didn't feel anything at all, she only felt incredibly tired, too tired to look down at her fingers feeling for the slots for her buttons.

But when she was ready to make her way out of the Room, he barred the doorway with his right arm. Like a boyfriend, she thought. *I will not let thee go except thou bless me.* "Before you go," he said in a low voice that now seemed to be filled with feeling for her, "tell me you're okay."

"I'm okay." But her voice was a new voice that she had never used before, the voice of a woman taking (with a great and detached medical calm) her own pulse, and then he – but with reluctance, she felt – let her pass.

"So I'll see you next week, then," she heard his voice say as she was walking toward the stairs to outside.

Without looking back she answered yes.

Going up the stone stairs into the sunlight, she warned herself to compose her face to meet the critical gaze of the caravan girl sitting in the open doorway of her beetle, but as she was stepping out into the day she could see only the long strips of stubble fields lying in the heat haze of the buzzing afternoon light.

So he had no one coming, then. There were only the two of us here. Although the children were still at the bottom of the garden, running at the windy edge of her attention like bright little flags. She got into the car and drove it carefully down the laneway as if she had to listen and feel her way over every bump and hollow. But when she got out to the highway she had to sit for several moments, unable to decide which way she should turn. But once she had remembered and turned and then was out in the flow of traffic the world ordered itself: highway, direction, fields, the city. Her neck hurt her and her back was on fire, but the ache in her arms and eyes was the worst. And where were her sunglasses? She reached down into her shoulder bag and felt her way among loose peanuts and pens and tubes of lipstick, but she couldn't find them. She could barely see, the glare of the day was so bright, but she neverthe-less drove on, squinting and now and then even whimpering a little while the car kept drifting toward the highway's soft shoulder. The only way she could bring it back on course once again was to think of the pavement as an asphalt conveyor belt, bearing her home. A summer's heat was also draining all the life out of the fall afternoon. It was as hot and sad as an after-noon in high summer, the white undersides of the aspen leaves blown back by the wind. She thought it must be the wind that was making her think of the trees as runners, their goal their obsession, not a person. She felt a dull envy of them; of them and of everyone with the good luck to be unlike herself and, lulled by them, she must have dropped off for a moment because her heart was startled by a flung scatter of pebbles against metal — in her dream, someone was throwing stones against her bedroom window — but then she understood that it was only the car's tires hitting a belt of loose gravel and then someone was saying "If you get my drift . . ." as in the startled drift of the car sideways, she was again jolted awake. But a few miles later she must have briefly dropped off again because she was all at once on water, on a canal, and the long moan of a tugboat was warning her away from another boat — a cry of green racing by her, outraged, its passing lights flashing.

At the first traffic light coming back into town she was more awake and all at once aware that she was being watched by someone in the green car stopped next to hers. She turned to see a sharp-nosed and sunburned fair man gazing over at her in dumbfounded wonder. But when he saw her see him, he looked quickly away. And then she did the same, as if the sight of his embarrassment had caused her to feel an unbearable discomfort. She was afraid to crane up to look at herself in the rear-view mirror after this, she was too afraid of the emotional disarray she would find there, too convinced that her face would look disassembled, hardly human.

When she got to the car-rental place and turned in the keys, the men behind the counter looked stunned by her too. After she'd turned away from them she could feel their joined gaze on the backs of her legs as she was walking through the open doorway and down again into the last of the hot sunlight. Then she could hear two sets of footsteps come down the stairs behind her and when she looked back at the rental lot from the first intersection she saw that the two men were carefully examining her car; one of them crouched down by a front tire, the other one inside it, hunched in an ominously listening way at the steering wheel. They think I wrecked it, she thought.

Children she met on the walk home stared openly at her too, but the adults she encountered, after the most furtive glances in her direction, looked away, their city eyes lit by circumspect city fear.

She needed to buy something to eat, but she didn't want to go into Habib's, she didn't want to be kindly observed, she couldn't bear it, and so she walked up the hill to the convenience store on the corner and in less than a minute she was breathing in the sweetish smell of darkly freckled bananas and old glassy candies wrapped in twists of antique cellophane. She wanted to buy a grapefruit, but the grapefruits were all dented and soft. She'd never once dared to buy anything canned here, fearing the ill effects from cans containing spaghetti and beans canned decades ago. The old Chinese woman who owned the store was behind the counter, and Claire, feeling shaky but also famished, bought a can of sardines from her, picturing tarnished silver fishes packed in ancient oil as she wondered how many years they'd been lying pressed in their tin in this dim little store.

Then at last home, where Dirk van der Meer, in his grey shorts, was raking the leaves from the grass on the front lawn. When he saw her he smiled. "Hey!"

"Hey," she said in a small reedy voice, reaching into her bag for her dark glasses. Which she now could find with no trouble at all, and so she put them on just in time to stumble into the deeper dark of the house.

Up in the safety of her own apartment, she lay in the stale dimness and let herself cry. She felt as if she could cry forever and never dry out. But then she recalled her mother, years and years ago, dressed in her pale pink satin dressing gown and carrying on shamelessly. Quilted silver satin lapels, her hair cut in a duck-tail — a varnished yellow on top, a chevron of dark hair beneath — her body writhing and bouncing around on the bed like a crazed little pony while she'd moaned at them, "I'm a terrible mother, I've failed miserably, you are all so terribly *spoiled*," Claire and her brothers cooing back at her in their frightened, appeasing voices, "No, no, darling Mummie, you're a good mother, you really are," then reaching out to take quick little pats at her, as if they'd feared she would give off a shock like the shock that came from the electric fences the farmers would put up to keep the cows in. I'd better watch myself, she decided, I'd better watch my step. But she lay on her bed and cried until the outside darkness turned the dim bedroom even darker, and sometimes, in spite of all the deadness coming from the loss of Declan and the loss of the world through Declan, there were moments when her tears seemed to spring from some hot spring of pure health as she cried bitterly, almost sweetly, with the worst pain in her throat.

The next morning she called the receptionist at the Institute and made an appointment to see Declan the following

Monday in town. And she wouldn't stay talking things over with him either, she would just go in and pay the receptionist in advance for the hour and then when they were alone she would make her announcement that she was leaving and then she would leave.

But on her way to the phone she detoured into her bedroom and unzipped her plastic storage bag and stood breathing in its unpleasant ether and taffeta smell for several minutes, trying to decide what she would wear for the final visit.

Getting ready for her appointment two days later and even knowing that everything was over and must be over between them forever from now on, she still carefully dressed herself in her beige drawstring blouse, sheer as chiffon, a miniature sampler of tiny x's stitched across its bodice, then pulled on her black pantyhose and her most narrow black skirt.

At the Institute the receptionist told her to go to the corner room at the back, the one whose windows looked out onto the park. It was the room she'd been shown into the day she first came to see Declan. Which seemed like yet another sign from fate or the beyond that she must leave him. But an ill tingle in her heart still seemed to be telling her that she was not yet convinced. All she could think was, How will we be with one another? She did know one thing: he would not make the sort of mistake that Steff, wanting forgiveness, would make: smiling a little boy's sheepish or jokey smile. He would know better than to do that, would know that it was not a situation that could be made light of, would know that to play their parts, a kind of convalescent dignity would be required. It also occurred to her that she must not be sitting, she should be standing and pretending to look out the window. And she did look out, both seeing and not seeing the beautiful park. She remembered his arm barring the way after he had hurt her, she remembered his voice, she remembered what he had said with it. What she could not remember (because at the time she could not bear to look) was his face. She thought, I can't remember what he looks like! But then his face, or the memory of his face, appeared before her and she saw (or remembered) his gallant impersonal sadness and the way it could turn him into someone she would feel she could absolutely rely on. Although not until the moment he stopped being sad for the sake of an idea or the world. But at this same moment she heard his voice out in the hallway, speaking to the receptionist.

So soon!

And her heart began to race as the capacity for thinking any thought at all left her.

He came into the room then and closed the door carefully behind him. She could see how drained he was looking, as if he hadn't slept at all since the afternoon she'd walked up the steps and out into the day. But his hair was shiny and soft – he must have just washed it – and he was wearing a long-sleeved white shirt, open at the throat, and whatever his thoughts were, he looked like a man who was doing his best not to think them.

Because she had just washed her own hair, it even seemed to her it was quite possible that they'd both been shampooing their hair at the same time last night, both of them thinking of this moment when they would see one another again. It made her feel that they must understand one another. She even had to remind herself that she was afraid of him. Because she didn't feel afraid. She only felt an almost unbearable pity for both of them. It was only to break the awkward silence between them that she finally said that she didn't think they could go on the way they were going.

He didn't deny it. He only stared down at her left hand, at rest on the treatment table.

She looked down at his hand then too, holding hard on to the rim of the table, so close to her own hand, and it did not seem like a hand that had hurt her. It looked like a beautiful and honest hand. A hand that knew (with all its heart) what tenderness was. It was only with the greatest effort that she was able to make herself say, "So I think I really will have to go this time."

As she said this she was sure she could feel his whole body listening. She had to remind herself that he had been trained to listen and so was able to listen with the humility of one who has learned how to listen. He was listening too much to say one single word to her.

So that she felt she had to be the one to say, "And not ever come back."

After a moment that seemed to take years he said, "And so we part friends then?"

It surprised her that he would ask her a thing like that. She couldn't even look up at him when she said yes.

He held out his hand then, not as if he wanted to help her up from the table, but as if he wanted to shake hands with her.

And so they shook hands. Of all the curious ways they had touched each other this seemed to her the oddest.

Then it was time for her to go.

He quickly went to stand in the narrow doorway. Did he want her to embrace him? If she did give in and do that she knew she would never leave him.

But as she brushed by him, it seemed to her that his eyes were painfully moist and that he wanted her to go quickly.

And so she walked straight through the Institute and out into the still afternoon and she didn't look back.

Walking down the steps from the Institute, she'd been light-headed with grief, and by the time she was walking in the cool fall air she was feeling the amazed and sickly effervescent euphoria of someone who's survived the funeral of someone deeply loved: I'm breathing, I'm alive, I'll never see Declan again.

She'd planned to stop off at the Sunshine Trading Company but when she got to where it was (or where it was supposed to be) it was no longer there. And so she walked back up Bank to the health food store near Gilmour.

As she stepped into the store a voice called out to her from down at the back by the grain bins, a voice belonging to a man she vaguely knew. Tom Lunman, his name was, he was a skiing pal of Steff's. He held up a steel scoop to salute her. "How you been keeping?"

"Pas mal."

"Pas mal, pas terrific?"

She gazed at him keenly, but he appeared merely to be making polite conversation. "C'est ça."

But after this it seemed to her that he was gearing his shopping to her shopping, and that he was matching her, peanut butter for almond butter, buckwheat for millet, tofu for tofu. They ended up together in the line for the cash.

Out in the street he offered her a lift.

"Wonderful. I've moved, though. Down to Ottawa South."

He said Ottawa South was perfect, he'd been planning to go out to the school of engineering at Carleton anyway, he could just drop her off down there and then nip over to Bronson.

She couldn't think of one single topic for conversation as they were getting into his car, but it was all right, he was talkative enough for the two of them, he was already telling her about a recent trip to Lunenburg and about a squash tournament he'd taken part in, in Wolfville, but when they reached her street he sat and stared straight ahead, all energy drained from him.

"Thanks so much, this was really great."

He roused himself then, to turn and stare at her with an awkward, almost ill-tempered hunger. "Do you ski?"

She gazed with a kind of dread at the green slopes of the lawns on her little street. What month was this?

"Not right now, of course," he reassured her. "But soon." His self-conscious laugh was almost a cackle. "When the snow flies."

She said no, she was too much of a coward.

"Coward?"

"Don't want to break my little bones."

"Do you swim?"

"No."

"Do you dance?"

"Not in public."

She could see his eyes watching her eyes, trying to figure her out. She could see him trying mightily to smile. He said, "In private, then."

She shook her head, smoothed her hand down her skirt while she could feel him looking toward some melancholy horizon of his own. But I'm trying so hard, she couldn't say to him, I'm trying so hard not to hurt you, can't you see that? I don't want to say no to you, please don't make me. And so she said that she'd been really incredibly busy at work lately.

Again he stared at her. Then at last giving up on her, he let himself out of the car, came quickly around to open her door, stood while she gathered her provisions together. She stumbled out, flushed, ill-equipped for his disdain but ready for it. If suffering his disdain was what it would take to set her free.

"Well goodbye, then," he said, and with surprising energy he walked around to his own side again, let himself with swift heaviness in, turned on the ignition.

Through the car window, another surprise: he made his mouth pucker up into a kiss.

It threw her. But as she was walking up the sidewalk to her door, she decided it wasn't a kiss after all, he was saying something to her, he was telling her to loosen up.

〜〜〜〜

Words from somewhere — but she couldn't remember where — words that were like a deranged chant in a children's game of hopscotch kept repeating themselves in her head: Once you have seen God (hop, hop) what is the remedy (hop, skip) what is the remedy (hop, hop) what is the remedy (hop, skip). She thought of how nearly insane this chant was (like any chant) and finally the only way she could stop it was to put in a call to Ottersee. But Declan wasn't taking his calls, his answering machine was on. And so she sat on her bed, her hands clamped between her warm thighs, waiting for him to pick up his messages and call her back. Her feet were chilled in red sandals that had the cracked-lacquer look of cracked nail polish, and she was fighting crying and knew she would lose control of her voice completely when she heard him say her name.

She waited half an hour, rehearsing her little speech with care, going over it again and again.

At eight-thirty she understood that she was getting cold and she pulled on a pair of socks and then strapped on her sandals again, snagging her dry fingers on the socks' dryness. She felt unattractive and knew she was breathing in an obsessed way, with a child's adenoidal and desperate harshness.

At nine o'clock she tried Ottersee again, but Declan still wasn't at home. At nine-fifteen she went into the kitchen to make herself a cup of tea and when she brought the cup back into her bedroom she felt chilled again and so took out her African robe and tied it on fiercely.

At ten o'clock she tried calling him again. This time she was prepared for the machine and left a more elaborate message: There are still things to be resolved and so I need another appointment. And so could you please call me back please, it's really important.

At ten-fifteen she went out to the kitchen to heat up a can of oxtail soup, then she went back to her room and sat down by the phone with her steaming hot mug of it. But the phone didn't ring.

Just before midnight she went to bed, but she knew she wouldn't be able to sleep. Thousands of thoughts came to her, the memory of a time she and Steff went to visit an old college friend of his in Montreal, and how Steff, shaking the ice cubes around in his glass of scotch, stared out the window to announce to the air: "I just don't find Claire all that attractive any more." Which had led his old school friend to study his own drink in speechless misery – poking the ice cubes around and around with a melancholy thumb – and then when they'd at last been ready to say goodbye and drive back to Ottawa the friend had stood at his door with his arm around her waist, he'd so much wanted to console her, if he could, for having such a husband. His hand holding her briefly clasped to his side could have held her only yesterday, she could still so much feel the tender impression his fingers had left on that side of her body. But even memories of kindness (or especially memories of kindness) could make her pillow wet. She kept bunching it up, trying to find a puff of it that wasn't damp, and every time she took in a deep breath she breathed in the smell of rubber from the hot water bottle she'd bought last week at Tamblyns – an unpleasant smell, almost a sour-paint smell, almost fecal.

At work the next day she thought only of calling Declan, she lived to get home and go straight to the phone. And this time she would leave a cooler message, no more imploring, imploring would only make him feel a saddened contempt for her. But her fear was that it would be the same despairing waiting all over again, he wouldn't call her back.

The patients were all in their own little worlds too, a polite galaxy, when a young woman and a small boy came in from the windy world of the street. Still holding hands with the child, this woman came over to Claire's desk. She was wearing a mini-dress made out of a harsh and wiry raspberry brocade and the bottom half of her body was young, hefty — her legs as heavy as an athlete's legs — but there was something about her mouth that was rodenty, elderly.

And yet she sparkled.

When Claire gave her a questionnaire to fill out, she noticed that the child was gazing up at her with a bright and fascinated look that also had childish dismay in it. At least until he asked her, "Why are *you* crying?"

She looked down at him, startled. He must have believed that only children could cry. "But I'm not crying," she told him.

"Hugo!" his mother sternly whispered down to him. "Go hang up your coat." While all around them the people who had too quickly looked up were now too quickly looking down.

Claire smiled at the child as he was being plunked down to sit — his little legs pointing straight out — on one of the chairs that lined the far wall of the waiting room. She wanted to go over to him and kneel beside him to whisper, "Don't be sad, Hugo. And don't even be puzzled. You're a very intelligent little boy because you understood that I was crying even though there was no actual evidence of tears . . ." But now the front door was opening again, and Zuzi Tenniswood was coming in. She had a friend in tow and she smiled at Claire, not really seeing her. "There's a *Vogue* magazine in here that we want to steal, okay with you, Claire?"

Someone who was more cheerfully on the ball than Claire felt she would ever be again might have said something to make these girls laugh. Something abusive and friendly, something like "Lay even one finger on those magazines and you will be shot," but Claire wasn't on the ball, not at all, not at all, and so she only said, "Sure, go ahead, Zuzi. Feel free."

The next night was again nearly sleepless and so, except for a drugged hour or two, was the following night. When she did sleep, she had terrible dreams: public-toilet dreams, a bad smell in the air. A dream about a frightening noise, a kind of scrabbling on the window-screen down in her kitchen while she was turning to say to someone "Now the sky is poisonous . . ." In one of her dreams she was living with Steff again. In her dream she sat down at a desk to write in a notebook: "Feel a compulsive need to check everything: ocean, rocks, etc." She also had a fever dream in which she was being driven very fast up and down little hills by her mother, but when she looked toward the front of the car, there was no one in the driver's seat.

She began to be afraid that Declan would go away for the weekend, leaving her to spend her whole two free days calling and calling him, and so she broke her promise to herself and called him on Friday night just past eleven.

But this time a real voice answered, a woman's voice, the voice of his wife. And how human she sounded, this envied woman. In her Ottawa Valley drawl that sounded so southern, she said, "Declan isn't here right now, but when he gets in I'll ask him to call you."

Claire thanked her and then sat beside the phone, feeling so faint she was afraid she might have to throw up. Her heart lopsidedly galloped. How strange life was, nothing ever worked out the way you imagined it would, and to prove it, here was this envied woman being sensibly kind to her, she was actually relying on her for her kindness. She planed her damp hands down the front of her robe, breathing, not-breathing, waiting, all African-drum heartbeat.

At twenty past eleven, the phone rang, and when Declan said her name, and in spite of the fact that she was immediately weeping, she said in a broken voice, "Why didn't you call me? I've been trying to reach you for the last three days."

He hadn't had time to pick up his messages.

"I feel there are still things to be resolved. I feel I need another appointment."

But he was completely booked up for the next two weeks. "If not longer."

She tried not to plead. "After that, then."

"After that, my wife and I are going off to Scotland for six weeks."

"May I write to you then?"

A long pause. Then (in either a sad or a dead voice): "If you like."

Late at night, before she turned off her light, Claire would read, sitting propped up in her bed. She would read hungrily, starved for words, starved for help with her feelings. And then would be surprised by how often there would be real help for her. One night she read in a novel that moved her: "He could explain if she would listen. Explaining was a way of getting close to somebody you had hurt; as if in hurting them you were giving them a reason to love you." There was also the familiar (but more than ever true) "Romance has no part of it, the business of love is cruelty . . ."

In the mornings she sat on the side of her bed in her nightgown, trying to psych herself up for the descent to her neatly stale kitchen, squinting too hard because the bright light hurt her heart. It was hard, too, not to recall that only a few weeks ago she'd been incredibly happy to get up in the mornings and blissfully stand trying to decide on a shirt and skirt for the day (if it was an Ottersee day), happy to hurry out into the mornings whose faint hint of melancholy (the melancholy of perfection) had only made her happiness happier.

She began to go for walks in the direction of the Institute. At first these walks took place while Declan was still away in Scotland, but after the six-week period was up, she only walked in the direction of the Institute on the days she knew he would not be in town. She would go as far as the park behind the Institute, but never beyond it — she did not, after all, want to see herself as an obsessive — and as she walked she would pass men with dogs on tight leashes and mothers holding the reins to haltered children made fat by puffy parkas, and sometimes, too, she would walk back and forth in that little citified wood waiting for the lights in the Institute to come on, waiting for the dog owners and the mothers and the babies to go home. Waiting and worse than waiting, pathetically lurking. How sad life is, she would think as she made her secretive way among the grey trunks of the trees, how sad for other people too, how filled with disappointment, how difficult to bear, just look at all the unhappy faces, then at last she would hurry home, not wanting to encounter anyone, either friend or stranger. Above all, not a stranger. A stranger, any stranger, would need to take only one look into her eyes to know everything.

In the evenings, she worked on her letter. A letter that was both conciliatory and accusing, but also contaminated by a kind of sickening pleading. And by two opposite kinds of longing: the longing for things to go back to where they were, and the longing for justice. She longed for Declan to explain himself to her in a way that could allow her to forgive him.

At bedtimes she brewed herself a powerful sedative tea made from the twigs of a tree that grew in the Amazon rainforest. She stopped measuring it out in tablespoons too – no, it wasn't twigs, it was the shavings of some tropical tree-bark that smelled as spicy and dusty as a wood full of cinnamon trees – and began to dump handfuls of it into her tea mug. Night after night she drank her spicy but bitter tea, at least until the night she found herself sitting on the floor of her clothes closet, pawing among her shoes and sandals and whimpering because she was under the impression that the movers would be arriving at sunrise and she hadn't even started to pack yet.

She was also often dizzy; the room with its pale-yellow curtains would spin and dip around her when she sat up on the side of her bed in the mornings, and when she went down to the kitchen she would feel too sick to eat. And yet eating, in the end, would seem to be the one cure for her condition. She didn't mention any of this to Dr. Tenniswood or call Dr. Hardy for an appointment, her symptoms felt too private. Instead – during the periods when she was feeling more stable – she would read through the index lists at the back of her holistic-therapy and doctor books.

The bad things it could be a symptom of frightened her. A disturbance of the middle ear, high blood pressure, any number of diseases that were either neurologically macabre or terminal. Unless it was simply that her diet was too alkaline. In a book on Vermont folk medicine she read that dizziness was a common symptom for people living in the state of Vermont, it was because of the high alkalinity of the soil there. Vermont was even *called* the Land of Dizziness. The cure was apple-cider vinegar, two teaspoons in a glass of water with each meal.

She tried it, and there were days when she even felt better. She also felt better if she could get out for a walk in the wind

or in the clear morning air. She noticed too that the spinning
and dipping sensations bothered her much less at work, which
made her wonder if at work she didn't get dizzy because she
was afraid to get dizzy. The book also said that depression
and exhaustion could change the acid-alkaline balance of the
blood and urine, that there could be a psychological compo-
nent to dizziness. And that sometimes the best cure for too
much alkalinity was to take a hot bath or go skiing. Or go out
for a walk. She went to the hallway closet to look for her
rubber boots, then turned them upside-down and shook each
one of them out before she poked her bare feet into them, a
precaution she'd also learned from a book: a girl in a novel
she'd read last summer aimed a bare foot into a rubber boot
and felt the plump barrier of a warm little mouse asleep in
the toe of it.

~~~~~
~~~~~

In the Rideau River there were long dying shoals of ice, sharks
of ice asleep under the cold dark river water, and everywhere
in the parks there was frozen mud-crunch and bracken. But the
March afternoons were as cold as the afternoons of November,
and on one of these afternoons on her way home from work,
Claire walked too far down the path that ran along one side of
the park behind the Institute and got so close to it she could
hear footsteps running fast down the front steps, then the gulp
of a car door someone slammed shut. She fled back the way
she had come then, her heart wild even long after she'd reached
her own street.

Her whole apartment, as she let herself into it, smelled of hardening lemons. She opened a window, then went up to her bedroom and sat down on her bed in her cold coat. She picked up the phone, then dialled the number of Declan's extension at the Institute, a number that she still knew by heart.

His recorded voice sounded tired. She waited for a few moments before she called back. Did he sound sad? She set the phone in its cradle and went down to the kitchen to pour herself a glass of wine, then went back up to her bedroom to call him again. And again tried to diagnose the depth of the exhaustion or loneliness in his voice, but the recording wouldn't ever give her quite enough time. She dialled again, listened again. After three more calls she went down to the kitchen, but while she was making a salad, the phone rang. She ran to it, almost in terror. She couldn't believe it could be anyone but Declan, reached telepathically through her strong bond with his recorded voice on the Institute phone. But it was only a wrong number.

That night she began a new letter to him with the words, "I always felt you had the kind of intelligence that would make a woman want to be honest with you in a way that would matter more (or at least matter differently) than honesty with a woman friend." But then she decided that writing this might be a mistake, he might think her disloyal to other women. Or a sycophant. And so she tore the letter up and got out a new sheet of paper, this time beginning with her need to see him again. But did the word "need" sound too hysterical? She was sure that it did, and so she crumpled up this letter, too, to make another fresh start. But *this* letter, although it began very much more cheerfully, was all too soon growing longer and longer, compounding itself, compounding banalities, compounding pleading, and so before turning out her light she tore the paper into pale-blue bits that looked up at her from her desk, tiny torn blue faces.

Progress (even great progress) has been made since the new year. And now that it's spring, Claire no longer goes for walks in the direction of the Institute, now she takes her evening walks down by the river, and on one of these evenings, as she's cresting a small hill a streetlight in the hollow below her begins to fade, then die. It blooms into weak life once again just before it fails utterly, casting the most scooped-out part of the path into darkness.

She's on the point of turning back, but then decides to go on through the dimness to the more illuminated parkette adjacent to Bank Street. But she's not quite halfway there when she remembers that Dirk van der Meer once warned her to never walk down by the river at night, and at this same moment there's the crack and rustle of someone making his way through the trees. She begins to run, sending small avalanches of pebbles in spurts ahead of her, then feels herself literally fly through the air to land on a sharp jut of rock. She cries out, the pain in her left knee is so extreme, but when she tries to stagger up, she discovers that her right arm (the one she flung out in an attempt to break her fall) has turned itself into the arm of a rag doll. It's only because there's a small maple tree nearby that she is able, with her good arm, to pull one of its lower branches toward her and use its swingy support to draw herself up. Behind her, in the dark woods, there's another rustle, but it's so busily delicate that she now decides it's a bird or some small forest animal going about its nightly business among the trees, and at last, hopping along with the help of a walking stick made out of a fallen branch and darting a look behind her every other breath, she reaches a gas station where the man at the counter calls her a cab.

Once she's back home again she uses her left hand to do everything: run a glass of water, swallow three aspirins, ease herself with exquisite caution down onto her bed. By this time her left ankle has begun to swell, but the ache in it is bearable; now it's her useless arm that's turned painful – in fact the intensity of the pain surprises her since in the beginning it only felt limp and moderately sore. But now she has trouble moving it at all, and so she just tries to let it rest beside her while she waits for the pills to do their magic. But they don't dull the pain, and a bit before dawn she pulls the phone to her with her good hand and pokes the numbers for a cab. It's easy to get ready to go out again, she's still dressed, and once more she hop-walks, this time down the stairs to the street.

The early-morning air is cool, effervescent as she crosses the lawn while the taxi, its lights dimmed, cruises down the street to her like a lover. She opens the cab's front door with her left hand and slides clumsily side-saddle in beside the driver so he can reach over to close her door for her.

The sleeve of his jacket, as he reaches across her, smells of fish and cigarettes. And something else, splinters or wood chips, something outdoorsy.

"I can't bend my arm, so I've probably broken it."

He gives a quick snort. "If you'd broken it, I think you'd for damned sure know it."

She does know it, but she can't be bothered to argue with him as they take off through a dawn that isn't quite morning. As they cross Billings Bridge the heavens are a grey and starless expanse of pre-dawn sky, raised an inch or two (like a window blind) above a band of burning red over the black huddles of trees in the river park.

An ambulance whines past them as they swing into the Emergency parking lot.

"Looks like you've been pre-empted." (This in an unpleasantly satisfied voice, a voice designed for use in addressing a malingerer.) "And so it looks like you'll be having yourself a nice little wait."

The gurneys are being run out to the ambulance as Claire pushes her way in through the Emergency doors. And it *does* turn out to be a long wait. An X-ray technician doesn't come for her until over two hours later and when she asks him about the accident he says, "Two dead, three in critical condition . . ."

After the film is developed an exhausted intern comes to show it to her. "It's definitely broken and it's going to hurt a bit more than an ordinary break because it's so close to the funny bone." He smiles down at her. "Just one of God's little jokes," he tells her, "to break your arm so close to the funny bone."

From a bright silver pail, the cast man lifts up several long gauze strips saturated in freezing wet plaster, then winds the heavy damp bands around and around Claire's useless arm. The wet gauze is so cold she's afraid it will give her rheumatism. She pictures the plaster stored in a dark holding tank, deep under cold ground. "You couldn't warm it up just a bit?"

"Your body heat will warm it."

The doctor on call (an intensely blue-eyed woman with a sharp nose and chilly fingers) writes her a prescription for codeine. "Just for the first few days. Because of its location, the break will be particularly painful, but the good news is that it's an unusually *clean* break —"

The pain, a deep ache that intensifies at times to an almost insupportable pain, is much worse and lasts longer than she would ever have believed possible. She begins stockpiling her codeine tablets so she can use them at night, she finds it so hard to sleep through the pain and also to sleep (as she must) on her back. At work she has to type with one hand and get the patients to help her when she tries to wrap the blood-pressure cuff around patient (and impatient) arms. Although she has also become something of a star at the clinic, with her broken wing. One guy, a sweet amputee from Arnprior, even teases her and asks her if he can write his phone number on her sling.

A week later, at the hospital, when the cast man is out of the room for a few minutes, Claire goes over to his work list and sees her own birth date. He's got the correct day, but the year is wrong. Then she sees that the name next to her birth date isn't even her own name, it's a man's name: Irwin Thorson. Her own name is below Irwin Thorson's name, then there's the day of her birth again, this time along with the correct year. Irwin Thorson, she sees, also broke his arm last Friday night. She finds this astounding, and while she's waiting for the cast man to come back she sits thinking about something she read once — was it a poem? It might have been a poem — in any case, something about someone (or everyone?) meditating on the extravagance of having a separate fate, and after the cast man has returned and cut off her cast to fit her out with a new sling, she sets out in search of her star-crossed twin.

A scruffy little man who's clearly been scratched and cut in a fight is sitting crouched in the anteroom off the X-ray room. Claire wonders if he's high on some blissful combination of a recreational drug and morphine because when she asks him if his birthday is on June the twenty-sixth, he smiles a curiously happy smile: "Yay-us . . ."

"And did you break your arm last Friday night?"

"Yay-us . . ."

"I really find that just so incredibly strange," she tells him. "That we were born on the same day and we broke our arms on the same day and we've come back on the same day to get our casts taken off."

Yay-us, it *is* strange. But his bright little eyes tell her that he has seen things a thousand times stranger. Then the nurse from the cast room comes down the hall to tell him he can go home now.

After the nurse has gone off again, Claire watches her doppel-gänger roll his green hospital gown into a loose bolt of cloth, then shove it up into the armpit of the arm that's been broken. He uses his good hand to tuck the gown's leftover sleeves into

his sling, and as a final debonair touch he grins at her, then
capes his windbreaker protectively over the whole arrangement
before he takes off down the hallway.

So there goes her twin, more or less to the tune of "There
Goes My Heart." Her handsome and toothless and tricky thief
of a twin. But couldn't there be astrologically mitigating circumstances? Their different years of birth as well as different rising
signs? And all the other planets aligned in different (or even
opposing) skies of the horoscope? Besides, this thief was a
charmer, she thinks, and she remembers the boy at the fish store
confusing her with someone who was another kind of double.
But if she should meet herself would she know herself? She tries
to imagine it. She tries to imagine seeing herself come walking
toward her along Bank Street. She would be herself but she would
also (is *this* fair?) be her mother. It would make her want to run.

That night as she walks along the grassy rim of the lake, worry
about the future makes her feel stuffed up in her sinuses. It
would only take one unexpected expense (probably dental) to
make the whole wobbling house of cards come toppling down.
She sits on a park bench and pictures herself seated in a bright
and bleak kitchen. But instead of Steff standing at the sink
and preaching to her about her deficiencies as a housewife,
she's married to Declan and he's standing at the sink and
preaching to her about the body and it's all very dreary. But
now something dead is being bobbed on the water: a dead gull,
or part of a gull. She watches it being washed to the edge of
the shoreline in the grey, evening-warm wavelets, the whole
lake softly grey by this time — both water and evening sky grey

with the lakeside, fog-grey of twilight – and only then does she see that the gull's head and body have been completely eaten away and what is being lifted a little on each incoming wave are its wings and its bone-cage, the bone-cage so white and washed clean it looks as synthetic as the bird people use when they play badminton.

She stands for a long time thinking about how beautiful its wings are, and how sad life is, and as if to confirm this, later in the evening she smells an odour of exhaust fumes contaminating the mist in the van der Meer back garden. She doesn't close the windows, thinking it will soon dissipate, drift past, but at the same time has a vision of the whole world filling up with toxic fumes until the air everywhere smells like an underground parking garage. And besides, the evil air is still lingering, and so – like a woman fearing a rainstorm – she at last runs from room to room trying to force down the windows with only one hand.

~~~~~

Although she's never been good at sports, that night she dreams that she's playing tennis on a red clay court, running and whacking the ball with such a brilliant ferocity that when she wakes up she feels how much more genuine her dream rage was than the orderly fury she used to pretend to feel when Declan would urge her to punch at a plump cushion he was holding in front of his genitals as he step-danced around her. It seems also to have something to do with her arm having been broken and then immobilized for so long. The rage has been building up with the mobility as if it's a future power she can count on.

A few weeks after her arm has healed again, Dr. Tenniswood tells her that while he's seeing patients for counselling on Friday afternoon he wants her to take his car and drive out to the village of Hoyt with a carton of syringes and a two-month supply of insulin for an old patient of his. "She lives all alone out there, and there's no pharmacy nearby that will make a delivery."

Claire gets out the road map, but discovers that Hoyt is well southwest of Ottersee – a disappointment – and so she'll have to turn off the highway at least forty minutes before she gets to Declan's town.

When she slides into Dr. Tenniswood's car and turns on the radio it's tuned to a station that plays classical music. But she decides she can't tolerate the show's announcer, a man who seems to her to be an archivist of his own voice. It occurs to her that this might be a clever thing to say at a party. But she no longer goes to parties. What she does instead is in fact exactly what Declan once told her she must do: she stays home alone. (Alone with her thoughts, alone with her body.) She's even become the sort of recluse who does nothing more original than sit and stare into space. Stare into space and think. What is the difference between grief and thought? There have been times when she's been convinced there is no difference.

But it's a damp windy day and as she drives, the old happy highway feelings come back to her. She also wonders if Declan ever drives along these same country roads. Whenever a car approaches her and it's black, she sits up straight behind the wheel and tries to make her face look alert and appealing. But each time the car blasts past her, its driver isn't even remotely like Declan, and so she tells herself to please just drive, don't even think of him, and besides, her right arm is aching and when she gives it a rest by driving with her left hand she thinks of the boy in *First Love*, peering around a street corner to see his father's mistress sitting in the big window of her little wooden house, the window as large as a stage for a puppet show, the boy's father, out on the Moscow street, pleading with her, then in frustration or longing bringing his whip with great force down on her shapely white arm, branding her, making her his forever. Then the mistress kissing the cut and passionately sucking it while the boy's father storms the steps up to her door, she at this same moment swiftly leaving her window to run into his arms. And then what the boy sees in his father's face afterwards: so much pity and tenderness.

But a very odd sort of grove now appears just ahead. In a great field there are four long stands of trees defining the four sides of a vast square. And at the nearest corner where the trees meet (or where they should have met) there's an opening, a breath. It's an absence that could be anything: spiritual, ominous, prescient, bleak. It's an absence that is, more than anything, presence.

After she's delivered the insulin, she drives back to the city on the same narrow highway, but she can't find her trees. They must have already appeared – since she's now coming from the opposite direction – as a boundary line of trees at the edge of an ordinary field, and she would have had to be checking constantly in her rear-view mirror to see their heartbreaking oddity.

A seagull flies overhead and a rosy light turns the tip of one of its wings pink and Claire can't get over how beautiful it is. The pink of the wing deepens, waves of burning gold threads define its ripple of feathers. Which is when she understands something terrible: it's not a rosy light from the sun, the gull is on fire. But then it's gone, it's flown over the roof and she wakes from her dream in the act of trying to decipher it. What can it mean? Gull for guile? Or gull for no guile? Or gull for gullible. Unless it means the bird has flown and you better get used to it.

While she's over at the stove, stirring her porridge, the phone rings. It's Steff, calling for no reason that she is able to discover. The last time she went out anywhere with him – in the fall of the year that ended with his moving out – they went to the ballet. All she can now remember about that evening is that Steff ate a quick dinner downtown before coming to pick her up, while she was too late getting home from work to make herself even a marmalade sandwich and so she'd dropped an orange into one of her coat pockets to eat as supper on the way over. And so then they had to be off, running out to the car with their coats open, and once they were on their way and she'd finished peeling her orange and was ready to section and eat it, Steff had flung out his arm and hit it down onto the floor of the car, where it rolled crazily around in the grease and the fluff. "Why can't you do things when other people are doing them?" he'd yelled at her. "There's a time to eat, and a time not to eat! When will you learn that?"

But now his voice (so much more friendly now) is telling her that he's just been given a big contract to work on a housing project in the Lebreton Flats.

"Well, that's *great*," she says, longing for the conversation to be over so she can read the Saturday papers, then using the porridge about to boil over as an excuse to bring it to an end.

When the phone rings again a few minutes later she thinks *oh no*. But this time it's Libi. Who never begins a call with "How are you?" or "Do you have time to talk?" or even "Hello"; her questions are instead tossed out of nowhere. But this morning she says "I wrote to you last week, but now I have news of fresh disasters." And only then does she go on to say "Did you hear that Herr Doktor is living out west?"

"I haven't heard anything," says Claire. "So how do you know he moved out west?"

"Because Emma, the daughter of my friend Jane, is living with him!" cries Libi and, really, it's a cry that's more like a wail.

Claire has to sit down.

"He moved out to the West Coast, to Chilliwack, five or six months ago and he's from some little town in Ontario. Jane thought it was called Rottersea but when I said are you sure it isn't Ottersee she said yes, that could be it."

Claire speaks in the flat and unimpressed voice of someone who so dislikes what she's hearing that she's not able to sound anything but distrustful. "And his name is Declan Farrell."

"*Yes.*"

"And so has he left his wife then?"

"He got separated from his first wife and now he's living with someone else."

"But I thought you said he was living with this Emma person —"

"No, no," says Libi, "Emma is living with *him*. With him and this new woman. Emma was smashed up in a motorcycle accident four or five months ago and after every doctor she saw had given up on her, Declan saved her life, he got her walking again."

All her old admiring feelings have come flooding back. But she only says, "I don't understand how so much could have happened. In such a short time." And he's left his wife! This is the thing that astounds her most, not the fact that he is now living so far away. Although the great distance certainly astounds her too. Like a child, she has been imagining him living in the same place with the same wife and the same children and the same car and the same garden. But all she can think of to say is "I suppose the new woman is young —"

"Early thirties, I think. But Emma says that although she's a terrific cook and very bright she's also just incredibly plain."

Claire wants to know how she means that.

"You know. Plain. Stocky. Hair that somebody cut after fitting a bowl over her head."

"What does she do?"

"She's a professor, I think. Emma told me what of, but now

I can't remember. Slavic languages, possibly. Or maybe some kind of higher math."

"Do you by any chance know her name?"

As a matter of fact, Libi says, she does. "Her name is Kris. And the reason I know this is because Emma is always going on and on about her. Kris this, Kris that."

"But how can so much happen in a person's life in such a short time?"

"Don't you want to know how much has happened in *my* life in such a short time?"

After too long a moment, Claire says, "Yes, I do."

But then Libi will only say, "Nothing ever happens, why do I even ask you to ask?"

After she has hung up the phone, Claire wonders what it meant, really, when the daughter of Libi's friend said that Declan's new woman was plain. For some reason she keeps imagining her as squat and shining and voluptuously hefty. A woman who must know how to grip a man's legs with her own fat little legs when they are in bed on a wanton Sunday afternoon of wild wind and rain. But she keeps seeing another version of her too: hair cut brutally short and half-shaved high up in the back, her face wearing a squashed and shrewd although unanimated look.

~~~~

The next afternoon the white of a letter gleams behind the eyelet petals cut into her brass mailbox. She warns herself that it will only be a bill from the phone company or her dentist, but it's been addressed by hand with no return address in a script that's scientific and small and somehow familiar to her. Once she's let herself into the apartment she slices the envelope open with a paring knife.

"Dear Claire," the letter heart-stoppingly begins, "Why haven't you written?" But when she quickly turns the page over to see that it's a letter from Libi, her disappointment is so acute it feels like betrayal.

As they are on their way down the dark aisle to sit in the front row, Claire spots a single seat up near the back and turns to whisper to Judy and Lynnie that she's going to take it, she might have to leave early. She should, too: she has to finish an essay for school. And so she excuses her way past a man who smells of beer to sit up at the back with all the popcorn eaters and lovers.

The movie – it's already starting: grey domes serene behind fog or smog – seems to be some sort of political romance, and everyone in it is photogenic and on the side of bravery and freedom and they are all artistic as well – some inane romantic *idea* of the artistic (they all have studios, there is a war) – and they are also all just so unsubtle and uncomplex, although of course they pretend to be deeply subtle and deeply complex, and they are lucky too, or if they are unlucky, then they are unlucky on a grand romantic scale, and after forty minutes have gone by she goes down to the front row to Judy and Lynnie and dips down beside them in the flickering light and so is able to see how young they've become, two young girls half floating,

half sleeping at the bottom of the sea, their skirts and sleeveless blouses bleached by the movie, the movie's headlights
shining down into their eyes, dazing them. And when she lowers
her voice to whisper, "Jude, I have to go now," Judy gazes up at
her with an almost frightened blankness, the gaze of a child
asking only to be allowed to return to her dream. "So I'll talk
to you tomorrow, okay?" Judy whispers yes, her eyes still held
by the movie, and then Claire tries to make herself very bent
and small, walking back up the aisle in the deep movie dark,
convinced that she must be looking as if she's just had abdom-
inal surgery or stolen something.

Dizzy from the stale popcorn and carpet smell, she steps
out into the warmer (and much lighter) night to discover that
her loneliness is waiting for her in the mild grey evening.
Loneliness, or the longing to see Declan again. But then that's
what the movies, even the bad movies – or especially the bad
movies – have the power to make you ask yourself: "Where is
my life?"

The phone rings just after she gets home from the movie,
and when she runs to it, it's Libi again, crying out in a bewil-
dered voice, "Do you know what Declan Farrell told Emma to
do? After she got her divorce from her awful husband? He told
her to make a quilt out of cut-up pieces of her wedding dress
and then when she was finished stitching it all together the man
who was right for her would come riding into her life."

When Claire doesn't respond, Libi says in a watchful voice,
"So is that the sort of person your Declan Farrell is? Does he
think like that? In terms of *myth*?"

Claire tries to picture a quilt made out of a wedding dress,
squares and petals in shining white satin and chopped-up

slivers of beaded taffeta and lace. An aerial view of a boudoir landscape: a virgin crop of white beads on white satin. She thinks of witch doctors, rain dancers. "He wasn't like that when *I* knew him . . ."

"And here's another thing Jane told me. There was a woman — someone twenty, twenty-one, someone Emma's age — who was working with Declan when she was first staying at his place, a sort of apprentice, and this apprentice-woman told Emma that once when she was alone with Declan he kissed her."

Claire looks out the window at the night, not wanting to know more. But she also can't stand not knowing more and so she has to ask, dry-voiced: "What kind of kiss?"

"A kiss is a kiss is a kiss," says Libi. But then she says, "Oh come on Vornoff, let's not kid ourselves here, it was a real kiss, why else would she bother to tell Emma about it?"

It's not possible to sleep. She doesn't even feel human. Or else she feels too human. She's all nerve and electricity, like one of the winter telephone wires of her childhood, strung along the highway with their strummed and irritating nerve song in the brutal (although often sunny) coldness. She wishes that Libi hadn't told her about the kiss.

Three hours later she's still awake. She can't seem to stop trying to picture the young assistant Declan so unwisely and allegedly kissed. But instead of being in Chilliwack they're at the house out in Ottersee, in the big churchy room where she so long ago checked out the books in his library. She imagines herself as his new woman, the quick-witted and stocky but voluptuously plain second wife; she's walking barefoot from the big ferny kitchen and on through the small cramped room with the bay window and the very tall wall rug and, swift but still innocent, into the room where the sorcerer is kissing his young apprentice. And when she at last sleeps she dreams she's sitting in the big cathedral in North Battleford waiting to see Declan. Where the hymn books should be, there are bright magazines: *Vogue, Mirabella, New Woman.* She's apprehensive and impatient as she keeps flicking pages, but toward morning she wakes up to the sound, somewhere nearby, of real pages being turned, and is frightened for a moment, thinking someone must be downstairs. But then she relaxes: it's not a literary intruder going through her books and magazines, it's the wind turning the pages of the newspaper she forgot to bring up from the back garden. Looking for something.

〰〰〰

People are hurrying home from work, pushing past one another. A worried, heavily breathing man runs by Claire, running in the neat way men run when they're wearing a suit, his jacket's blunt tails divided, a hand in his right pocket. And then as she's turning off Sunnyside onto Bank, she meets a woman in a white raincoat carrying a bouquet of freckled tiger lilies, and she has a sense of the ordered and elegant house this woman is hurrying home to, her ungrubby life. I should buy flowers too, she thinks, try to live my life with more gracious hope, and she is all at once overcome by a longing for colour, posters and flowers and views saturated with colour: blues that are Mediterranean or cobalt and deep pinks with wells of red flaring up, small fires flickering up the insides of the bells of the flowers. But it's a

cold and mistily raining evening for May, and the plastic pails
standing in rows out under Habib's wet awnings are stocked
with green tulips that haven't begun to open out yet, their green
beaks so tightly closed they have a blind look, as if they've been
uprooted from the gardens of aliens.

A little after seven Judy comes over to ask her if she wants
to go to the movies again, and ten minutes later they are already
on their way in the hazily cool spring evening, rain over, and now
that she's actually out, away from the apartment, Claire feels all
at once bathed in the particular pleasure of going out to a movie.
To go out with a woman friend is also wonderfully pleasant,
nothing to worry about except will the movie be a good movie,
nothing to look at but the chartreuse haze on the willows and
aspens growing on the embankment down by the river, or the
way, when Judy shifts gears, the peacock eyes of her green shawl
are revealed, a spilled family of blank-eyed blue moons falling
through the shawl's shifty glitter.

In the movie the husband, an American senator who loves
his wife, is tempted to have an affair with his stunning although
somewhat neurasthenic assistant. The wife tries to woo him
back by making love to him and then huskily whispering in a
tumbled, flushed moment, "You have exactly five minutes to do
something wonderful to my body. . . ."

Claire can't focus on the movie at all after this. Is it some
kind of joke then? A joke everyone knows? Or did Declan see
this movie and then decide to try a variation of this line out
on *her*? Either way, she finds his lack of originality painful. It
seems sleazy and sad, unless she can come up with a new way
to think about it. Still, his having borrowed the idea from a
movie is better than his having picked it up from a joke. She

sits hunched down in the dark and listens to Judy laugh at something the senator has just said to his adoring assistant. Whatever it was she missed it and doesn't even care that she missed it. The air from the air-conditioner is also freezing her feet in her flimsy sandals and one of her breasts aches. She thinks of Declan carefully weighing her left breast, her right breast, trying to decide if her breasts were pregnant breasts.

"Have you ever heard that before?" she asks Judy as they are crossing the parking lot to go back to the van. She's walking with her cold hands shoved into the clasp of her armpits. "That you-have-exactly-five-minutes-to-do-something-wonderful-to-my-body? I mean, is it in the public domain or something?"

Judy turns to smile at her, then smiles up at the night sky as if it's her lover. "God! If it isn't, it should be!"

They drive home along the canal, its hundreds of lights in dark water, but now the beauty of the night has been contaminated for Claire, there isn't a street here that she hasn't walked along thinking her unrealistic and foolish thoughts, and as they are swinging along Echo Drive she turns to Judy to say, "I'm thinking of moving away from this city."

"When did you come to this decision?"

"A little while ago, actually. I've been meaning to tell you."

"Claire, if you don't mind my saying so, this sounds completely deranged. Do you even know where you're going?"

She doesn't. But she says in a voice meant to prove that she does, "Toronto. After all, where else can you move to, in this country? If you want to find a job."

"Do you even know anyone there?"

"My brother Felix is there."

"You'll never find an apartment like the one you have with *us*. Not ever."

She knows it. She knows it, and she loves the apartment. She loves *them* too, God knows, and she really does feel a deep regret at the thought of leaving her back garden and the way the afternoon light falls on her stunning walls (mikado yellow) and her upstairs and downstairs, and her view out over the garden to the beautiful park.

"Not in Toronto, you won't. And not at that rent."

But Claire is remembering a visit she made to Toronto with Steff, the year before they broke up: the way people walked so incredibly fast there, the smell of the lake in the air.

When they get back to the house, they sit silent in the van until Judy says "So are you giving me notice then? Is that what this is all about?"

Claire says there are things she has to do first. She has to talk to Felix, she has to find a job there.

When she phones Felix the next night, he confirms Judy's story about the rents being sky-high. "And the vacancy rate is practically less than zero. But here's the scoop . . ."

This is so like Felix that she has to smile. Her youngest and most cheerfully conspiratorial brother, he's always saying things like here's the lowdown, here's the scoop, but he actually does know of a place near High Park, it just so happens, and it's about to be vacated by the best friend of Lola, a friend of Felix's. "So first you should talk to her. Her name is Becca, and she's going off to teach at an über-posh boys' school in Nairobi for a year, but winning Becca over is only the first step. The real challenge, and this challenge, I warn you, is going to be fucking mythic, is to win over the demon landlady, an apparently ghastly little creature everyone calls Dotty Dot, although I seem to recall that her real name is Dot Simone."

The courtship of the demon landlady begins in earnest in the early weeks of a tropical June. Claire has by this time become telephone friends with Becca. Like military strategists, they've plotted the timing of Becca's giving her notice to Dot Simone, but Dot Simone has not yet been willing to reveal to Claire that Becca's apartment will be free in September. Instead she shrieks at Claire, telling her that her tenants are quiet business people, people with cars and jobs in banks, telling her she might be "better off" in one of the apartment complexes closer to down-town, telling her that if she doesn't have a car she won't want to be living "way out here in the west end." But Claire persists, says she would love the west end, says she is a quiet person herself, and finally Dot Simone relents and gives her a date at the end of June. "But get here before the sun goes down so you can see what the place looks like in daylight." And then, almost as an afterthought: "What sort of job do you have here?"

"I'll be working with a group of doctors in an allergy clinic on College Street, west of Bathurst."

"So you're a nurse then."

"Yes." And to distract her from even the thought of asking for proof of her credentials, Claire quickly tells her she'll be taking the train from Ottawa in the early afternoon of the following Sunday and that she'll be arriving in Toronto a bit after five.

"Get here before the light goes," Dot tells her. "I don't show apartments after eight o'clock."

~~~~~

Somewhere outside Kingston the train stops in the middle of a field of mustard flowers, then for an endless time it simply sits, waiting.

Eventually a porter makes a noisy entrance with the trolley of drinks. "One of the passengers two cars down had a heart attack. Now what we're doing is waiting for the ambulance people to come."

Another hour passes before there's a surge toward the windows to look down on two ambulance attendants carrying a stretcher through the tall grasses flanking the train. Then another wait until the stretcher-bearers inch back again, carrying their cargo, a man whose face is partly hidden by an oxygen mask, but whose dome of bald head reveals an ashen tan.

The passengers all return to their seats, and then almost everyone coughs just a little, drily, from such close contact with misfortune. Claire tries not to keep checking her watch. If she should lose the apartment! She's convinced that Dot Simone is waiting for any misstep at all on her part to deny her the right to live within the walls of her kingdom.

In spite of the lake, and the occasional breeze from the lake, Toronto is under the siege of high summer, and Claire, coming out of Union Station, walks into the hot breath of the city to hail a cab.

In the taxi she opens her window to let the warm wind blow back her hair and feels a tinge (no, more than a tinge) of excitement. The fast-moving bazaar of the city even makes her feel as if she's auditioning for a new life instead of only going off to an audition for the horrendous Dot Simone.

At the house where Felix lives she can only stay long enough to leave her overnight bag with him, then she has to be off, anxiously hurrying through the muggy twilight to Marmaduke Street.

"You're *too late!*" Dot Simone's voice shrieks at her over the intercom although it's still only ten minutes to eight. "Somebody else has just been here to look at the apartment and she really loves it and so she's going to take it!"

"Someone on the train had a heart attack!" Claire cries back, nearly weeping. "We had to sit out in the middle of a field for over two hours!"

But there is no reply.

What will happen now? Will the harridan even come down? Claire stands tucking her shirt into her tailored skirt and praying.

A tiny woman eventually arrives, parading like a tin soldier on the other side of the glass wall. A bony and powdered little person, she's heavily made up and wears her white hair swept up into an elaborate concoction. As for her slacks, they are prim and tailored (either navy blue or black, it's hard to tell in the lobby's weak light) and her top is green satin with a sprinkling of what looks like green sugar on the left shoulder. She looks haughty and vulgar. But after peering at Claire through the glass door she condescends to let her come in, and while they wait for the elevator she tells her she has another apartment on the floor above the apartment Becca had. "And it's a lovely apartment too."

Claire has already decided that she's willing to be shown anything at all inside this building. Rising up in the elevator she even says to her, "Oh, Dot – is it okay if I call you Dot? – I love your outfit – it's really adorable. . . ."

And the terrible little woman wrinkles her little nose up at her sweetly and says in her terrible voice, "Everyone calls me Dot, dollie, and you're right, isn't this just the cutest?"

On the sixth floor Claire follows her into a small hot north-facing apartment with a brown shag rug on the floor. She pretends to judiciously look all around her. No, she really does look. God, if she should have to end up in this ugly box. Two giant evergreen trees stand close to the bedroom window, adding to the room's air of dark claustrophobia. "Dot," she says. "Thanks so much for showing me this, it really has possibilities, but I don't think it'll do –"

Half an hour later – after Dot has taken her down to her office to fill in an application form ("Just in case that really lovely lady decides to change her mind") and has introduced her to her almost poisonously alert adolescent son – "This is Claire, from Ottawa, she's a nurse" – and Claire has laughed at the harsh jokes the son has made about hospital closings and the fools at Queen's

Park – Dot shows her the apartment on the fifth floor. "No harm in just showing it to you, is there now?"

No harm at all.

After the grim forest up on the sixth floor, coming into Becca's apartment is like coming out of a dark wood into a sunny Alpine meadow. Claire walks all around it, praising and praising it. "The tenant must be really sad," she says to Dot Simone, "to have to give up such a terrific apartment."

"She's got other plans. She's going to Africa."

"What a long way to travel."

"She's a missionary, she told me."

"Amazing," says Claire.

But then Dot tells her that there are actually four people who are all in love with the apartment. A single man, a single woman, and a married couple. She will let Claire know her decision in the morning. "Call me in the morning just before seven, dollie – I'll let you know then."

"I can't bear to lose it," Claire tells Felix that night as they sit together in the upstairs leafy parlour of his house, drinking beer. "But I don't know how to make sure I don't –"

Felix cups a hand beside a hip pocket and waggles his fingers.

"Slip her a bribe? But how much should I offer her?"

"But would you really do that, Claire? It's illegal."

"I have to have a place to live!"

She spends a sleepless night on the couch in the parlour. At five to seven she pulls her coat on over her nightgown and goes out into the cool kitchen to put in a call to Dot Simone. Who says to her, "You know what, dollie? I was sitting here with my husband and son last night, right here in my kitchen, and I said to them 'I've got these four lovely people all wanting the same apartment, which one will I give it to?' and do you know what my son did? My son spoke up and said 'Give it to the nurse.'"

God bless the young.

Her blouse, a pale-green shell made out of what she thinks might be shot silk, looks as if it's been left out overnight in a frost. But now she can feel the force of the late summer's bright chill burning down on it. There's also a cold burning on the backs of her legs as she walks down her street. But when she lets herself into her apartment, it's as warm as a honeycomb in the hot sunshine, there's even a wasp buzzing all around it, and after she's opened the kitchen window to let the crazed creature fly out, she carries a Pyrex bowl of cold cooked potatoes into the front room with her. She sits on the sofa and eats the potatoes with her fingers as she reads the morning paper, the way she so often does since there's no one to see.

She has to pack, she needs to begin, she needs help, but she won't be able to rely on Judy to help her because the van der Meers have cleverly gone camping in Algonquin Park and won't be back till the end of next week. But at this moment her phone, as if it plans to rescue her, starts to ring.

She knows his voice at once when he says her name.

"Hello, Tony," she says.

He tells her he saw her yesterday, as he was driving along Wilbrod Street.

"Was I walking along looking terribly grim?"

"I couldn't quite tell. But then I wasn't taking notes, I was just driving by."

She smiles the smile she wants him to hear in her voice. "It's just that it makes me anxious to have people see me when I don't know they are seeing me. Even when I'm dead I don't want people to look at me," she tells him. "I want my coffin to be closed."

"But Claire. How could this matter? You'll be *dead*."

"My self-consciousness is posthumous. Or will be posthumous. Or whatever the correct tense is."

"So," he says. "As a matter of fact, it *did* seem to me that you were looking quite grim. Which is why I've decided to call you and invite you out to dinner tonight."

She says she would love to, but the problem is she's moving away and her apartment is in chaos. The movers are already coming the day after tomorrow.

"Where're you going?"

"Just to Toronto."

"Oh," he says, and his voice even sounds a little flatteringly forlorn.

"If, on the other hand, you'd like to come and help me *pack* —"

"Sorry, but I can't." And they both laugh when he says

he has just this moment remembered that he has other plans.

On her last day at work there are several new patients: a hypertensive woman whose jacket has droopy pockets; an embittered man with a neck injury; a beautiful grey-haired woman whose eyes shine with a frightened glitter as she holds her baby daughter tight in her arms. As much as possible, Claire has to try to keep her own eyes free of pity when she talks to this woman: she has already seen her blood tests and knows she has leukemia. There's also a musician, a Miss Middlemiss, a morosely dignified woman caped in an assortment of paisley shawls and mauve and fuchsia silk scarves. She has had a colostomy – the smell she brings with her into the examining room is so distinctive: a smell that isn't so much fecal as it's the sweetish sick smell of cooked blueberries beginning to go bad. Wrapping the blood pressure cuff around the musician's disciplined but loosely age-freckled arm, Claire vows to herself to swallow (every morning, do not forget this) her flax seeds and bran.

On her way home from work, Claire walks along the canal. Final walk home. Last rites and last nights. She breathes in the night air and looks out over the black water at the way the warm wind is distorting and multiplying its lights.

The night before the movers are to come she sorts and packs until close to sunrise, although the dawn looks dark. At ten to five she's still sneaking peeks at articles in magazines she's been planning to read some day when she gets a free moment, she still can hardly bear the thought that she won't ever read them, that she'll have to die without reading them when in fact there might be something in them, some information that could change her life, even save it, but now she'll just have to let them go, although maybe just *these* three, these three she should keep, how much weight can they add to the official ballast after all? And she tosses them into a box, then sets the alarm for eight and washes a Valium down with a teacup of cold water.

The movers, three fat men from Hull, arrive at four-thirty, their last call for the day, and as Claire runs down to meet them, she prays for them to like her so that they won't overcharge her. But with each unready room they enter, she can see her stock falling with them. She needs to appease them, serve them something, and so a little after five, when she's scooping vitamin bottles and debris off the two bottom shelves of one of the kitchen cupboards and hears footsteps behind her, she calls out in her not very good French that there's beer in the fridge.

But a voice that's not one of the movers' voices careens into a little dance step behind her. "C'est si bon . . ." and she turns to see Tony O'Bois.

"Thought I'd just drop by, see how things are coming along." He hugs her, but it's a utilitarian hug, while from his voice she can feel his gaze being aimed over the top of her hair: "So show me what still needs to be done then."

And so now there's nothing left to do but drop the keys for the van der Meers in through the mail slot of their door – it's a moment, a small moment in history, *goodbye, goodbye* — then drive out to the road that runs along the canal. The sky has turned dark by this time, stormy, there's a big wind building in the trees down by the Rideau River, and Claire feels very small in the world driving up her street with Tony in his car.

The aroma of fried bananas and the crash of surfy music — surf and some kind of tinkling, imitation Bach — greet them as they come into the restaurant, and as they are helping themselves to casseroles of curried tofu and potatoes and to tofu quiche and to salads containing pickled beets and tofu chunks, Tony whispers to her, "Does *everything* here have tofu in it?"

"Everything."

Squeezing past the long refectory tables (with only a few late diners finishing up their tea) they also pass by the worthy smell of platters of sliced rye bread, sliced whole-grain bread, a dried-out smell reminiscent of something unpleasant. Sanctimony, perhaps, or chicken feed.

"Even the pumpkin pie?".

Even the pumpkin pie. But they both help themselves to wide slices of it.

And then while they're eating it, Tony asks her if it's good to be getting away from this smug little town.

"In some ways." She takes a neat bite of the phenomenal pie. "In many ways," she says.

He leans back in his chair. "Tell me about the West."

She tries to think of some aspect of the West that would especially please him. "Well, it's sunny a lot," she tells him. "It's very sunlit, very wide-open country. There's hardly ever a grey day, it's either sunlight or storms. And the storms can be shockingly violent."

"Tornado country," he says, in the tender voice of a foreigner. "Yes."

"It sounds pretty amazing."

"It is," she says. "Pretty amazing and boring." But then she talks about elk ranches and a pelican colony her brothers liked to go to on Worthington Lake.

"Pelican colony or penal colony?"

"Pelican colony."

"Pelicans in work gangs. With their big yellow shovels."

She laughs, although she's afraid that any minute now she might spin right out of control. But now Tony is talking about his own childhood: all the towns he lived in, being an army brat, his father a captain in the Falklands war. The stints in Germany and Cyprus.

"This must be why you are as you are."

"And so how am I then?"

"Well, you're very observant," she tells him. "And very generous too, a generous listener." But she finds herself hoping he won't get withdrawn, now that she's praised him so much. "A very open, observant, tolerant person." She should stop right now, she shouldn't say more. Men got anxious if you praised them too much, they thought it meant you weren't attracted to them, they thought you were trying to make up for your lack of interest in them by saying something kind. "But I'm sorry, I know all this must sound very banal."

"Not that banal."

"And God knows, you're not an egomaniac."

"You don't know me, love . . ." But then he says, "Tell me about the town you grew up in."

"We actually lived out in the country. Almost halfway between Turtleford and St. Walburg. And the really big tourist attraction in St. Walburg was – and, God knows, probably still *is* – the end of the tracks . . ."

"The end of the tracks . . ."

"Yes," she says. "You walk down to the end of the tracks, and then you actually do get to the actual end, the actual end of the steel. And then there is nothing. Or everything. Then there's the world."

"Do go on, Fräulein Vornoff. Please do tell me more about this nothing . . ."

But she can't, this is not the way she can afford to let the evening come to an end, and so instead she says, "But the thing that fascinated me most about St. Walburg when I was a child was a house called the Catalogue House. It was a house completely constructed from a do-it-yourself kit ordered from the Eaton's catalogue."

This, she thinks, should be of interest to the historian in him, but he surprises her by saying, "You must remind me never to go there." And when she laughs he surprises her again: "What about that shrink you were seeing? The psychodrama person?"

"That's over now."

"What *was* this guy anyway? Some kind of crazed flirt?"

She shakes her head to let him know she really can't talk about it.

It's a little after eleven when he drives her, in a light rain, to the bus terminal on Catherine Street. But in spite of the terminal's airiness she feels ill from the prospect of moving on, the transitory but deep humiliation of moving being not only a matter of strangers having the right to look in at her unready life, but also her sense of being fated, moved like a pawn across a bright and dangerous landscape. And she's afraid then, that he'll see the terminal as too sad a symbol of her diminished world, after all she's not leaving the city by car or plane or even by train but by the most pathetically economical form of transportation, the way students or people who have failed in the world travel. And isn't it possible that he (being the only one seeing her off) will conclude that she doesn't even have any friends?

He buys her an apple and also a magazine for the trip, then as they're waiting for the boarding time to be called out he flips the pages, makes snide remarks about the models. A male model dressed in a white linen suit and a white fedora is holding a glass of champagne in one hand while he gazes out over blue water. "He's looking at the sea as if he wants to make love to it."

But now the Toronto bus is boarding, then Tony is walking with her to the end of the queue, where at the last possible moment – the other passengers having by now all already boarded – he pulls her quickly to him to hold her face pressed against his buttons as if in forcing her to gaze into the view within the depths of his jacket, he's sparing her a view of her even darker future. There's then another small but interminable wait before the driver releases the brake, then the bus is backing out of the terminal while Tony continues to stand looking up at her window, holding up his hand in a clowny half-wave, and she waves back, trying not to let him know how much she can see that he's trying not to look worried for her sake. Then, just in time, she has an inspiration and holds up the page with the photograph of the man in the white fedora, and he smiles up at it and holds up his own invisible glass of champagne, using his free hand to shade his eyes against an imaginary sun, then the driver swings the bus away from him in the rain, they are out of the terminal, they're on their way, her throat is aching, and in no time at all they've passed the final jumbles of lights and are already roaring out into deep country. She had hoped to leave early enough to see the bleached fields and dark trees, the distant hedged farms in the misty and slightly sinister light of dusk, but it's by now after midnight and there's only the endless rainy dark. How can she ever have imagined that she could live out in the country? If she moved out here — or to a place somewhere like here — she could no longer be the person she believes herself to be. And she thinks of all the despair out here: the abandoned, boarded-up barns and houses, the listless hearts of the towns, so many announcements of loss. She would have to buy herself a gun. And she would never sleep. Now it's cities that feel safe to her. But in her childhood she was under the protection of her father and so was never afraid. Cities were the places that frightened her. Even little Saskatoon, which was never much more than an overgrown town, with its fast-moving cars and its Hutterite cowboys looking like the cowboys in *High Noon*. One early evening the spring she turned fifteen, walking by the open door of a saloony bar stocked with red lamps and dark bottles, she saw a cowboy in a black Stetson and a long coat reaching down to the spurs on his high-heeled black boots, the reddish light turning the coat into an evil bronze taffeta raincoat. And in the summers, the girls in their sleeveless blouses would pour out of the not-very-tall office towers at noontime, each girl with her shrill voice and her sexless little walk going nowhere in a bossy hurry, all the women who were charmers – all those opportunists of the voice, of the eyes – having long since made their clever escape to the cities.

The rain doesn't stop until nearly sunrise, a hundred kilometres northeast of Toronto. But coming into the city isn't a thrill on the bus, it's not like coming in on the train, hugging the shoreline of the lake's vast grey plain of water, instead it's just grey city, poor city, grey city, poor city, until it's all at once rich city, towers of black glass, lilac glass, gold glass, mirrored glass, all of it gleaming with a hallucinatory splendour after a night of no sleep.

The cabbie who holds open his taxi door for her as she's on her way out of the terminal has an amused, lethal look. Long-nosed, early thirties.

"I'd like to go to the Polish district," she tells him, but then can see that he is (with difficulty) repressing a smirk.

"On Roncie?"

"On Galley Avenue, close to a street called Roncesvalles."

"In these parts, we call Roncesvalles Roncie," he tells her. And on the way to Felix's place on Galley Avenue, he calls back to her over a shoulder, "So how you think you gonna like the big city?"

"You can tell I'm not a native, then."

"Sure," he says, and she can see his eyes watching her eyes in the rear-view mirror. Then he says archly, "The Polish district."

She looks out the window, smiling or almost smiling, but she keeps blacking out, just for brief instants. Here she is, in the huge and violent city. She asks him if he's ever afraid, driving at night.

"Not often, but then I mostly pick up women." He laughs. "That's what I do. At night I pick up women . . . my shift is just about over anyway, I usually stop between six and seven." And during the day he goes to school. His doctorate.

"What's your field?"

"Linguistics."

This brings a self-conscious end to the conversation until he decides to tell her it's a city of educated cab drivers.

She smiles again, then looks out the window. How beautiful the early-morning lake is, off to their left and bright with its pre-breakfast glint and sparkle. She says in the dreamy voice of someone young enough to think of the future with pleasure, "I'm moving here. From Ottawa. My furniture is in a truck on its way here right at this moment."

"Good, then," the doctoral candidate briskly tells her. "Because in spite of much evidence to the contrary it's really not such a terrible place."

Once inside the house where Felix lives, Claire walks stealthily up the carpeted stairs and across the cold red linoleum. The whole house is asleep, except for the cat. Does he remember her? He comes to her as she's moving about the upstairs kitchen with small clinks and creaks, sniffs at her ankles.

She pours a little milk from three different cartons onto her corn flakes because she doesn't know which of the cartons belongs to Felix, then she pours a quick stream of milk into a saucer for the cat before she carries her bowl of cereal into the parlour.

Felix has already made up the couch for her. How sweet this is, having a brother in this city who's made up a bed for her. But her head is simply swimming from exhaustion, and the moment she's finished her corn flakes she crawls between the sheets in her T-shirt and underpants to discover that her head won't stop spinning, it's on a collision course with the walls, she'll never sleep, over and over again the walls keep coming straight for her.

Toronto is hard, hard and pitiless and endless, it just goes on and on. It makes Ottawa seem hilly and verdant and even little. A small city, Ottawa, as small as Ottawa once made Saskatoon seem, long ago. The thousands of people climbing up the subway stairways and being borne up on the escalators seem not only to be the displaced, but the displacers. New immigrants, true, thousands and even hundreds of thousands of them, but also the new generations. Every day Claire feels more disposable. And every day in this city she runs: from work to home, from the streetcar down subway steps to the eastbound train, from the eastbound train to the northbound train, from the northbound train to Wilson Station, from Wilson Station to the express bus out to York and her classes.

She lives to get home and make soup and tea. Then she lies back on the sofa with the phone and a plate of salted crackers beside her so she can have something to nibble on while she talks to Felix. She's forever trying to dream up some pretext or other to put in a call to him, legitimate requests. It helps her so much to talk to him, to hear his honest brotherly voice. If he's not in a rush to go back to his lab he even likes to give her advice. Sometimes they talk about life in Toronto and they both get very scathing. "And everyone seems so driven in this city," she says to him from her sofa one Thursday evening, where she's lying on her back with the phone lifted off the coffee table and propped up on her belly.

But on this particular evening Felix, instead of joining her in her nightly tirade, says, "I know things are sometimes hard for you here, Claire, but you've got to stop calling me so much, okay?"

She apologizes to him. "I know I do it too much."

〰〰〰

Walking downtown late one Saturday afternoon in September she sees surreal scenes: six pairs of black knee-socks and seven pairs of black leather gloves scattered about on a sidewalk in front of one of the big old bank mausoleums and just after this, a very long line of people high up in a row of tall lighted windows, pedalling hard toward the window glass on their long line of stationary bikes. At times like this, Toronto excites her — it's such a mad mix of the bad and the good: so much money, greed, architecture, lake light, so many lanes and enclaves that look as if they've been rescued from the nineteenth century, so many tiny lights in the trees. Or she walks through the theatre district with its nostalgic posters and its air of twinkling corruption and feels as lonely and lost as a tourist.

One mild grey Sunday afternoon in October she sits out on her tiny balcony and writes a letter to Tony O'Bois, a thank-you letter that feels a little falsely upbeat even as she's writing it, she's so eager to make her new life here appear to be happier (and certainly more exciting) than it really is. She gives short shrift to her job at the allergy clinic, but a good deal of attention to Dotty Dot who is, she writes, "a legendary snoop. Everyone I've talked to in the building has at least one horrible Dotty Dot story to tell. Last week in the laundry room the shy science student who lives on my floor told me that Dotty Dot even walked right into his apartment one night when he was lying in his bath, he was just reaching for the soap when he looked up to see Dotty Dot peering down at him." She also tells him about her plans to go to the Winter Garden Theatre to see *A Streetcar Named Desire* and her plans to visit the islands out in the harbour – it's all *plans* – but by now the weeks of the golden fall are too quickly passing by bus windows, streetcar windows, and when she goes downtown on Saturday afternoons to visit bookstores she's aware, like any unmoored person, of turning the pages for news of only one thing: her loneliness as it's experienced by the character she would get to care about most. But at other times the nervy abundance of the city bathes her in happiness; she has a sense that she's a traveller in a new world. Some of the places she's heard about for years really surprise her though – Philosopher's Walk, for instance; she used to imagine that taking a walk down Philosopher's Walk would be like going for a walk inside an etching. But Philosopher's Walk turns out to be much too Canadian for that, too open and green and haphazard with even a row of spindly trees running along one side of it, like a row of trees on a boundary line far out in the country.

One afternoon when she's been walking along breathing through her mouth and so hasn't noticed until it's too late that she's been inhaling a cloud of exhaust fumes, she passes by the source of it: an idling white car parked outside the open door of her neighbourhood fruit store. Its toxic vapour blows in over the banks of plums and baby tomatoes while she's paying the cashier for her gassed bananas. She wants to hold her breath forever, not breathe the fumes in, and so claps the tail of her scarf to her nose before plunging out into the brighter light, at the same time raising her free hand to the offending car as if to stop it in traffic, then making a furiously erasing gesture while glaring at the driver over the blown silk purdah of her leaf-printed scarf. But the woman in the white car only stares at her in such hostile wonder that she decides to stop and tap on her window. This leads the sourly glamorous one to slip over to her with an expression of imperious doubt, then to roll her window minimally down for her.

How very afraid of the world the rich are, thinks Claire as she bows down to the narrow aperture to make her small speech on behalf of the air. "I'm just wondering if you would mind not running your car engine? If you're going to be parked outside this store?"

Can a person hoot in utter silence? The sports car owner seems to: laced up to the tops of her thighs in exquisite suede boots, she looks stupid and vain as she leans fluidly over to roll up her window. The engine, meanwhile, keeps running. But then she apparently decides to speak after all, her eyes have a brimmed look, meaning she must have thought a thought she considers wonderfully witty, and so she rolls her window down again, although just a crack: "Honey, why don't you just go fuck yourself?"

And Claire walks home despising her, her liquidity. But doesn't liquidity have to do with silks? Or is it money? And even though she also knows she shouldn't take refuge in something as trifling as private anger, she does take refuge; she takes refuge in railing against the way, from century to century, the wrong people prosper.

It starts raining lightly the next afternoon just after lunch — a tonelessly grey city rain, miserable, listless — and not long after she's left the clinic for the day, she walks west on College as far as Little Italy, planning to pick up flowers because Felix has at last agreed to come over for supper. She stops at a flower stall, attracted by the petalled blazes of yellow — what are they? forsythia? but isn't forsythia more of a spring thing? — then changes her mind and decides on a bouquet of chilled white snowdrops being bobbed by the rain. She's asking the shivering Korean boy who mans the stall how much they are, when she happens to glance up and see Declan, in a tan raincoat and already five people away from her, beyond her and walking fast, and by now she's already hurrying after him, but why would he have come back east again? And if she does manage to catch up with him, will their conversation only be awkward? If he asks her how she is, she's afraid her eyes will humiliate her by filling up with tears, she's so afraid she won't be able to give a good account of herself, and in a panic she tries to remember the ways she has done well here. That she's been going to school (but for only two courses), that she has a job (but it's a very dull job) and yet even this unimpressive and very short list seems to be a list that must belong to some more impressive woman's life. Or it's a list for an exam, of only two rules, but she keeps forgetting what they are. She follows him down one block, down the next. If he turns around, she'll hide behind her umbrella. The need to see him again is after all overpowering, and so she only walks faster, her heart out of control, and is soon just behind his right elbow. But at this same moment the traffic light changes, and he decides to cross the street to the right instead of straight ahead. And of course he's not Declan at all, he's not even his double, he's a short-nosed man with a self-important look, and even — on this rainy dark day — dark glasses, his appearance one of the harsh tricks of hope and the city.

So. She has been spared pain. And possibly great pain. She should be grateful. Now life can go back to being ordinary again. But for the next few hours it's not ordinary at all, it's unendurable.

Late on the following Saturday afternoon here Claire is again, more or less restored to the world and hurrying down into the subway station at Dundas West, then riding the train east, racing across the high bridge over the wide cloud-shadowed valley bordering the Greek part of the city, past Donlands, past Greenwood, then at last up the steps into the hot afternoon and a part of the city a bit north of the Beaches where she's going to meet Libi who's flown to Toronto to stay with a cousin of hers on Coleridge Avenue.

The two women embrace lightly, then sit and drink beer out in the back garden with the cousin, a harsh-faced legal secretary who wears a fine gold chain around one ankle and an armful of noisy, insistent bracelets. But at last they are able to get away and walk along the leafy streets to Woodbine station, then they are fleeing west back to the city to take the escalator up into the hot October sunshine. Libi seems to have brought summer back to the city, she smells so of suntan oil. Her hair even looks as if she's combed it with suntan oil. She's also wearing a green midriff blouse and a dark voile skirt with thumbprints of tobacco and leaf-green on it.

Claire says, "For tonight I've got us tickets for a Chekhov play at Hart House. *The Cherry Orchard.* It's a student production, but I've read reviews of it that said it was good."

The production of the play *is* good, as it turns out, and as the curtain falls for the final time Libi and Claire are invited out for a drink by the man who's been sitting to Libi's left and who rushes, at play's end, to help her into her jacket. Claire foresees a drab end to the evening, but as they come out into the night they can see that the performers are mingling with the audience outside on the steps, and then Libi's new friend calls out to the actor who played Lopakhin, and after introductions and a bit of cheerful but awkward talk about the play, Libi and Claire set off with Lopakhin and the admirer (Avi) for a bar somewhere on Bloor, detouring along Philosopher's Walk, a warm wind ruffling the leaves, the lawns of the campus falling steeply away into the dimness to their right. Avi and Libi are walking along quickly, and so Claire and Lopakhin are soon left behind, Claire telling Lopakhin that she once lived next door to a seamstress who worked at the National Arts Centre. "And this seamstress was married to an actor."

"They all are," says Lopakhin with a smile. "All the pretty little seam*stress*es."

"And this actor at some point in his career got a role in *The Cherry Orchard*, although I don't even think he played Lopakhin. But after that, no matter what play he was rehearsing, whenever he wanted something to eat he would come to the door of his wife's sewing room and bleat like Lopakhin."

Lopakhin bleats three loony *baaaaa*s, but now Libi and Avi have turned around and are walking back toward them. "We've changed our minds. We're going to go the Boulevard Café on Harbord Street." And so they are off again, this time leading Lopakhin and Claire in the opposite direction. As they walk and talk, Claire begins to understand that what she's dreading most is that Lopakhin will ask her what sort of work she does here. Is there any way she can truthfully answer this question without making what she does sound deadly dull and even pathetic? She sees herself at work: raising little hives on arms by scratching them with allergens. As if swarms of orderly bees have stung the skin into perfect little rows of telltale bumps.

But now the moment is actually here, Lopakhin is actually asking her what sort of work she has come to Toronto to do.

"Environmental testing," she tells him. Which is, after all, more or less the truth. But at this same moment she slips and loses her footing. Lopakhin holds out his hand to her, and so they end up walking hand in hand as they follow Avi and Libi. Soon, though — in fact almost immediately — Claire has the feeling they both want to stop holding hands but that neither of them wants to be the one to do it first, particularly in view of the fact that neither of them apparently wants to be the one who *doesn't* do it first. By the time they reach the Boulevard Café (where Libi and Avi are waiting for them as if they've been waiting forever) their hands are slippery from the sweat of being held in one another's lacklustre grip. But here at last they can let go, to climb single file up the stairs, and once they've found themselves a table they get into a discussion about a nephew of Libi's who was once a lover of Avi's. This must be what they were talking about during the intermission. Libi then talks about flying here, last Friday night, to go to her high-school reunion in Guelph. "And it was awful. Awful beyond words."

Avi says, "Tell us about it anyway."

Lopakhin then tells them that three summers ago when he had to drive out to Vancouver he heard an interview with a writer whose name he didn't catch and this writer was talking about going home for his high-school reunion. "And one of the things he said was that everyone was exactly the same. The class beauty was still the class beauty. She was hideous, of course, but she was still the class beauty."

They all roar with laughter at this, Claire warmly glancing over at Lopakhin because even if the story isn't his, he's been amused enough by it to remember it for so long, and when he offers her a cigarette, she accepts it, telling him how much she used to love being a smoker, and how hard she found it to give it up. "Not the nicotine, but the hand gestures. I just really miss the whole choreography of it."

Lopakhin's quick eyes glint at her. What is he thinking? Who knows? He's an actor. He says that that's the whole dilemma in life, isn't it, the choice between choreography and dying.

Avi then tells them what he says is a famous story: the poet Anne Sexton liked to give her readings in a red satin dress with little red buttons all down the front, partly unbuttoned (halfway up, halfway down) and as she was reading she would kick out a leg with such force that the dress would keep undoing its buttons. He impersonates her reading at Harvard when he was a student there, taking little kicks out at the side of the table, then he does her ghoulish voice croaking "Little girl, my stringbean, my lovely woman . . ."

Lopakhin then speaks of a reading that a poet friend of his once gave, telling Libi and Claire that she wore a beige dress that looked like beige sugar. "It only went up over one of her shoulders . . ." (he shrugs up a shoulder) ". . . and her hair fell over the opposite eye . . ." (he shakes his hair over his opposite eye) ". . . and before she started to read she stared at the audience for at least ten seconds . . ." (he stares at Libi and Claire for at least ten seconds) ". . . then in a voice as deep as a man's she said 'I hate sex.'"

Claire asks Lopakhin if *that* made all the men in the audience sit up and take notice.

And Lopakhin sleepily smiles at her to say, "Darling, they were riveted."

One dark morning in early November as she's on her way to work, Claire pulls a pale-blue envelope out of her mailbox. An airmail envelope with French stamps. When she tears it open she finds a letter with a postcard folded inside it, and on this postcard a photograph of a street of houses walling a canal or river in a city called Ljubljana (a city that looks too beautiful to be on this earth) and on its back the words, "This place is like Prague, but without the tourists. And seems — incredibly — to be far removed from the carnage to the south. Will write a real letter from Belgium . . . Love, Tony." Then the letter from Belgium, dated two weeks later (October 24) and beginning in Brussels: "Skipped the lace museum and the beer museum; even skipped Rembrandt and Rubens and Franz Hals and Breughel at the Musée de l'Art Ancien. And why? Because I've just decided to squeeze in a quick trip to Paris . . ."

Which is where the postscript comes from, dated two days later: "Didn't actually do much once I got here but visit Montmartre and the bookstalls along the Left Bank, and then yesterday spent an hour or two in the cold but sunny Luxembourg Gardens . . ." He also writes that he might be coming to Toronto for a week, "late in the spring, in early June, to a conference of historians. I'll call you . . ."

It's nearly sunrise when Claire finishes her essay for her Woolf course. No point in going back to bed, and so she takes the elevator down to the street and goes for a walk down Marmaduke Street, the small houses and their narrow gardens still held in mist and sleep, then continues on to High Park. She has a headache that makes her head feel zingy but clear in an insane sort of way. She walks carefully, taking deep breaths and trying to calm herself. By the time she gets to the park there are delivery trucks out on the streets, upright white vans out of children's books, the odd small dark car beetling south. She climbs the path to the Lodge, passes the cairn where its architect's grave is. Ten minutes later – she's now on her way down again – there are joggers and people on early morning walks with their dogs. She even sees – and it's a startling sight against the great yellow lawn of the park – a man walking a baby polar bear on a leash. How can this be? On the way home she tells herself she must have been hallucinating. Either that or it was an abnormal dog.

There's a mosque farther along, high walls precede and also partly conceal it, and there's no snow anywhere, the winter's snow has already been and gone, it's already March, the mosque and the barren parks and the bright cold days have all turned this part of the city into something Middle Eastern, foreign, but Claire's feet are still freezing in her low little boots. She wants to hurry home so she can make a start on her essay on Lord Byron. She even makes notes for it first thing when she gets back to her apartment, from the chair she sinks into, still in her cold boots.

After her supper she sits on her sofa and opens her English Poets anthology to the Byron chapter and reads from a letter Lord B wrote to Lady B: "You don't like my 'restless' doctrines . . . ," then underlines the words "I can't bear to see you look unhappy." She makes notes until nearly midnight, then on her way to her bathroom looks out the dark windows and sees that it has begun to snow heavily. But this is completely insane, it's almost spring.

A snowy night breeze also blows in to meet her as she hurries (still wet from her shower) down the hallway to her room, the curtains are belled by it, but on her way to get her robe she's jolted by a deep thud against the far wall and when she hurries over to her window to look down she sees a man in an anorak aiming a snowball straight for her window. As she winds herself into one of her grey denim curtains she also sees that he doesn't have the power to make the snowball fly high; it rises toward her in a majestic great arc, then drops in a straight drop to fall out of sight. For a moment she even imagines that he must be someone she knows, perhaps even one of her neighbours from the apartment upstairs, but no, he's a stranger, she can sense his embarrassment from the way he shrugs, then holds out his arms in a way that seems to sing up to her, "So I'm a bad boy! So *sue* me!" Wrapped in her ungainly sari of grey denim, she stands at her window (trying to loom up) until he turns to trudge away into the snowy darkness.

The next morning she's in her kitchen scooping jam out of a jar and enjoying the foggy Sunday feel of the day (fog after snow) when her phone rings.

"Listen," says Libi. "I have something to tell you . . ."

"What is it?"

"Declan Farrell is dead."

Claire sets down the jam jar, then holds onto the rim of the counter while she pulls a chair toward her from the next room and as she sinks down on it she whispers, "But how can that be?"

"Shot himself. Yesterday at lunchtime."

How quickly words turn everything into something that's always been true, once they've been spoken. Because she has always known this. She accepts it because she has always known it. It's also the very last thing she would have believed, if anyone had ever predicted this for him. He's had the last word then, he's made everything be over.

She has to stand again. "But why would he do that?"

"A former woman patient of his in the village he was living in, near Chilliwack, went to the police, wanting to charge him, but the police decided not to, there wasn't enough evidence. But then some other woman out there apparently charged him. That's all I know. I don't know the details . . ."

Claire has to take a sip of water or she won't be able to speak. "But where did he shoot himself?"

"In the study of his house. Oh, you mean where on his body. The mouth. Apparently only romantic fools shoot themselves in the temple."

She really did mean where in his house. She can't imagine a bullet going anywhere into his body. But if it was lunchtime out in Chilliwack, what time would it have been in Toronto? It must have been three, and she recalls the way yesterday at three she was wandering around her apartment so puzzlingly at loose ends, her head aching as she was barely able to zip up her boots and set out to get her hair cut. In one of those moments a life (a life she knew, or thought she knew) came to an end. So he's killed himself then. What a cruel thing, to do that. He is all at once not attractive at all to her, being dead. The dead are the dead. But now a pain begins to burn behind her eyes and she wants to cry out, Oh my darling friend, have you really been that alone? Separated from him by time (and by thousands of miles), she's grown accustomed to feeling free of him, but now that he's dead he seems to have come near. "The thing was," she says (still in the dry voice), "he was such a romantic about change. He believed he could change people utterly. But you can't. People are who they are. He thought he could make himself unassailable, and then when he found out he couldn't . . ."

"Life caught up with him," says Libi, not unkindly. "It accrued."

I've always believed that I seduced and abandoned *him*, thinks Claire after she's said goodbye to Libi, but this isn't entirely true either, she has just as often believed the absolute opposite.

She also can't seem to stop thinking: He who lives by the body dies by the body. But that's totally mad, doesn't everyone die by the body? At the same time she keeps having thoughts that are so guilty they make her feel that he must still be alive, and if not still on this earth then hovering somewhere close above it, looking down on her, noting how much she even feels he deserved the end that he came to. At these times she tries to defend him against herself, and so decides that his miraculous attentiveness was so extraordinary that it must have made him long now and then to take refuge in a kind of brutal detachment. Her gratitude to him used to stay the strong thing, it would stay so profound that even his unkindness would seem to have sprung out of kindness. His death has always been out there, she thinks, an event that has always already happened, all it was requiring was for someone, and – life being life – the most improbable someone (someone who never approved of him, someone who didn't even know him) to bring me the news of it.

Since hearing of Declan's death she has thought of nothing but him; this is really the first moment in which she's stopped to wonder if any other subject will ever be large enough to engage her attention. She picks up a book, tries to read, goes through the motions of reading, but almost at once finds herself thinking of him again and wondering if he'll be cremated, and if he's cremated will his ashes be flown east to be cast over the lawn out at Ottersee. Or will his new woman carry them, hugged in an urn, up one of the coastal highways to scatter them to the winds over higher ground? And she recalls a picnic supper at the edge of a graveyard years ago and how after she'd packed the leftovers away in the picnic basket, she went for a walk with Steff among the graves and almost at once they'd come (as if led to it) to a small flat stone shoved at a slant into the green lawn of the dead. A kind of footstone. But a footstone that had her own initials carved into it. She had stared down at it, transfixed, convinced that she was not long for this life. Even now, years after that walk among the graves, she can all too clearly see the carved letters in the long-ago stone: C.V. And how ironic, really, that she (who has done so little with her life) should have initials that also stand for *curriculum vitae*. Soon she will be forty. She must do something with her life. Because people die.

But what made him decide to bring his life to an end? Weeks of not being able to sleep might have led up to it, but she also pictures one of his children coming home crying from school at lunchtime (one of his daughters) after being taunted about her father's lost reputation. He would not have been able to bear it, it's the one thing she's absolutely sure of about him, he would not have been able to bear being the cause of pain to his children. But would he even have known about their pain? He was living at the other end of the country from his children. But what was he thinking, this is what she can't seem to stop longing to know, what was he thinking during the final hours of his life? And at this, as if to answer all questions at last, he comes to the doorway of the Room, and she feels drugged by sunlight, by the smell of mowed lawn, although not too drugged to hear him say, "But it all comes from the same place, good and bad, can't you see that? It all owes its power to nothing more harmful than my scandalous willingness to be misunderstood."

It's snowing again, but how can it, it's already April, then it rains non-stop for six days, day after day of dense rain followed by an early spring chill, the streets at last laid bare, the industrial air hazy with smoky spring evenings.

On one of these cold evenings a moving van pulls into the driveway five storeys below Claire's bedroom window and within a few minutes the new tenants, who look like college boys — she's not sure how many, but there are at least five — begin to walk back and forth over the hardwood floors above her ceiling in the hob-nailed workboots students so love to wear. Bumps and crashes come next. Furniture being dropped or shoved across floors. But the final and worst assault is the music, pounding so relentlessly down that her little apartment is horribly transformed into a washing machine that agitates her heart with drumbeat, not water. She runs up to the apartment above her and knocks on the door, and although the student who answers it dismisses her with the sullen fury

of his gaze, the sound (at least overnight) is turned almost
bearably low.

But the next morning the volume has been turned back up
again, and to an even more relentless pounding than before.
New boots have arrived. Fascist boots. And so it's up the stairs
again to talk to a new guy who's coldly handsome and openly
combative. This time the sound is turned down only slightly,
but now, as if to take revenge on her, there are new torments:
bottles (beer bottles?) bounced on the floor and the sound of
boots being stamped vengefully hard on the floor above her
kitchen, and even what sound like the thumps of people spitefully jumping from chairs down onto the part of the floor that's
over her bedroom, a trick to make her afraid to come back up
and complain to them ever again.

When she goes down the stairs to speak to Dot Simone,
Dot (dainty, in her tin-soldier way) only looks terrified and
tells her that she refuses to involve herself in arguments between
tenants. And so it's back up to her own place again where she
grabs her jacket out of her coat closet, locks her door, races
two steps at a time up the stairs to the music, pounds furiously
hard on the door with both fists and then, suddenly frightened
herself, runs all the way down to the lobby and out into a night
whose cold wind she fiercely walks against, crying with rage
because she made the move to this city. When there was really
no need for her to move anywhere at all.

Two young men are getting out of a pickup truck just west
of the main entrance of her tower when she comes back from
her walk. They both have such a young male glow, such an

exuberant strut as they come walking in fast tandem toward her across the parking lot.

The taller one, who's wearing a wine scarf tossed over a shoulder, holds the door open for her and then presses the bell of the painfully shy science student who lives on her floor. And when he speaks into the intercom she hears him say: "Let us in, man, we're hookers . . ."

The boy with blue hair then takes his turn: "This is Satan, and I'm coming to get you —"

After a stunned social silence, the disembodied voice of the science student comes out of the wall. "Oh," it says. "So," it says. "Do you guys want to come up?"

"Yeah, man, buzz us in."

The boys grin at Claire as they rise together in the elevator. They make her think of her brothers and, by extension, of all jokey young men, and so make her (however briefly) forgive the beer drinkers who live up above her and who've made her life an eternal torment.

The next morning as she's pulling on her jacket she hears a scuffle out in the hallway. Once it's quiet again she opens her door to peek out. The corridor is deserted, but an envelope, as square and white as an envelope containing a wedding invitation, has been left on her doormat. She takes it inside before she tears it open. A note is loosely written in red ink on the lined piece of paper she pulls out: "Will you please stop bothering us. We have to live our life. Thank you and go to hell."

But one square white envelope turns out to be the forerunner of another: an actual wedding invitation appears in her mailbox the next afternoon.

Beneath her windblown veil, the bride's bowed head is capped by a bonnet planted with dozens of rows of miniature pearls. She looks as if she is trying not to be aware of the communal gaze of the wedding guests, standing out on the Tenniswood sundeck in the May sunshine and gazing down on her as the photographer arranges her near the big maple tree at the bottom of the garden. They are watching him kneel on the grass to fuss with the heavily embroidered long satin skirt that in some lights is greyly silver and in brighter lights white, and they are still watching as he rises and begins to walk backwards with his cameras, making large and irritable beckoning gestures with both hands and calling out to the bridegroom to tell him to move a little closer in behind his new bride.

The bridegroom (whose name is Junzo) quickly comes forward and obediently kisses the nape of Zuzi's neck, and as he does so, she inclines her head demurely.

But the photographer, still unhappy, calls out, "Closer!"

And so Junzo brings his straight arms stiffly forward and locks his hands in a V in the folds at the front of the long beaded dress, then bends his knees slightly and tilts his pelvis close in behind his new wife. Now what he most resembles is a golf instructor trying to teach a woman in a wedding gown how to play golf. But there is no golf club. And so the pose (even if only on demand) seems exquisitely sexual.

Zuzi must think so as well because she turns her face sharply away from him. But then she appears to have second thoughts and swivels within his embrace and throws her arms around his bowed neck to lock him into a very long and show-offy kiss. People turn their smiles toward the house, but Claire decides to stay behind for a bit, out here in the warm sunshine. She leans on the railing and watches the younger woman begin her slow promenade down the long lawn, and as she watches her she thinks of her own wedding, held at the wrong time of year, and of how sacrificed and anxious to please she had felt: the skin above her chest shivery but itchy from her wedding gown's insets of spidery but coarse bridal lace.

She really does not want to go into Dr. Tenniswood's noisy and shaded hacienda and do the right thing and mingle. *Go,* she tells herself. But for another two or three minutes she stays where she is, watching the photographer arrange and rearrange the bride and groom to his liking, then she sees Zuzi hold out a hand to Junzo, and now they are beginning to walk fast away from the photographer, but at the end of the garden they turn in slow unison to face him once again. But while she continues to stand looking down on them a little gust of warm wind lifts Zuzi's veil to turn her bride's bonnet into a helmet of pearl bullets.

Ottawa must be Canada's Shangri-La, thinks Claire as she climbs the stairs past two watchful but glowing Ottawa women wearing dull gold Egyptian bracelets pushed high up on their darkly freckled arms. And Toronto is Illness City! But when she steps into the powder room it's to discover that another wedding guest is also in here, seated at a low table and drawing on a pink lipstick while staring at her own heavy and humourless face in the glass.

To her surprise, Claire knows this woman's shrewdly mournful eyes and her marvellously shining and healthy pelt of dark hair. "Della Dwyer," she says to her.

But the woman turns from the mirror to stare at her with such disapproval that she feels obliged to say, "You're not Della Dwyer?"

"Della Greer," the woman (now looking heavily pained) manages to say to her.

Is this a different person then? Someone who shares with Della Dwyer a first name and the same lustrous hair and lugubrious features? "But you used to be Della Dwyer?"

"Della Greer."

And then she remembers, she did hear this name once, and she wants to say to her, "Look, it was a mistake made out of innocence, not out of any kind of reactionary dogma." The fact that she's kept Steff's name has never meant she wants to go back to him. She simply prefers Vornoff, as a name, to Ulrich. But when she says "I'm Claire Vornoff," Della Greer coldly replies "I know," then stands to draw the narrow strap of her beaded and tiny black evening bag over a shoulder that looks as if an eagle has recently flown in to perch on it but then right away decided to fly off again, leaving behind the imprint of his talons in black sequins. And without giving Claire so much as a sideways glance, Della Greer and her shining black hair make a grand exit.

Which makes Claire decide to stay up here a few minutes longer, she so much needs to collect herself after having been made to feel wrong. She goes into the washroom, a room that smells of its new plastic shower curtain, ferns incised on clear ice, and the curtain's plastic smell seems to be the smell of loneliness, a smell that comes from hiding, being judged. She looks at herself in the mirror and sees a face belonging to someone that someone has given a quick push to, a face bobbing in a lake of cold water.

In the powder room she looks at the world through a window that opens out into the sad and warm afternoon, and feels even more alone, a tiny woman trapped alone inside a corsage, the smell of the powder room is so synthetic but at the same time holds within it such a fresh floral scent. But has she changed at all, she wonders. And just look at what a small ration of contempt it takes for her self-confidence to flap right out the window.

Halfway down, the stairway changes direction, passes by a tall window that looks down onto an aisle of green lawn. So this is Ottawa then, the real true Ottawa, hard-hearted paradise. Long ago she must have done something to offend the vengeful D.D. (or D.G.), but, if so, she's not at all able to recall what it was. She supposes she might even need her coldness, something to hate, ever since last night on the ride into town, she's been in love with Ottawa again, its inlets and the sun on all its big and little bodies of water, its long views of blue hills. All she needs now is to find someone who'll do her the service of saying to her, "Della Greer? God, pay no attention to that woman, she's totally deranged."

And now here D.G. even is, at the foot of the stairs, talking to a stooped fair man who has a melancholy and unreliable look. An academic, surely. While D.G. herself now only looks serious, earnest, a judiciously matronly woman with nothing at all to indicate her coldness but her sequined talons and the black sandy glitter of her evening bag as Claire swiftly slips past her. Unnoticed, unscathed.

There's music when she comes out into the world again to get into the reception line – music, high anxiety, shrill laughter, sunshine – then she's next, but Zuzi does all the work for her, hugging her with a squeal and then turning to say to Junzo, "This is Claire, my very most favourite person from my childhood. Remember how I was always coming into the office to pester you, Claire? For these teeny-weeny bitty little baby bandaids for my dolls?"

"Those poor little dolls of yours, Zuzi. You were forever mutilating them."

~~~~~

The wedding dinner is served on long tables out on the lawn. The air smells of cut grass and mayonnaise and salads already beginning to die in the sun. The plump librarian on Claire's left has just returned to Canada after five years in Kenya. Claire tells her that early in her marriage she and her husband let out a room to a graduate student from Nairobi. "Wachira. A Kikuyu." While Wachira was living with them she couldn't hurry naked down to the shower in the mornings, and after he left Canada to fly back to Nairobi, she and Steff had only one week of privacy before her mother invited herself for what turned out to be a difficult visit. The night she'd flown back to Saskatoon the house began to breathe again, was theirs again, and in honour of her mother's departure Claire had washed her hair in the shower, turbaned it in a luxurious black towel, her sunburned arms turned into long flushed gloves of hot skin. She'd felt like a nude debutante (a nude debutante from a country where the women were sensationally graceful: Liberia, Namibia) luring Steff into Wachira's room to have sex first on Wachira's bed, then on their own bed.

While more wine is being poured, there's talk of renovations, gardens, talk that moves Claire to picture a house with red clay tiles on its floor. Red tiles and a door opening out into a garden. Small dark oil paintings hanging low above fragrant arrangements of flowers. Blowsy peonies. And vistas, long views, the pure air of the morning.

When she goes over to the buffet she finds herself standing next to Mitchell Kinkaid. He appears not to have seen her yet, but when he bumps into her as they are both serving themselves from the same quiche he gives her a boozy, quick kiss next to an eye, his skin warm from wine or the sun.

Last spring after his divorce went through, he tells her, he married his second wife. "A woman with two kids of her own."

Claire looks back at his table to see a slim fair woman standing to serve two children lemonade. Testy and elegant, she seems to be the kind not to stand for any nonsense.

Claire then remembers to praise the house. "It's lovely, Mitchell." Which it is, really. Although she's afraid it's walking on tricky ground, praising it.

"Thanks. It's pleasant enough. Of course we were just doing what the man wanted, that was our job here: this is the house that Jack built."

After Mitchell goes back to his table, Claire talks to a woman named Evelyn da Gamba, one of the violinists who played in the wedding quartet at the cathedral. They are moving side by side down the length of the long buffet, heaping their plates with smoked salmon and a banana-and-bean salad, when Evelyn shakes out her right arm. "I've been having some trouble with my playing arm, but the therapist who could really help me with it left his wife last year, then moved out to the West Coast."

But now Jack Tenniswood has all at once appeared between them and is naming and diagnosing the delicacies for them. "My dear friends, you really must try *this* – it's mushroom risotto made from wild mushrooms picked on the banks of the Miramichi. And *this* is a spinach souffle quiche. And *here* we have bits of goat cheese on shiitake mushrooms, we've gone a bit ethnic here in honour of the groom. . . ."

And so the two women help themselves to a little of everything until he moves on to another group of guests.

"For a while I even thought he might be coming back this way, but now I know for sure that he won't be, because four or five months ago he shot himself."

"If his name was Declan Farrell, I was for a time a patient of his . . ."

Evelyn peers at her, over her risotto. "And you did know that he shot himself . . ."

"Yes."

His death, Evelyn says, caused a lot of controversy in these parts. "Even though he didn't live around here any more . . ." But she and her husband (the cellist) found him only dedicated, helpful. "On the other hand, for some people it was a real Dr. Jekyll and Mr. Hyde situation: a friend of mine who knew him extremely well, and who also knew his children extremely well, told me that as a father he was also just terribly demanding. The children confided in her, so this wasn't just hearsay. And according to her, the boy in particular was in a deep depression . . ." She takes a mouthful from a deep baked meat dish, then says, "You've got to try this, I swear it's prehistoric meatloaf, they've put some kind of weird and amazing combination of stuff in it, onions and prunes and apples and rum . . ."

Claire breaks into it with a serving spoon and it crumbles greyly while an ancient meaty odour rises up from it. She still has such a clear memory of the little girl coming down to the car, and such a clear memory too of her apple breath as she gave her directions to Newbliss, but now she has to pay attention to Evelyn again because Evelyn is bringing her even more news: how her friend told her that there were layers and layers and layers to Declan, and that if you went down deep enough you found something – "the word she used was 'maniacal' – I don't know if that rings a bell with you . . ."

It does ring a bell, being the word Claire has most often wanted not to think when she's had unhappy thoughts about Declan. She also doesn't want to remember the way she used to dream of meeting him again some day, and the way, when they met, or re-met, they would fall in love, real true love out in the world, years after their sad farewell at the Institute, two wiser people, now that time – in its wisdom or unwisdom – would have turned them into legitimate strangers. But now Evelyn is narrowing her eyes to seriously tell her, "You should talk to this person, if you ever come back here. But then Declan Farrell was an extraordinarily beautiful man, wasn't he? And we do tend to more easily forgive the beautiful people –"

How elitist obsession is. Even now, Claire wants to be the only one who was perceptive enough to have been aware of his beauty. It makes her feel how corrupt adoration is, how it doesn't change a thing. But after a moment of doubt, and knowing it will make it less true if she says it, she makes a confession: "I was, in a way, quite in love with him . . ."

"Were you?" Evelyn studies her with a bright, almost cold curiosity. "Oh well, don't despise yourself for it, you were merely one among many . . ."

Exactly.

"So," says Evelyn. "And how's life in dear old Toronto? Any good men at all down there?"

"The only men who ever ask me to go out with them are men with allergies."

And Evelyn smiles at her as if she has just said something hilariously clever.

But now it's time for the concert, and Evelyn (in jewelled sandals and a short brown tunic that exposes her bare arms and sunburned knees to even more sun) is playing the violin while her long-bearded husband sits beside her and saws at his cello, the two of them seated with a comically prim formality under a chestnut tree, the clear tumbling sound of the music liquidly trickling while the words "maniacal, maniacal, maniacal" can't seem to stop playing themselves over and under Claire's thoughts. Maniacal, manacle, miracle, monomania, love, tenderness, unearned tenderness, ruin.

After coffee and dessert, louder and more percussive music, younger music, blasts from speakers mounted high up in the foliage, and it's dark now, or nearly, already there are vines of lights trembling in the breeze, they're dangling down from where they've been flung like twinkling stockings to hang from the railings of the upstairs balconies, and the bride and groom are still moving in and out among the dwindling islands of wedding guests, being kissed, thanking.

But now there's dance music and Claire sits at one of the empty tables watching Mitchell dance with his sternly elegant wife. As he's dancing, the taller of his new little daughters is hanging onto the backs of his shoulders. He tries to hitch her up, get her to ride piggy-back, but she's too big for it, her legs in her white stockings are too long to lock themselves around his waist and so they simply hang down, swaying slightly at his back, as if she's swaying to say, "Your time is running out darling Mother and Stepfather dear, soon the hour of puberty will be here . . ." and at last he's obliged to give up and turn from his wife to dance with his new daughter. Whereupon his wife turns to dance with the little boy, a fastidious, serious child who looks to be about seven. But because they are a family and the only ones dancing there's also something quite sad about the spectacle, as if it's time for the music to turn foreboding and tinny.

But it doesn't, it only gets better to dance to, so much better that it sends Mitchell over to Claire to ask her to dance, and so they do a slow jive, or a parody of a slow jive — is there a difference? — while she feels just tired enough and just drunk enough to dance well. And as they are dancing, leaning coolly away from each other's stylized grip, then prowling around each other for the rhythmic kill, it occurs to her that the guest room she'll be sleeping in tonight is a room whose dimensions Mitchell, perched on a high architect's stool, once drew on a big blank sheet of white paper.

Three hours later, up in her corner of the blank sheet of white paper, she snaps out the light, hoping to at least doze until the early-morning train, then lies in the dark, thinking of Declan. Was he bizarrely intuitive or a doctrinaire hoodlum? But there is no answer, there's never any answer, and at last she sleeps, dreaming or half-dreaming a kind of geometrical vision: a galaxy of half-erased equations and triangles are sparkling through the cloudy slate of a night, the fragments left behind after the mathematical windstorm of plunges and hard dents made by a stick of chalk, the purged sensation that comes from having leapfrogged across a blackboard to the perfect solution.

~~~~

Hot sunlight is pouring onto laps as the train swings close to the lake, and Claire reaches into her shoulder bag for an orange and then sits in the sleepy heat eating it while the slowing-down clacks are already announcing the uninflected granite light of

Union Station, everyone already at work by now, then she's on her way north from Union Station to St. George and west from St. George to her home station, where she climbs up into a city wind sifting through the morning's debris and gritty litter.

But the morning, just in time for her emergence out into it, is contaminated by a toxic taxi rattling by. Holding her breath, she hurries to the row of cabs across the street, then slams herself into the lead cab to take in great restorative gulps of the stale nicotine air.

"Where to?" asks a voice with a Scots accent.

She gives him her address, then tells him that she's just arrived in the city from Ottawa on the early-morning train.

"So what's the big attraction in Ottawa?"

"A wedding. In a swank part of town. Up in Rockcliffe."

"Up where the toffs live?"

"Yes."

"So how was it?"

"It was fine. The bride was too young though." She looks out the window at the green of High Park. "Only twenty," she says. "But then that's the age I was when I got married too."

In the rear-view mirror, she can see his eyes glancing back to catch the look in her eyes.

"And it didn't work out is what you are saying."

"No, it didn't."

"Take me: I'm twenty-nine and still free as a bird."

She smiles and looks out at the birds in High Park. Are you free, birds? The early-morning streets skip past them, under the trees. "The wedding was sort of complicated though. I heard upsetting news about some people I used to know."

"Departed friend?"

How can he know this? How can he know that although she's used the plural, she means the singular?

~~~~

How small her apartment feels, with its boxed-in sunlight, after even this quick trip away from it, but the clean morning sun is already illuminating the clear glass jug of dried grasses while a burning blue square mosaic of rug absorbs the hot light. As she walks into the kitchen she breathes in a scoured but still somehow sour odour. Something she was thinking about coming back on the train: that somewhere she's read that the line between wanting everything and wanting nothing is a very fine line.

And then at the clinic what's left of the morning passes by her in overheard scraps of conversation that, when she dozes off for a second or two, turn disembodied, ringing. Each time she dozes, then wakes, she makes herself stand and pretend to look animated.

It rains after lunch, but stops just before three, and by the time she comes out onto College Street the air is sickly fragrant with its city mix of car exhaust and blossoms. Although there's still just enough sweetness in the day to make her decide not to wait for a streetcar, and so she instead walks to the subway station on Bathurst in the cool spring sunshine.

She turns onto one of the local small streets, a street of trees whose sidewalks are matted with what the rain has rained down: spinning tree propellers from the maple trees, thousands of them, rained onto the pavement like tiny footprints. Then it's down the steps to the train, and on the train west the usual: hope, guarded hope, no hope, fatigue (a lot of this), a blouse that's almost transparent on a brown arm (a kind of stencilled membrane), a short dress whose pattern is repeating rows of stick figures on terracotta chiffon.

At her own station she pushes through the turnstile to come out into an even sunnier afternoon. Again she decides to walk, it's not far in the warm day.

In the waxed cool of her lobby, the elevator is (for once) waiting on the main floor. Rising up in it she thinks of a phrase she can only partly remember: something that begins with "The shock of . . ." But the shock of what? The new? The shock of something. She thinks of Declan's funeral, sees the two wives walking tightly arm in arm on that far coast in the endless and stormless coastal rain, rain on the funeral flowers, rain on the graves. Unless it was sunny. It so often *was* sunny for a funeral. She feels it too, the sadness of sunniness, coming into her sun-blocked apartment. She also understands Ottawa now, and why in the taxi last night on the way to the station it made her feel sad. Because in Ottawa his absence was everywhere. It was more than the effect of racing fast beside dark water on the way to the train; it had to be, because she used to imagine herself going back there, a woman whose life had organized itself into some kind of triumphant order. They would run into each other on Bank Street. Then she would know what he meant to her. How much or how little. Who can know when it will die absolutely, this part of her that can only dwell on his commanding and dangerous and loving dark spirit? Because tender or brutal or dead or alive (or whoever he was or wasn't) she knows what she will always keep on remembering most is the exact temperature of his skin.

ACKNOWLEDGEMENTS

The reference on page 173 is to "My Melancholy Baby" (lyrics by George A. Norton, music by Ernie Burnett). I also gratefully acknowledge John Updike for a somewhat reconstituted (or perhaps not all *that* reconstituted) quote from an interview in which he spoke of going home for his high-school reunion, and Czesław Miłosz for a reference to a poem in which he wrote "everyone meditates then on the extravagance of having a separate fate." The line "God has his merciful, if daft, devices" on page 112 is from a book by Alden Nowlan. The references to "Herr Doktor" and "Herr Enemy" are from Sylvia Plath's *Ariel*, and the excerpts from letters that Lord Byron wrote to Lady Byron that appear on page 319 come (most recently) from *Touched with Fire*, by Kay Jamison. An excerpt from Bernard Malamud's *The Assistant* appears on page 261. On this same page, and also on page 239 there are either references to (or quotes from) "The Ivy Crown" by William Carlos Williams.

I would like to express my gratitude to the Canada Council, the Ontario Arts Council, and the Toronto Arts Council for their support during the years I was working on this novel. I'd also like to thank the institutions where I was writer-in-residence during the years 1993-1999: Concordia University, Carleton University, the University of New Brunswick, the Ottawa Public Library, and the Saskatoon Public Library.

I am very grateful to my family and friends, and to my editor, Ellen Seligman.

Many thanks, too, to my first readers: T, Barb, Nadine, Sandra, Carole C., Carol K., Faith, and N.B. I would especialy like to thank Doris Cowan.

And many thanks as well to Lisan Jutras, Anita Chong, and Dafydd Watkins.